Lost and Found

by

Charles Samuel Betts

authorHOUSE®

AuthorHouse™
1663 Liberty Drive
Bloomington, IN 47403
www.authorhouse.com
Phone: 1-800-839-8640

© 2011 Charles Samuel Betts. All rights reserved.

No part of this book may be reproduced, stored in a retrieval system, or transmitted by any means without the written permission of the author.

First published by AuthorHouse 1/14/2011

ISBN: 978-1-4567-2146-6 (sc)
ISBN: 978-1-4567-2147-3 (dj)
ISBN: 978-1-4567-2148-0 (e)

Library of Congress Control Number: 2010919598

Printed in the United States of America

Any people depicted in stock imagery provided by Thinkstock are models, and such images are being used for illustrative purposes only.
Certain stock imagery © Thinkstock.

This book is printed on acid-free paper.

Because of the dynamic nature of the Internet, any Web addresses or links contained in this book may have changed since publication and may no longer be valid. The views expressed in this work are solely those of the author and do not necessarily reflect the views of the publisher, and the publisher hereby disclaims any responsibility for them.

Dedicated to my children
Leah Saunders
Charles Ross
Craig McCandlish

Prologue

This is a story of people who have
lost love and happiness
and found both
again.

Chapter 1

JONATHAN MCCANDLISH WAS 25 YEARS old, and here he was standing in the middle of Madison Square Garden. It took him five years to get to this location. He wondered about those years as he looked around at the large arena. It all started right after he graduated from high school.

His father and he lived on a small ranch on the St. Augustine Plains. It was about 35 miles west of Socorro, New Mexico. His mother had died when he was 4 years old, and when he became 6 years old, he was sent to school in Socorro. He lived with his uncle and went through all his grades in the Socorro school system. During the school terms, he had only his weekends to be with his father. His father had a hardscrabble ranch, and they just barely made it all through those years.

In his sophomore year of high school, he began to notice girls and was particularly attracted to a very beautiful young girl called Mary McGregor. She had no interest in him as she was very actively involved with Tom Carlson. Tom was a son of a very successful rancher. He had a very large ranch that bordered the Rio Grande River and was considered by many to be the largest ranch in New Mexico. When his class graduated, they had a prom. He didn't invite any girl because he was only attracted to Mary. He knew she was going with Tom. He went to the prom, however, and waited to see Mary come and dance with Tom. Mary did not show up, and no one knew, what happened to her. She just disappeared.

Jonathan had always been a happy, go-lucky fellow. He loved rodeoing, but it wasn't important to him whether he won or lost. He just enjoyed the sport. He just managed to have enough points to be invited to compete in the National Rodeo that year, which was to be in

Madison Square Garden. All the other participants didn't expect him to win anything.

Mary McGregor was a very attractive young lady. She was 5 foot 6 inches tall with brown hair and light blue eyes. She was sitting in her office and wondering about what she could do about her life. As she wondered about this, memories of that terrible night came into focus. She could see herself sitting at home ready to go to the prom with the man she intended to marry.

She and Tom Carlson had been sweethearts since her sophomore year in high school. She knew that his father did not approve of her, but she felt that in time they could overcome his bad feelings. She looked at the clock, and it was 9:00 pm. Where was Tom? At 11:00 pm, she went to bed.

It was the next day that she discovered that Tom had been told by his father that if he continued his relationship with her, he would be disinherited. His not coming gave her the answer of how he felt about her.

She talked with her father about this disappointment, and he told her about his relationship with Tom's father, Clyde Carlson. They had been close friends at one time. Both had come to New Mexico together and had planned to establish a ranch in which each of them would be equal partners. During the process of acquiring land, Mary's father felt that Clyde was doing dishonest things. He confronted him about this, and they had an angry exchange. They broke their partnership, and each went their separate ways. Her father said, "I think that this probably is the reason for his anger regarding their relationship." She asked her father, "Why have you never told me about this problem?" He replied that he wanted to let bygones go away, and he didn't want his history to interfere with her relationship with Tom. They discussed what she should do at this point in her life. She said she could not face her friends as she felt humiliated by the lack of commitment of Tom for her. They decided that she would immediately leave and enroll in the University of New Mexico in Albuquerque. She still had the same thoughts and feelings of that night -- anger, fear and despair.

At the University, she took a business course. After graduating with honors, she went to Harvard Business School. She graduated and was immediately offered a position in a New York City firm that dealt in stocks and bonds. She had just finished her first year on that job and had received a bonus of $25,000.

She didn't like the work she was doing and felt very strongly she should form her own company and be her own boss. As she was pondering this in her apartment, she read in the newspaper about a rodeo being held in Madison Square Garden. It was for the national championship. As she read the clipping about this, the name Jonathan McCandlish stood out. She puzzled over this as she knew that name. Finally, she realized that he was that cute little boy with curly hair who seemed to be always looking at her when she was in her last two years of high school. The article seemed to imply that he was a very talented rodeo participant but never seemed to have the competitive spirit. For some reason, she felt she had to go to that event.

While she was there, the crowd warmed up to the event. The odds were presented on a board before the audience. She saw Jonathan's name, and the odds were 50 to 1. Without thinking, she took her $25,000 and placed it on Jonathan McCandlish to win all four events. As it turned out, she was the only one that placed a bet on him.

When the board announced the odds, Jonathan looked up and saw that he was 50 to 1. This meant nothing to him, but then the board reported that a person had bet $25,000 for him to win all the events. It troubled him. Who could that be? Something seemed to change inside of him. There seemed to be a surge of wanting to win; a surge he had never experienced before.

With the trumpeting of the band and the parades across the Garden, the announcer said, "The rodeo will begin. The prize is $150,000 for the participant that wins all four events." The people, who were running the event, didn't expect McCandlish to win anything, and they didn't want the ones that were expected to win to be eliminated by the first event. So, they gave the worst and meanest bronco to McCandlish to ride hoping that this would solve their problem. McCandlish knew that this horse was a vicious animal, and he had some idea why he was chosen for it. Instead of being concerned about this, it excited him. He mounted the bronco, Black Terror, tightened his grip on the rope halter, gritted his teeth, and he told them to open the gate. This crazy horse leapt out into the arena and started bucking in all directions. He twisted to the right and to the left. He leaped high into the air and with his all four legs stiff, he hit the ground hard. This jarred McCandlish severely, but he just seemed to laugh and continued spurring Black Terror on his sides trying to make him buck with more energy. The bronco tried every trick in his repertoire, but nothing worked. McCandlish rode him past the time required and kept riding. The owner of the bronco became very upset by this extended ride. He feared that McCandlish would possibly break the animal, and he would lose a big source of income. He complained to the authorities. The crowd was very excited by this ride and was shouting and loudly expressing amazement at the skill of this rider. They were demanding them not to stop the ride. Finally, when it became obvious the bronco was in distress, they lifted McCandlish off the bronco, and the animal nearly collapsed. The crowd was in an uproar. Mary couldn't believe her eyes. She had no idea of how capable Jonathan was. None of the contestants matched this ride, so he won the first event.

The next event was the calf roping event. His time was so short that no one could compete with him, and he won his second event. The skeptics that thought he was not capable of winning anything took a second look at him. They were amazed at what he had done up to this point.

The next event was bull riding. All of the animals that were being assigned to the participants had been selected prior to the rodeo, so here again Jonathan had been given the worst bull, El Diablo, to ride in this event. The skeptics felt, "We will really see what a fraud he is when he gets on this animal." The crowd had a different idea. They thought they were seeing a new champion. Mary who had made this ridiculous bet was beginning to think maybe this was going to change her fortune. Maybe if he wins this and the final event, she would have enough money to start her own business. Her heart was pounding, and she was frightened about what she had heard about this bull. The crowd was very excited because here was their young hero riding the worst bull that had ever been brought to that arena.

Jonathan was in the chute seating himself upon this angry animal. He grabbed tightly the band around the animal and strapped his hand tightly to it. After settling himself on the bull, he motioned for them to open the gate. The bull charged out twisting, turning, and doing so many different motions that it seemed impossible for him to stay on board. The bull began the most difficult part of the ride by bucking in tight circles.

The tight circles created centrifugal force that would usually throw off the rider. Jonathan stuck through these turns like glue. The crowd was roaring. They had never seen a ride like this. The bull was becoming heavily lathered, and his tongue was hanging out. It was obvious he was doing the best he could to unseat this creature on his back, but to no avail. He rode the bull past the time that he was supposed to and continued. The crowd was in ecstasy. They had never seen a ride like this. Finally, two horses went beside the bull and lifted Jonathan off. The bull was still raging and was charging around the arena angrily defying anything that got in his path and throwing his saliva in every direction. The crowd could not stop shouting. They had finally found a new champion. The final event of bull dogging was easily won by Jonathan.

Mary was stunned. She had impulsively bet on Jonathan as an expression of her despair of her inability to progress with what she wanted to do. Now, she suddenly had a large sum of money ($1.25 Million). She couldn't move. She was fixed to her seat. Slowly, she got up and walked in the direction of the payoff window. When she arrived there, she was greeted by an IRS official, and before any money was exchanged, they took their share of the winnings. As all of this was being settled, a young man walked up.

Jonathan was overwhelmed by the crowd's joy. He walked into the middle of the field, took off his hat and bowed to the crowd. They roared their appreciation of his effort. The ceremony of presenting the check was given by the appointed official, and he was escorted off the arena floor. After he had posed for all of the TV's and other duties that were required of a champion, he ran immediately to the pay window for wagers that had won their bets. He wanted to see who this person was that bet $25,000 on him.

He arrived just as Mary was finishing up with the IRS agent. He recognized her immediately as Mary McGregor, and his heart did a flip flop. He went over to her and said, "Mary, I had no idea you bet on me." Mary was so excited about what had happened that all she could do was hug him tightly and thank him for the opportunities he had given her. He didn't understand what she was talking about but was excited about being close to her.

After they exchanged their excitement, Jonathan said to Mary that he didn't know what he could do with all the money he had just earned.

He knew he had to invest it, but he had no knowledge about investing. Mary felt some responsibility for him and told him she would help him invest it and only charge him .25% for her services. He was grateful for this, not so much for the management of his money, but for the opportunity of having some contact with her. He asked, "Mary, will you have dinner with me." She agreed. Nothing really came of this, and both went their separate ways.

Jonathan when he left New York City intended to continue his rodeo experiences. While he was resting at a hotel in Calgary, Alberta, Canada, he received a telephone call from his father stating that he had received a draft notice. The notice ordered him to return to New Mexico for a physical. This shocked Jonathan as he was 26 years old and didn't expect to be drafted. As he was driving back to New Mexico, he had many thoughts in his mind. He began to question this ambition of his to be a rodeo rider. He knew that this activity usually ended with injuries, and he began to think that he needed to go back to college. He had finished two years of petroleum engineering at Texas A & M when he abruptly left. The urge to rodeo overcame his willingness to study. He remembered his impulsive behavior and told himself that he would reenter college and finish his degree in petroleum engineering. Even though these mature thoughts gave him a new direction, he was about to have an interruption in his life.

It was January 11, 1967, when he arrived in Socorro, New Mexico. He received his physical and was sent to Camp Pendleton, California, for basic training in the Marine Corp. After six months of training, he was sent overseas to Vietnam. It was late in the year of 1967, when he arrived in Saigon and was shipped north to Khe Sanh. This was poor timing on his part as towards the end of that year, he was actively engaged in combat. In early January, he and a group of men were shifted to the MACV headquarters (Military Assistant Command, Vietnam) in Hui. Their duties were to defend the headquarters. On February 3, 1968, the massive TET offensive began, and Hui was rapidly overrun. It was only his group of 200 American soldiers and marines that held out south of the capital. The fighting was fierce, and Jonathan was severely wounded. The next few months were all lost to Jonathan. He was air evacuated to Saigon and then to the United States. He had severe head trauma and multiple wounds. He was hospitalized in the U.S. Naval Hospital in Bethesda, Maryland, for six months.

During this period of time, he realized that he would no longer be able to be a rodeo cowboy. He made plans to return to Texas A & M. He started in September, 1968. All during this period, he had limited contact with Mary. She was concerned about his being wounded, but there was no emotional connection between them. She just continued to manage his finances. She had stopped charging him for her service and had over the past year increased the value of his portfolio to $200,000.

Jonathan had written her during his recovery period, but the letters were mostly about his finances and his trying to understand how she managed his investments. He wanted to be able to successfully invest for himself. When he left the hospital in August, 1968, he wrote Mary a letter stating how much he appreciated her taking care of his estate, and he thought now he was qualified to manage it. Thus, it seemed that his relationship with Mary was over, and he was now going on his own way and she hers.

Chapter II

After receiving this amount of money from her rash bet, Mary sat down and tried to decide how she was going to develop a company for herself. After she quit pondering, she began to remember the Indian women of New Mexico. They seemed to preserve their skin remarkably well considering the harsh conditions under which they lived. She wondered if maybe they had some special herbs or salves to help shield their skins from the harsh climate they experienced. She left New York and went back to her home in Socorro. There she sought out many different Indian women questioning them as to how they kept their skin from deteriorating. She didn't discover any new ways, but she did have a clear idea of the direction she was going with her new company. She was going to develop a cosmetic corporation, and she was going to be particularly interested in skin care.

Over the next two years, she struggled with this problem. She talked to many dermatologists and went to many medical meetings involved around skin care. She took courses in chemistry at the University of New Mexico and began to explore the ingredients that would possibly be of benefit for skin care. It was towards the end of her second year that she had a breakthrough and found a formula that worked well in taking care of skin that was exposed to harsh environmental conditions. After many tests of this product with no bad side effects, she decided it was time to move into the production and promotion of her company. All of this period of time paralleled the period of time that Jonathan was in the Marine Corp, his hospitalization, and Texas A & M.

In the fall of 1969, Jonathan graduated from Texas A & M. Mary was just beginning to start selling her products. On graduation, he took his $250,000 as he had increased it $50,000 and formed a production company. He was determined to explore New Mexico for the possibility of discovering new oil fields. He used his experience in geology and toured the state. Regardless of the places he went, his mind kept drifting back to Socorro. He knew that the Albuquerque Basin of which Socorro was a part of, had produced oil and gas, but it was scattered and difficult to find. He set up his company in Socorro and began acquiring land and leases in the surrounding area. He would spend days and weeks exploring the geology of this area. He finally located what he considered the best location for wildcatting. He was down to his last hundred thousand dollars when his production company started drilling. These were desperate times for him as he knew that this was his last chance to really accomplish the making of his company.

Drilling was slow and tests along the way were not encouraging. At the 6,000 foot level, they hit a pocket of gas, but it didn't seem to be enough to make a well. He decided to go further, and he was at 6,500 feet when they struck oil. It flowed well enough for him to have a significant well. His company was on the road to being very successful. Over the next few years, he had many successful productions and became a multimillionaire.

By 1975, he was thinking about acquiring land to build a home outside of Socorro. As he was searching for this, he read that an auction was to take place at a large ranch a few miles outside of Socorro. In the mid-70's, the cattle business was in a deep depression. Many ranchers had lost large sums of money. The ones that had established feeding centers for cattle had suffered the most. This ranch was owned by a Clyde Carlson. He had a large feeding operation and had lost heavily. He had mortgaged his ranch and had been unable to meet the loan requirements. The bank foreclosed on his property and put it up for auction.

Jonathan pondered this. This was the same Carlson family that he had known when he was going to high school in Socorro. Clyde Carlson had been a successful rancher. He had been contemptuous of the small ranchers of which Jonathan's father was one. He decided to bid on this property and was determined to buy it. At auction time, he drove up to the ranch house of this property. There he found a large crowd who were mainly interested in buying the equipment of the ranch. He saw the agony in Clyde Carlson's face. For the first time, he felt some pity for him. Next to Clyde was Tom Carlson. He had married a local girl, and they had two children. He wondered what would happen to them.

After the sale of all of the equipment, the auction of the property was announced. Most of the people had left, and there were only a few bidders left to respond to the auction. The opening bid was set to begin at $500,000. This ranch was approximately 100,000 acres and bordered the Rio Grande River for at least 6 miles. It was only moderately desirable as a ranch, but Jonathan was aware of the possibility that this land might cover a large gas and oil field.

He was determined to have this land. The bidding went up from $500,000 to $600,000, and then there was a jump to $1 Million. Jonathan made one bid -- $2.5 Million. This squelched all the bidders, and the land was his. As he was up signing the check for the property, Clyde Carlson came up and said, "Don't I know you?" Jonathan said, "No, you don't really, Mr. Carlson. I knew your son, Tom, because we were in high school together, but we were never friends and only casual acquaintances." Clyde continued saying, "You know you really got a bargain. This land was worth over $5 Million. I worked all my life developing it, and you are getting it for less than 50% of its value." He was angry and despaired. Jonathan chose not to answer this and walked away. He told the auctioneer that he would give the previous owner one month to leave the property. This was very kind of him, but Clyde saw it as an insult and was enraged.

Chapter III

MARY'S COMPANY STARTED OFF VERY slowly. She was having difficulty promoting the product even though she knew it was a very good product. Promotion was not one of her skills, and she knew she had to do something to overcome this deficit. She pondered about this, and while she was thinking about promotion, she remembered her roommate, Elizabeth Horne. Elizabeth had taken a business course at the University of New Mexico with Mary and had decided she would go into promotions. They had lost contact with each other even though they had been roommates for four years.

She decided to try to find Elizabeth and ultimately found her located in Dallas, Texas. She was working at a company that promoted products. It was a dead end street for her, and she was thinking about quitting and trying to find something else. When she received Mary's call and learned what Mary was trying to do, she immediately said, "Can I come and help you with this?" Mary was delighted and said, "Yes, come and work with me, and I will give your 10% interest in my new company." This offer was far more than Liz thought possible and said, "I'm on the next plane to Albuquerque."

This combination was what the company needed and in a few months, their product was being sought by more and more people. By the end of 1975, Mary had a very prosperous cosmetic company. She was now 35 years old, and she was tired. She was wondering what she should do with the rest of her life. She had not been interested in any kind of relationship with another man and had all through those years avoided dating. Now she was wondering about the wisdom of this. She had always wanted to have a family and children, and now she was approaching the critical age for having children.

One Monday morning, when she came to work in her large corporate building in downtown Albuquerque, she called Liz into her office and said, "Liz, I'm going to sell my company and go in a different direction. You own 10% of this company, so I'm telling you this to see how you feel about it." Liz was very surprised and didn't know what to say. She asked, "Do you have a buyer?" Mary said, "No, the thought just came to me over the weekend, and I wanted you to be the first to know my desire to get out of this business." As Liz thought about this, she realized she was also tired of the demands of this business and thought maybe retirement would be good for both of them. She laughed and said to Mary, "Well, you need a good promoter to sell your business, and I am just the one for it." They both stood up and hugged each other. They realized that this would separate them and somehow sadness was felt by both.

Over the next few months, Mary and Elizabeth explored many options concerning the sale of her company. Many pharmaceutical companies had cosmetic divisions and were interested in owning the formulae for the products that Mary's company had developed. So, there was much bidding in regards to the purchase of this company.

On December 15, 1975, Mary finally came to terms with a prominent pharmaceutical company. They offered to buy her company for $500 Million cash and one million shares in the acquiring company stock. The deal was to be closed on the 17th of December, 1975. It took all day for this to be accomplished, and it was late that evening that Mary closed her office and went down into the garage. She got into her car to drive to her home on the western outskirts of Albuquerque.

She was very tired and found it difficult to drive the five miles through heavy traffic. Christmas shoppers were everywhere, and the highways were crowded. As she approached the intersection of Interstate 40, she entered the western approach. As she was accelerating to enter, a truck lost control and crashed into her car. Mary was seriously injured and had to be removed from the car with the Jaws of Life. She had many fractures and was unconscious. She was unconscious for several days and there was concern about whether she would survive.

It was Christmas Eve, and she slowly opened her eyes. She looked around bewildered. Where was she, she asked herself. It was a room that was all white, and she was lying in a bed. She reached up with her hands to her head and found it was covered in bandages. Her right leg was suspended, and her left arm was in a cast. As she became more and more conscious, she became aware of severe pain. She could hardly speak out, but a loud moan did come from her lips.

She was in an intensive care unit at the Albuquerque General Hospital. There was a nurse's station just across the corridor from her bed, and the nurse saw her move and heard her moan. She rushed to her side and said, "Try not to move. I know you are in pain. We have an order for pain medication as needed. It will only take a few minutes for me to give you a shot, and you will feel better." The kindness of her voice reassured Mary, but all she could feel was confusion and pain. Finally, she was able to ask the nurse, "Where am I, and who am I?" There was a puzzled look on her face, and there was fear in her eyes. The nurse said in a gentle reassuring voice, "Mary, you have been in a terrible accident. You have been unconscious for over a week, and you have had many fractures. We feared for your life. Your awakening now has encouraged all of us, and we feel you are going to be okay."

Mary was puzzled by this. She called me Mary. "Mary, what?" she said to herself. There were so many questions that came to her mind that she didn't know what to ask. All she could do was be quiet; big tears rolled down her cheeks. The nurse felt she had given her too much information and told her it was best she go to sleep. When she awaked, she would probably feel much better. The doctor had some concern about sedating Mary as she had a brain concussion, so there were limited things they could do to help her go to sleep.

Mary just lay quietly in the bed and tried to see if she could remember anything that had happened to her. It seemed that all of her past memory was lost. She seemed to be starting her life from this moment. What had she been doing? Where was she going? Why did this accident happen? All these thoughts hammered away in her mind. As the pain medication took hold, she drifted off into sleep.

She was dreaming that she was back in some strange place. She knew she had been there before, but it was strange to her now. She could see an old man there. He seemed to be sitting on a porch of an old house. Who was that man? The dream echoed in her mind. Suddenly, she was wide awake. She knew the face of that man must be something important to her memory. She tried to grab hold of this face in her dream, for she felt that this might give her some clue of her past memory. Struggle as she may, nothing came into focus. She finally drifted again to sleep.

Chapter IV

After a month's time, Jonathan moved into the ranch house that he had purchased. It had been called The Carlson Ranch. He changed its name to The Lost and Found Ranch. He knew that he didn't want to live in that house as he had no fond memories of the Carlson family. He wandered about the ranch looking for a location on which to build his home. As he wandered close to the Rio Grande River, he found a high bluff. He knew that here was where he would place his home. This was quite a distance from the highway that ran along the western border of his ranch. He decided it would be worthwhile to build a good road to this location and immediately started to work on both projects.

Jonathan's personality had changed a lot since that day he won the big rodeo in New York City. He now found himself as an impatient man driving, not only himself, but also others in any project he undertook. He built a 6,000 square foot ranch house. He had designed the house himself, and he spared no expense in the building of it. He converted the old ranch house into a house for his ranch manager and started developing a cattle business.

He had just finished this project on December 24, 1975. He had all of his newspapers delivered to his front gate. That morning he walked down to the front gate to get his morning paper. For years he had taken the Wall Street Journal as he now managed his own stocks and bonds. There was a lead article on the front page of the Wall Street Journal. It said, "Mary McGregor, the recent owner of McGregor Enterprises, was seriously injured in an automobile accident on the 17th of December, 1975." It was reported in the paper that she had serious injuries and not expected to live.

This news was like a knife plunged into his heart. He had forgotten or not thought about how much he loved Mary, but this news overwhelmed him. He said to himself, "What can I do? I can't lose this woman." Nothing came to mind. The only thought was he had to go to Albuquerque. "I can't stay here and not be a part of what happens to Mary."

He called Bill Williams, his ranch foreman, and told him he was going to leave the ranch in his hands for at least several months. He called the manager of his production company, David Fremont, and told him to continue his geological survey on his new ranch and keep the rest of his business operating as best he could. He said, "I will be involved in an important issue for the next several months. I will be available to you on my radio phone, but don't call me unless something is very important."

With this, he packed his belongings, threw them in the back of his Mercedes 500 convertible and was off to Albuquerque. When he arrived at the hospital, he immediately contacted the doctors who were taking care of Mary. They told him they could not discuss the case with him as he was not listed as a relative. He refused to listen to this rejection and insisted on going to the ward where she was located. He had trouble there because he was not a relative. By this time, he was quite angry. He recalled several years ago that he had donated a wing to this hospital. He decided to go to the Administrator of the hospital. He knew this man because he was involved intensely with him during the building of this wing. When he walked into the office of Joseph Smith, the administrator, he was greeted warmly. Jonathan was still angry about the rejections he had received and immediately demanded the administrator do something about the problem he had. This behavior surprised Mr. Smith as he felt he had been a friend of Jonathan's for several years.

Joseph said to Jonathan, "Please tell me what's troubling you. I don't understand why you are so angry." In a rambling, angry voice, Jonathan explained what had happened. He said, "I have known Mary McGregor since high school. She has always been very important to me, and she helped me start my career. Even though we had not been close friends, I have felt indebted to her, and I want all of the best care that can be given to her. I want this hospital to be on alert of the importance of this patient to me, a patron of this hospital. I want the staff to understand that I intend to stay here as long as she is in this hospital, and I expect this hospital to make it as comfortable for both of us as it possibly can." Joseph was taken aback by this demanding tone, but he knew he was dealing with a very disturbed angry man, and he also knew that he would lose a patron if he didn't handle it with care.

He said, "Jonathan, please sit down, and let me find a way to make all of this happen as you desire." He got on the phone and asked if there was any relative of Mary's in the hospital. The charge nurse on the intensive care unit informed him that no one had appeared to claim any kind of responsibility for her. They were concerned about this lack of information and were pleased at least someone had come wanting to help her. Joseph reported back to Jonathan what he had discovered and told him that they needed to get in touch with a relative of Mary's in order for him to get permission to be with her. Jonathan was surprised that no one was there to take care of Mary. He knew that Mary had a father, but he didn't know if he was alive or not. He immediately got on the phone with people he knew in Socorro and began to try to find who might be a relative of Mary's. He finally found her father who was alive. It took several days for Jonathan to locate her father. He had left his small ranch at the age of 60 and retired to a retirement center near Phoenix, Arizona. When Jonathan called him, he was shocked to hear that Mary had been injured and told Jonathan that he would immediately fly to Albuquerque.

Jonathan met the airplane that brought Andy McGregor to Albuquerque. Andy did not know that Mary had any involvement with Jonathan and was surprised to find him so interested in her. Jonathan immediately told him about his connection with Mary. He didn't say he was in love with Mary. He just simply said that Mary had been very important in starting his business career, and he was very concerned that she have the best of care. He told him about the problem he was having in helping her. He said, "I looked for you, Andy, with the idea that both of us could see that she got the best of care. When they arrived at the hospital, Andy was surprised at how much respect the staff showed Jonathan. They were very anxious to please him, and they immediately went to the floor where Mary was. Jonathan waited outside while Andy went into the room with Mary.

Mary had been removed from intensive care and was on the general surgical floor. She had a private room with 24 hour nursing care. Andy rushed over to the bed and hugged Mary. Mary drew back from him and almost screamed. She said in a high pitch voice, "What are you doing, trying to hug me? Who are you anyway?" This was a great shock to Andy. He had no idea of the severity of her brain damage. He sat down by the bed dumbfounded. He just looked at her for a few minutes, and then he said, "Mary, don't you know, who I am? I am your father, and I love you very much."

This statement startled Mary. This was the first time anyone had come into the room claiming that they knew her. She was excited about this but fearful because she didn't really think he was her father. After a few minutes, she said to him, "Please leave me. I don't know who you are, and it is upsetting to me when you claim to be my father." Andy slowly got up and walked out of the room. He was utterly devastated. Jonathan was outside the door waiting for him and recognized immediately the change that had come over Andy. He told him what had happened. Jonathan put his arms around his slumped shoulders and guided him to a small room where they could have a few private moments with each other. Jonathan told Andy that he was going to do everything in his power to help Mary regain her memory and be a normal person again. He said, "Andy, you don't remember me, but I was in high school with Mary. I was in love with Mary and have kept these feelings all these years. Mary was in love with Tom Carlson. I became friends with her when I helped her win her wager on me. I won a national championship at a rodeo in New York City in December, 1966. We connected up with each other for several years. She helped me manage my winnings, but she was never interested in me emotionally. She developed her company, and I developed mine and neither one of us thought we would have any connection again. When I read about her accident, I knew I still loved her. I couldn't stand by and see her die and not be taken care of. The hospital tells me I cannot be involved with Mary's care as I am not a relative. They say that if she has a relative that agrees to my taking care of her then they would agree to my being in attendance with her." Andy was quite touched by Jonathan's statements and told him he would certainly sign anything that would permit this to happen. The necessary papers were signed, and Jonathan now had access to Mary.

Jonathan felt he needed the best advice he could get in order to find a way to engage Mary. He knew several prominent physicians in New York and called them asking if they knew anyone that specialized in memory loss following trauma. One physician referred him to a Doctor Samuel

Jones. He was located in Ann Arbor, Michigan. He was a professor in Neurology and Psychiatry at the University Of Michigan School Of Medicine.

Jonathan called him and told him his problem and wanted to come to Ann Arbor and consult with him. He left Albuquerque and told Mary's father his emergency phone number. If anything happened to Mary that was serious, he was to call him immediately. The flight to Detroit was approximately 4 hours. He had many thoughts during that flight. The threat of losing Mary was very painful to him, and he forced himself not to consider this. These thoughts kept hitting him back and forth, so when he finally arrived in Detroit, he was very tired and emotionally drained.

He rented a car at the airport and drove to Ann Arbor. He had made an appointment for 2:00 p.m. on December 31, 1975, with Doctor Jones. He arrived early and was waiting when Doctor Jones came to his office. They went into his office, and he related to Doctor Jones the reason for his being there. He had brought all the medical documents that were available regarding Mary's injuries including x-rays and CT scans of her brain. Doctor Jones listened carefully to what Jonathan had to say and looked at all of the medical records that were available. He told Jonathan that there had been marked swelling of Mary's brain, and it would be difficult to know if any permanent damage had been done.

Jonathan became impatient with Doctor Jones and said, "I didn't come here to hear any bad news about Mary. I came here to find out if there was any way I could help restore her memory. I was told that you were a memory doctor, a doctor, who helped restore people's memory. I want to know what I can do to help Mary." Prior to this, Doctor Jones had been a professionally withdrawn doctor, but the emotional reaction of Jonathan stimulated him to be more attentive to Jonathan. He said, "Jonathan, may I call you that? I am sorry if I appeared to be less than human with you, as I was talking about someone you love. I hope you will forgive my error and let us get down to the business of how to restore her memory." They had a long talk about what areas of the brain were involved with memory and how one went about trying to establish contact with past memory. The main point he was making was that the persons involved in this process had to be very patient and caring. These two words would be the primary stimulus that would encourage Mary to fight through this fog of memory and, hopefully, recover everything that she had lost.

He said, "Jonathan, you have to first become a familiar person to Mary before she can be able to trust you enough to begin this process of exploring. Somehow, you will have to develop a relation with Mary where she will want to work with you in this regard. I have no way of telling you how to accomplish this. This is something that you have within yourself that somehow must connect up with what's inside Mary."

Jonathan left Doctor Jones with the understanding that in the future he could call him whenever he felt it was necessary. They both seemed to have developed a warm relationship with each other. Doctor Jones was impressed by the love that he sensed in Jonathan, and he told him on leaving that he thought he had a very good chance of recapturing Mary.

The flight back to Albuquerque was very strange for Jonathan. It was a mixture of hope and despair. He could not conceive of anything inside himself that could possibly attract Mary. He saw himself as two people. One was an immature fun loving guy who was so shot up in Vietnam that he had to completely change the way he looked at the world. He was now a hard minded business man who had not looked at a person as a human being for a long time. The feeling of caring had not been in his life for many years. He knew that he must somehow develop this ability to express caring, or he would never be able to reach Mary.

He was very tired as he flew back, and he slowly fell into sleep when he was about two hours into the flight. He didn't dream and didn't become aware of anything until the stewardess shook him and said, "We are landing in Albuquerque." This brief sleep seemed to refresh him, and he felt encouraged that maybe he could do something that would help Mary trust him.

Mary awakened the second time, and this time she seemed to be more aware of her surroundings. She wasn't the helpless, crying child she seemed to be the first time she awakened. She seemed to somehow be stronger in her thoughts and more demanding in her attitude. With a stronger voice, she called the nurse. She said, "I somehow have no memory. I don't know where I am or who I am. Can you help me?" The nurse repeated what she had said before, only went into more details about her injuries. Mary had always been a strong person who was capable of enduring many difficult situations. She was determined that this situation would be one that she mastered.

When the nurse answered the question "who am I?", Mary McGregor felt no response at all within herself. It was just a name. The question "where am I" was answered with a statement that she was at Albuquerque General Hospital, and she had been there for two weeks. Mary's next question was what happened. The nurse said, "I have only read the police report, which stated that you were entering the west bound lane of I-40 when a 16-wheeler lost control and rammed into your car. They had to use the Jaws of Life to extract you from the car, and you had multiple injuries -- mostly bone fractures and a brain concussion. It was your brain concussion that has caused your memory loss. The swelling has gone down, but we still don't know how much damage was done to the memory centers of your brain."

Mary thought for a few moments and said, "Has anyone come here claiming to be a relative of mine?" The nurse responded with a no. She said, "However, there was a handsome man who had come to see you, but the hospital had initially refused his right to be a visitor. Apparently, this man was very important because the hospital administrator was bending over backwards to please him." At the present time, she was told this man was trying to find her father. As far as she knew, he had been unsuccessful up to this time. This puzzled Mary. She had a father that she didn't know about, and a strange man was interested in her. What did all of this mean? She was given a shot for pain, and she slowly drifted away.

This time she dreamed many dreams. She dreamed of a beautiful lady who ran a business. The business was strange to her, but she seemed to be very successful. She was unhappy. She was troubled because she couldn't seem to find a husband. This was such an aggravation to her that she immediately wakened and shook her head in disbelief. She couldn't stop the thought of the young lady longing to find a husband. Was she looking for a husband when she had this accident? Was she engaged to some person, and the engagement was not going well? Was this man asking about her, engaged to her? What was he in her life? There were no answers to any of these questions, and she just drifted off into another dream state.

She had just awakened when suddenly this man rushed into her room and started hugging her, claiming he was her father. She felt like screaming, but all she could do was harshly push him away. It was very unsettling to her because she had no feeling for this man and did not think he was her father. She lay there listening to him talking about how much he loved her and stating over and over again that he was her father. All it did was agitate her so much that she asked him to leave. When he left, she told the nurse to never let that man in again.

Andy McGregor was devastated by the way his daughter responded to him. He could find no comfort in anything that was said to him. He found himself being very dependent on Jonathan. When Jonathan said he was going to Ann Arbor to interview a memory specialist, he was excited and pleased to realize how much Mary meant to Jonathan. He was further reassured when Jonathan gave him his phone number. When he was told by the nurse that Mary did not want him to come in the room again, he again felt despair. He left the hospital and went to a local motel and called Jonathan. Jonathan was at the airport ready to board when he received the call from Andy. When Andy told Jonathan what had happened, Jonathan reassured him that he was going to do everything he could to help him and Mary. He suggested that he try to take a nap, and he would come by the motel and pick him up as soon as his plane landed in Albuquerque. With this reassurance, Andy lay down on the bed and slept. It was a deep sleep with no dreams, and he was awakened with the knock on the door, and there was Jonathan waiting to take him to the hospital.

Jonathan and Andy stopped at the local restaurant and had a late meal. They talked about his conversation with Doctor Jones, and because of the positive attitude of Jonathan, both felt much better. The drive to the hospital was uneventful. They both realized that they would make this drive many times before they left this area. Jonathan didn't like the idea of spending all this time in a motel, so he had his ranch manager call around and find a deluxe furnished apartment for rent. He signed a six month lease. Neither one at this time realized that Mary had a large home in Albuquerque and that her father could have moved into that home immediately. This information didn't matter to them as they both planned to live in this apartment together.

Chapter V

THEY ARRIVED AT THE HOSPITAL and consulted with the ward doctor and the attending nurses. Jonathan discussed with Mary's attending physician the information that Doctor Jones had given him regarding how he was to approach Mary in helping her to restore her memory. He emphasized to this physician, Doctor Jim Hunt, that he would require the ability to visit Mary as much as she would tolerate. He asked Mary's attending nurse to tell her that the man who had been waiting to see her was still waiting. He wanted to be with her any time she wanted to see him. When told this, Mary said no, and she stated further it was too early for her to consider what this man might be in her life.

The nurse returned to Jonathan with this information and he said, "I will be here every day, and each day I want you to tell her that I am here. I want to see her as soon as she is willing to see me." This state of affairs lasted for about a week.

It was a Sunday afternoon, and the nurse went in to see Mary and said, "That man is here again. Do you want to see him?" She said it in such a negative tone that she was sure the answer would be no. To the surprise of both Mary and the nurse, she found herself saying, "Yes, I want to see this man." When the nurse came out and reported this to Jonathan, he felt a sudden fear. This was his first opportunity to see her. He had wondered if he could show enough caring that she would be interested in seeing him further. He looked inward, and all he saw was a hard business man who had abandoned all of his caring ability. He was not a happy person and was not a person that made conversation easily. How could he overcome these handicaps was the question when he walked towards the room and opened the door.

He walked slowly into the room, and it was obvious he was hesitant and unsure of himself. He was not a threatening person at all, and Mary recognized this immediately. She saw that he was afraid of something. It didn't occur to her that it was fear that she would reject him. She suddenly felt sorry for him. He looked so forlorn and helpless. She saw him trying to talk and realized he was having a great struggle to say anything. She wasn't afraid of this man, but she wondered why he was so afraid. Since he wasn't able to talk, she said, "The nurse tells me that you have been waiting to see me for over a week. At first, I didn't want to see anybody, much less a person I didn't know. Your persistence intrigues me. I wonder who you are and why you are interested in me. Can you talk with me?" These words were like a shock to Jonathan. He had no idea it would turn out this way, but he was greatly relieved that she didn't ask him to leave. He didn't want to overload her with his feelings for her. He wanted to say something that would not threaten her.

"Mary," Jonathan said, "May I call you Mary?" He waited for her response. She thought a few minutes and decided that maybe it was safe to talk to this guy and she said, "Yes." He continued by saying, "I have known you for a long time. We were not close, but we did keep in touch for a period of time. I have always been fond of those times. When I heard you had this serious accident, I felt that I had to come if it only meant that I would be near you." This kind of talk amazed Mary. This man obviously cared for her but was afraid she was going to reject him. Why would he feel that way? They talked on for about 20 minutes about casual things. He looked at her and saw that she was tired so he said, "I know you are tired, and I am going to leave now. I hope you will let me come back again." Mary pondered this and was silent for a few minutes. This statement was a caring statement, but she didn't know whether she wanted to continue with this man. During this silent time, she realized that no one had come to see her. This was the first person that seemed to care for her. She thought that maybe it would be wise for her to continue to see this man. She told him yes. She would like for him to come tomorrow.

Jonathan didn't know how to say goodbye. He struggled with what he should say. He finally realized the best way was to say nothing. He managed a slight smile and gently waved as he closed the door. As he entered the hall, he found Andy anxiously waiting. He wanted to know everything that had happened. Jonathan said, "Let's go to our private room, and I will tell you all I can remember." He related word for word what had transpired. Both realized that this was just the beginning, and all in all it was a good beginning. The beginning was very fragile and would require much patience on their part. For a while, both were silent and were in their own deep thoughts.

Jonathan suddenly became alert and said to Andy, "We must begin to find out about Mary's life. First, let's consult a lawyer about how we should proceed in order to get you her power of attorney. Then we will go to her office, collect all of her materials and find out where she lives and go there. We must learn as much as we can about her life prior to her accident. Mary has just closed a large business deal. She sold her business for 500 million dollars according to the Wall Street Journal." Andy was shocked and could not absorb all of this information.

Jonathan realized that Andy was overwhelmed by what he had just said. He knew that Andy would have to make many important decisions, and he felt that he would need all the information that he could get. As he thought about this problem, he realized that Andy would need to know more about him if he was going to be able to feel comfortable about his intruding into Mary's life.

He said, "Andy, I need to tell you about me. I want you to trust me, and the only way one builds trust is by being totally honest with each other." He started off by saying, "I am thirty five years old, and I have loved Mary for twenty years. I have always longed to be with her, and my intentions now are to find a way to get Mary to love me. I want you to know all about me because I want to be a part of yours and Mary's life. I used to be a happy-go-lucky kind of guy. I loved rodeoing, and I didn't care if I won or lost. Achieving was not important to me. One day, when I was rodeoing in New York City for the national championship, Mary made a big wager on me to win. I suddenly wanted to win, and I did. This win helped Mary and me. It gave me a feeling that if I was ever to have a chance to attract Mary, I must be more serious about my life. The Vietnam War interrupted my life. I was drafted, and I was severely wounded in the battle for Hui. I was in the naval hospital at Bethesda for six months. I went back to Texas A&M and graduated with a degree in petroleum engineering. From 1969 to 1975, I have been developing a production oil company. I have been very successful and now my assets are valued at over a billion dollars. I currently own and live on a 100,000 acre ranch near Socorro, New Mexico. I also own an oil company. I consider myself a successful business man, but interpersonally I fail miserably. It took finding Mary again for me to consider what a cold efficient person, I had become. I didn't care about other people except in the way I could use them in my business. It frightens me to consider how limited my assets are in showing Mary how much I love and need her."

Andy was amazed by all of this self analysis. He already knew that he liked Jonathan, but he had no idea how important he must be in his business world. He had always been a man who had a modest income, and he never was very ambitious. He had seen how greed had destroyed his relationship with Clyde Carlson and had decided that he would be modest in his demands towards others. After having these thoughts, he turned to Jonathan and said, "I appreciate your telling me all of this, but I wonder why you felt the need to tell me." Jonathan replied saying, "I know that you will need help in getting acquainted with Mary's personal and business structures. I want to be a part of this, and I want you to trust me enough to let me participate." Andy replied, "You have already shown me how much you love Mary, and your caring for her and me has been a great comfort. I am so grateful to have you by my side as I try to get back with my daughter. What must we do now?"

With this exchange of confidences, Jonathan said, "We must first get you power of attorney so that we can do whatever needs to be done. We also need to find out about her activities. As we get more time with her, we will be sensitive to any memories she might retrieve."

With this, they left the hospital and went to Jonathan's personal lawyer. Even though Don Wright, his lawyer, was very busy, he stopped what he was doing and saw Jonathan immediately on his arrival. Jonathan was, not only an important client, but also a very close friend. They had known each other in Socorro and had been in Vietnam together. It was thru Jonathan's efforts that Don's life was saved during the battle of Hui. In fact, Jonathan received his severe wounds saving Don's life. They were brothers, and now they looked out for each other. Don had no idea why Jonathan was here with, of all people, Andy McGregor. Don's father and Andy had been close friends. Both had lost their wives about the same time, and they both had retired and moved to Arizona at the same time.

They lived in the same retirement center. His father had written about Andy's daughter and her accident, but Don thought no more about it.

Jonathan opened the conversation by thanking Don for seeing them so promptly. He continued by saying, "I know you are very busy, and it would only be an event of such great importance to me that would lead me to disrupt your day. Don, we are close friends, but I have never told you about my feelings for Mary McGregor. Since I was a kid in high school, I have loved Mary. As you might remember, Mary had eyes only for Tom Carlson, and I knew that I had no chance of being with her. All of the past 20 years when I was alone and not working, my thoughts would turn to Mary. When I read about her accident, I immediately came to Albuquerque General hospital and have been as close to her as possible. Mary has a severe brain concussion and has lost all of her memory. She doesn't know her name and nothing about her past. She does not recognize her father and refuses to see him. I have recently been able to visit her, but my relationship is tenuous. I have advised Andy to get power of attorney so that he can manage her affairs. We need your help and advice."

Don was surprised about Jonathan's feeling for Mary, but he was glad that he had found a woman that he loved. He had always been concerned about the sadness and the loneliness he knew existed in Jonathan's life. As his surprise abated, he gave Jonathan a big smile and came around his desk and hugged him and told him how pleased he was that he had found someone he could love. With that he sat down and told them about the process necessary to get a power of attorney in this type of case. He indicated that he would personally see that this was accomplished and would notify them when Andy would have to come in to sign the papers. Jonathan told Don that time was important as it was critical that he know as much about Mary's immediate past, as she had just completed a sale of her company. Also, Andy was concerned about her home as he felt that it was not being taken care of. Don assured them he would grease the tracks as fast as he could. All Jonathan could say was, "Thanks, Buddy".

Chapter VI

MARGARET CANADAY BAKER OF WACO, Texas, was sitting on a couch in her day room. She was finding that she would day dream a lot these days. It was one year and three months ago that Edward died. It was not a sudden death as both had been expecting it for a long time. Eddie, as she affectionately called him, had a long protracted fight with congestive heart failure. Being alone in a large house wasn't her idea of having fun. She finally got up from the couch and looked at the mess that was confronting her. When Eddie was with her, she enjoyed the house, and she made it pleasingly neat. Since Eddie's death, she had felt empty and didn't want to do anything. She knew that she was depressed, and she knew that she should be active, but life had no meaning for her. As she wandered around, she saw a stack of Wall Street Journals. She hadn't stopped Eddie's subscription to the Wall Street Journal, and they had continued to clutter up her house. She never did like this newspaper, because Eddie would bury his head into it, and she wasn't to disturb him. She went over to the stack and angrily began bundling them up. As she was bundling up her first stack she glanced at the headlines. She read a prominent C.E.O. of a large cosmetic company, Miss Mary McGregor, was hit by a large truck as she was entering interstate 40. It was at the last West Albuquerque exit. It was reported that she was seriously injured and was not expected to live. She ripped open the bundle and grabbed the paper anxiously looking for the date it was published. She read December 18, 1975. It was now January 11, 1976. She collapsed in the nearest chair and started crying. It was a loud almost screaming type of crying. This continued for a long time. Finally, she became quiet and began thinking about Mary. Margaret and Edward didn't have any children. They had desperately wanted children but none came. Mary was the closest thing to a daughter that they had.

Margaret and Nancy were sisters, and they were very close to each other. Margaret was two years older than Nancy, and she was the typical big sister. She was very protective of Nancy, and this sometimes caused them problems. On the whole, they loved each other deeply and did many things together. They both went to the same college, and Margaret graduated two years ahead of Nancy. Nancy's last two years of college was fun for her. She was free of her sister's supervision. Nancy, during those years, met and dated a handsome young man, and they fell in love. Andy McGregor was in his last two years of college and was planning to go to New Mexico with a friend when he graduated. Just before they graduated together, they were married and left immediately for New Mexico. Margaret had come to Nancy's graduation and was surprised, to put it mildly, when they announced their marriage, and their intention to leave immediately for New Mexico. She never forgave Andy for taking Nancy away from her.

When Nancy had Mary, Margaret came and helped with the baby. She was so happy that Nancy had a child that she almost forgave Andy. When Mary was six, she started spending summers with Margaret and Edward. They dearly loved Mary and took her all over Texas. If she came early enough they would drive to the hill country to see the blue bells. When Mary was twelve, Nancy suddenly died. Margaret was shocked, and all she could feel was anger. When she came to the funeral, all she could do was rage at Andy. She blamed him for Nancy's death and expressed all of this in front of Mary. When Margaret exhausted her anger, she found Mary crying. She went over to comfort her, and Mary drew away from her. She would never forget what Mary said to her, "Aunt Margaret, I love you, but I never want to see you again. My father and I are frightened and scared about not having my mother. We wanted you to come and help us, but instead you came and attacked my father. Please leave us and never come back. We will take care of mother and go on with our lives without you." Nothing that Margaret could say or do could change this. She had lost Nancy and Mary. The pain of this loss came back just like it was 23 years ago. Remembering this brought back tears and she quietly wept.

The day dragged on, and she was finally able to mobilize her best defense, anger. When Margaret got angry, she could do anything. She said angrily to herself, "I will not lose Mary again." She immediately packed some clothes and got into her car and drove to Dallas. She caught a plane to Albuquerque and arrived about 3:00 p.m. She got a cab and told the driver to get to the Albuquerque General Hospital as soon as possible. When she arrived, she jumped out quickly, and the driver had to run to catch her in order to get his fee. She hastily paid him and gave him a big tip. She rushed into the reception area of the hospital and hurried to the reception desk. She anxiously asked if Mary McGregor was a patient in this hospital. The receptionist slowly went thru her roll-a-dex and said she was seriously ill and only relatives could visit her. Margaret felt a relief and said, "I am Mary's aunt, and I want to see her immediately." The receptionist referred her to the administration office as she could not give her permission to go to Mary's floor. This enraged Margaret, and she stormed over to the suite that said Administration. She opened the door and slammed it against the wall. This startled every one, and she went to the nearest desk and demanded to see the Administrator or anyone who had authority to let her see her niece, Mary McGregor. Margaret was making such a loud noise that Joseph Smith, the administrator, opened his office door to see what was causing all of this disruption. Margaret immediately went over to him and said, "I am Mary McGregor's aunt, and I want to see her immediately." Smith brought her into his office and called the floor that Mary was on and asked the nurse to get Mr. McGregor on the phone. When Andy came to the phone, Smith told him that a woman named Margaret Canaday Baker was in his office and was claiming she was Mary's aunt. Andy said, "I will be right down to see this woman."

Andy walked slowly back to the room where Jonathan was working and said, "A bad apple relative has appeared out of the woodwork. I will go down stairs and deal with it." He didn't explain it further and slowly walked to the elevator. When he got to the administrator's office he walked in and said, "Hello, Margaret." As he stood there, both of them were remembering their last meeting.

Margaret opened the conversation by saying, "Andy, let's put the past behind us. I behaved badly, and I lost 23 years. Mary is seriously hurt, and I want to help her, and you all I can. Will you please let me in your lives again?" Andy was surprised and pleased by what Margaret said, and told Smith she was a relative and should have the same privileges as he and Jonathan. He took Margaret's arm and took her to Mary's floor. He brought her into the room with Jonathan and introduced him as a close friend of Mary's. When Margaret sat down, Andy related the problems that Mary was having. He said, "She has lost all of her past memory and doesn't even know her own name. Presently, she will only let Jonathan be in the room with her. She doesn't recognize me and has strictly forbidden me to come into her room."

Jonathan looked at his watch and realized that it was time for him to visit Mary. He left and hurried to Mary's room. Mary was awake and seemed pleased to see him. Jonathan sat and waited for Mary to talk. After a while, Mary said, "I had a horrible night. Every two hours I would have this horrible nightmare. I seemed to be falling into a black hole. I was helpless, and several times I awakened screaming. I am afraid of the night." This sounded to Jonathan like the nightmares he had when he was recovering from his wounds. He was at the U.S. Naval hospital in Bethesda, Maryland. He said, "Mary, I had similar dreams when I was recovering from war wounds." "You had dreams like this?" she asked. He replied, "Yes, I had wounds all over my body just like you have." "What did you do about it?" Mary asked. He said, "Mary, in those days there was a bunch of guys on my ward with similar wounds, and all had gone through the same nightmares. When a new guy came in and had these nightmares, one of us who had gone thru these nightmares, would stay by this guy's bed all night. If he started showing signs of struggling, we would touch him and gently reassure him that it was just a bad dream, and he would be okay. If this didn't work, we gently awakened him by saying his name. We would tell him we would stay with him until he felt better. This worked for me." Mary was silent for a while and said, "I don't even know my name."

For a while they were silent, and Mary asked if he would come back at seven tonight. She said, "I am having a lot of pain, and I want a shot. I need to go to sleep." Jonathan got up and said he would be back at seven.

When he returned at seven, she had a smile on her face. She said, "When I went to sleep, I started having that dream, and I dreamed you were with me. You were gently talking to me, and the bad dream went away. I slept fine and awakened a few minutes before you came." She continued, "Oh, Jonathan, thank you for telling me of your experience. It was a great comfort for me." Jonathan didn't say anything, but he had a big smile on his face. They were silent for a while, and Mary started talking about what she had been thinking.

She opened the conversation by saying, "I know now I can trust you, and I want you to visit me as much as you can. I particularly need you at night. Would you stay as long as you can this night?" Without hesitation Jonathan said, "Yes." This time when she had pain she didn't want him to leave, and he stayed until supper. He fed her and gently cleaned her face when she finished eating. He told her that he had to leave for an hour, but when he returned, he would be able to spend the night beside her bed. She said, "Thank you," and smiled.

During the next hour, Jonathan met with Smith and instructed him to get a small bed moved into Mary's room and to have a comfortable lounge chair placed next to her bed. He further requested that two "like" meals be brought to the room every time food was served. He wanted the trays to be identical. After this conference, he hurried to get with Andy and Margaret. He told them what had happened, and all were greatly relieved. He told Andy to take Margaret and find Mary's house. They both should set up headquarters there, for tomorrow, they would go to Mary's old office and get all of her possessions.

He also suggested to Margaret that they start exploring the house and try to familiarize themselves about how Mary lived. He grabbed himself a sandwich and hurried to Mary.

When he entered the room, he saw a troubled look on Mary's face, which quickly changed to a welcoming smile. The two trays of food arrived, and Jonathan fed them both. When they finished eating, he gently cleaned her face and without thinking kissed her lightly on the forehead. Mary smiled and said, "Don't you know that kissing is for the lips only." A second kiss was immediately applied. They both looked at each other and realized that they had crossed major boundaries in their relationship. Jonathan sat in his lounge chair, and they silently looked at each other.

Mary was wondering what was happening to her. She had all her adult life never invited a man to kiss her. Maybe Jonathan was right when he said that they had known each other for twenty years. He also said that they had never been close emotionally. She knew now she desperately needed a caring person, and Jonathan certainly was that person. As her thoughts continued, she started looking at him carefully. He was a tall, slim, and muscular man. He had light brown hair and it curled all over his head. He had brown eyes and he definitely was a handsome man. She thought that it would not be hard to fall in love with him. This thought pleased her, and she started to smile.

Jonathan had been in his thoughts. He was excited that Mary had let him kiss her. He hoped that this closeness would grow into Mary loving him. His thoughts were not searching like Mary's as he knew he loved Mary. As he sat quietly looking at Mary, he noticed her suddenly beginning to smile. He asked, "What are you thinking?" Mary continued smiling and said, "Jonathan, I was having pleasant thoughts about us. I had never realized how much I have needed a person in my life who really cared for me."

Jonathan got a big smile on his face and had a hard time keeping himself in his chair. Mary raised both of her arms toward him, and he jumped up and gently embraced her, and they had a long and tender kiss. Mary felt just tender caring, but Jonathan was greatly aroused and got back into his chair. Mary knew what had happened, and was pleased by it.

Eight o'clock came quickly, and it was time for Mary to get her pain medication. She found herself saying to the nurse that she didn't think she would need it. Mary still had pain, but now it didn't seem to bother her. She knew that she was not afraid of the night as Jonathan would be with her. She wondered a lot as to whether her reaction to pain related to her fears and her loneliness. She found herself drifting off to sleep, and the last thing she saw was Jonathan. Her last thought was, "I will not have to think more about fear and loneliness." During the night Mary had three episodes that would have lead to her nightmares. Jonathan was awake, and he would gently rub her leg and talk in a soft voice reassuring her that she was okay, and she went back to sleep. Each time this happened in her dream, she would see Jonathan, and she would slip off into a deep sleep. Her last beginning nightmare was at three o'clock. By that time Jonathan was very tired and fell asleep. Mary continued to sleep and had no further trouble. She awakened at six thirty and looked over at Jonathan. He was curled up on his left side in a lounge chair. There was a peaceful expression on his face. To her, he looked boyish, and she felt motherly feelings towards him. These lasted for only a few seconds, and she found herself having sexual thoughts about him. These two thoughts surprised her. How could this be? As she was pondering this, Jonathan awakened and looked anxiously at Mary. He saw her smiling. A slow smile came on his face. He asked her about her night and she said, "This was the best night I have ever had. I know I am exaggerating, but it is so nice to have you with me. I felt so safe." At this moment, the breakfast came, and he fed both of them. It was only the second meal together, but they both expected to have a fond kiss. After they finished Mary said, "I am supposed to have a conference with my orthopedist. His name is Doctor Bates. I did not choose him as my doctor. He was on emergency call that night of the accident, and he did the initial emergency care of my arm and my right leg. Jonathan, I am uncomfortable with this man. Will you help me? He will be here at ten o'clock." He responded with an eager yes and told her he would have to leave as he had a meeting with her father. Mary flinched. "Please, Jonathan, don't talk about that man. I still can't accept him as my father." Jonathan realized his mistake and said, "I am sorry I said that. Will you forgive me?" She replied, "No apology is necessary. This man is just one of the many memory problems I have, and all I can do now is keep things as simple as possible. It took me almost three weeks to accept you, and I am so glad I did." Jonathan smiled and waved goodbye saying, "I will be back shortly."

    Jonathan walked rapidly to the elevator and hurried to Joseph Smith's office. He caught Smith just as he was about to leave. Saying he was sorry that he had to interrupt his exit, but it was very important that he consult with him. This greeting of Jonathan's surprised him as Jonathan was usually abrupt, and the request to consult with him was very unusual. Without further ado, Jonathan got quickly to the point. He said, "This Doctor Bates is meeting today with Mary at ten o'clock. He is planning to do surgery on her right leg. As you know, it is shattered in several places, and she has been told that a rod must be placed in her leg bone. Is this man a qualified doctor to do this?" Smith replied, "Jonathan, I am a hospital administrator, and I am not supposed to discuss the qualifications of any doctor that is on our staff. I will say this, however, this doctor in now under investigation as to two procedures he has done. I can't tell you anymore."

    This irritated Jonathan, and he left abruptly without saying another word. He immediately called Don Wright and asked if he knew a Doctor Bates. He replied that he didn't know him, but he knew that he had two malpractice suits filed against him. Jonathan asked further if he knew who was the best orthopedist in Albuquerque. Don, without question, replied Doctor James Wilson. He continued by telling him of a friend who had a serious injury, and he saw Doctor Wilson. He had a remarkable recovery. This was all the information Jonathan needed. He thanked Don, and as he was about to hang up, Don asked about Mary. Jonathan said, "I will call you tonight, but I have to get to a ten o'clock appointment." Don said, "Hurry," and hung up. Jonathan rushed to the elevator, and when he got to the second floor, he ran to Mary's room.

When he opened the door he saw a worried look on Mary's face, which changed into a warm happy smile. They just had time to say hello when in walked Doctor Bates. Doctor Bates was a pompous man with a middle age spread. As he approached Mary, he purposely ignored Jonathan. He didn't realize that this was a bad move, for he found himself standing in front of a strong, angry looking man. This man was telling him his services were no longer needed, and it would be best for him to leave the room immediately. He tried to ignore this man and looking over his shoulder asked Mary if this was her desire. She replied with a firm yes. He backed away from Jonathan and in huffy tone said, "I have never been treated this way by such an ungrateful patient." Jonathan's eyes turned a dark shade of brown, his lips tightened to a straight line, and he told him in no uncertain terms that he would not have his fiancé, he caught himself and said, dear friend, be insulted in that way. Jonathan said, "If you don't get out of this room immediately, something serious is going to happen to you." Doctor Bates almost ran out of the room.

Several nurses were standing in the hall outside of Mary's room heard the exchange. They smiled and were glad that for the first time, Doctor Bates had been told where to get off. Mary was very pleased to be championed by Jonathan, and said, "You must have found out some bad things concerning Doctor Bates." Jonathan was silent for a minute and said, "Mary, I don't know what came over me. That pompous fool really triggered something in me. Yes, I did find out some bad things about his ability to do orthopedics. I also found out the name of the best orthopedist in Albuquerque, and I will get him to see you when he finishes surgery." Jonathan continued saying the company that she sold her business to, wanted her belongings to be removed from her former office. They told me that they agreed to give you 30 days to do this, and they wanted for me to start doing it today. He didn't say that it was her father who had been called, for she had told him not to mention that man. She was puzzled by this information and said, "Jonathan, I don't know what you are talking about. I need to see a lawyer. I want to give power of attorney to you as you are the only one I can trust. My lost memory makes all of what I am hearing seem bizarre." Jonathan said, "I will get a lawyer to come to your room after we have met with Doctor Wilson."

After lunch, Dr Wilson came in. He was a tall thin man, who was in his mid fifties. He had a kind face and introduced himself to both of them. He shook hands with Jonathan and went over to Mary's bed. He asked about her pain and asked if anyone explained what needed to be done to make her well again. She said, "No one has really talked to me about my injuries. They seem mostly to be interested in controlling my pain. Since Jonathan has come back in my life, I don't have as much pain. Now I don't take pain medication." Dr Wilson was impressed and told her so. He looked over at Jonathan and said, "You must give me some lessons in pain control." They all laughed. He continued, "I have looked at your x-rays, and it is time we operate on your right leg. You have fractured your right leg, your tibia, to be medically correct, in three places. The only way I can set and hold the fragments in your leg in the proper alignment is by using a small metal rod. With this operation you will heal well. I will cast your leg up to your mid thigh and make it into a walking cast. This allows us to ambulate you and start your physical therapy. Tomorrow we will operate and later on today I will take off your arm cast and put your left arm in a sling. I have talked to your head doctor, and he will remove your head bandage late this afternoon. Do you find this agreeable with both of you?" Mary spoke for both of them and said, "Thank you, Doctor Wilson, for coming into my life. I now have two men that I trust." She pointed to Jonathan and him. When Doctor Wilson left, Mary raised both arms to Jonathan and said happily, "Come give me a big kiss." He needed no encouragement. The neurosurgeon came and removed her head bandage and said he would be available if she needed him, but other than that, he was needed no further.

When Jonathan called Don Wright and told him of her desire to have him as her power of attorney, there was a long silence. He said, "I will talk to Andy and this will be no problem. Because she has a brain injury and has a loss of memory, she will need expert opinions as to her competence to request this." He said, "I will come over immediately and bring two people who could make that judgment." He hung up and Jonathan related what he had said. Mary smiled and indicated that this was no problem for her because she had Jonathan and nothing fazed her. They sat in silence, and Jonathan wondered if Mary had caught his calling her his fiancé. Mary had tried on fiancé and was not sure she wanted to go that far with Jonathan, but she felt he was a darn good candidate. She decided to let it pass for the time being, but she definitely was interested.

In about an hour, two professional men appeared along with Don Wright. Don introduced the two men as Doctor Edwards and Doctor Bucklin. He asked both men to tell Mary their qualifications. Mary was impressed by what they said.

Doctor Edwards had a PhD in Clinical Psychology from Stanford, and Doctor Bucklin's PhD in Clinical Psychology was from Vanderbilt. Mary was interested in their training and asked questions about it. Some of the questions were profound and amazed them. They both asked her many questions and did mental status evaluations. In front of Don Wright, they stated that except for her loss of memory, she was sound of mind and had the ability to make good judgments. They found Mary so interesting to talk with that they lingered and had to be reminded by Don Wright that they had to appear before the Judge to give their report. He just happened to be waiting for them. They hurriedly left, and she and Jonathan were alone.

For a while, they just looked at each other. Jonathan broke the silence by saying, "Mary, you really impress me. Those two Doctors really liked to talk with you." Mary smiled and said, "I like to please and impress you." She continued asking how he was able to get such fine men to come so soon to help her settle her problem about her power of attorney. Jonathan answered, "To answer this, I would have to explain my relationship with Don Wright.

Don and I were drafted in February, 1967. We were assigned to the Marine Corp. and had basic training together. In November, 1967, we were sent to Vietnam and were replacements for the marines stationed at Khe Sanh." Pausing Jonathan asked, "Are you sure you want to hear all of this?" "Jonathan, you are becoming very important to me, and I want to know as much as I can about your life," Mary answered. Jonathan continued saying, "It was very hot and humid in Vietnam. It seemed to Don and me that all we saw were jungles, swamps, and rice paddies. Shortly after we arrived, Don and I were sent to the town of Hui. We were assigned to be a part of the marines and soldiers who were to guard the MACV [Military Assistant Command Vietnam] headquarters in Hui. We didn't know what all of this meant. All we knew was that it was located south of the River Perfume, and we were in defensive positions around these headquarters. I will never forget that day. I was on night patrol around the headquarters, and at exactly 3:40 a.m. on the 31st of January, 1968, mortars and rockets exploded all around us. Most of the initial attack was north of the river, and we had time to gather whatever men available and make a defense of our headquarters. Fighting was intense, and the North Vietnamese troops were trying to establish a beach head across the Perfume River in order to assault our headquarters. Don and I were in the group of men trying to push them back into the river. We were not strong enough to do this, so we were ordered to fall back so that our artillery could fire on the bridgehead of the North Vietnamese troops. As we were falling back, Don fell wounded. It looked like he was going to be killed by the advancing enemy troops. I turned back and stayed by Don fighting off the advancing troops. That is all I remembered. I was told later what had happened. Apparently I stood off the attacking soldiers until our forces counter-attacked and rescued Don and me. I woke up one week later in Bethesda, Maryland. You know the rest. Anyway, we spilled blood together and have been blood brothers since. I would do anything for him, and he feels the same about me, hence all these people here today." There was silence as both were thinking about this story.

Jonathan broke the silence and said since she was to have surgery tomorrow he needed to break away and take care of some business. Mary anxiously asked if he would be back for supper. He said of course and gave her a gentle kiss. After leaving the room he hurried to the nearest phone. He called Andy and Margaret and said he would be at Mary's house shortly and got directions for it. He called Don and was told the hearing went well, and he would have power of attorney in the morning.

Chapter VII

Andy and Margaret did as Jonathan suggested and went to Mary's home. Mary had a housekeeper and a yard man. The property was in excellent shape. Andy had brought a camera, and they took pictures of the entire house. They picked out their bedrooms and settled down to get acquainted with this lovely home. As they were hurrying around, Margaret got into her natural mode and started ordering Andy around. This irritated Andy, and he stopped and said in a firm voice, "Margaret, come here and sit down. We need to get something very clear before we go any further. I remember your telling Nancy that I was a weak person who could not stand up for his rights. I am sensing that you might still have that same idea in your mind." While he was talking, Margaret was looking at his face. His angry look scared her. Andy continued saying, "When Nancy was alive, I wanted to get along with you for Nancy's sake, but this time that is not an issue. If you are going to stay here, you need to understand that I will not tolerate you bossing me around. If you want my help, you ask for it and not demand it." He asked her if she understood him. She said yes meekly. She had no desire to use her anger defense, as at this point she was really scared of his anger. With this exchange, they got busy with what they felt needed to be done.

Later on Margaret asked Andy if it would be all right for her to do the cooking. Andy smiled and said, "Yes, Margaret, as I remember, you were a fine cook." With this Margaret went happily into the kitchen and started supper. It was then that they started receiving calls from Don and Jonathan. Don explained Mary had requested Jonathan have her power of attorney. Andy had no problem with this. His only hurt feeling was that Mary didn't believe he was her father. A short time later Jonathan called and said he would be with them shortly as he had important things to discuss. Andy said, "If it is about the power of attorney, this is no problem for me." Jonathan thanked him for his understanding but said his business had nothing to do with that.

They hung up, and Margaret saw tears in Andy's eyes. For the first time in her life, she felt real concern for Andy. She went over to Andy and put her arms around his shoulder. In a worried voice, she asked if Jonathan had told him some bad news. Andy saw the concern in Margaret's eyes and told her about Mary wanting Jonathan to have her power of attorney. He didn't really object about the power of attorney. It was the fact that Mary didn't recognize him as her father and didn't want him around her. Margaret couldn't think of what to say and just stood holding him close to her. It surprised Andy that he felt comfort from Margaret holding him.

A short time later Jonathan arrived. He was surprised about the size and the beauty of Mary's home. Her house was surrounded by an eight foot high rock wall. He entered thru an iron gate and the drive ended in a circle in front of the house. The house was built in a Pueblo style. It was rectangular with very few outside windows. All of its windows opened to an interior garden area. When he entered, he was in a large room that opened directly to the inner courtyard. It was a two story building, and the upstairs had a wide porch that went all around the interior garden. The downstairs had six large bedrooms and opposite the entrance across the garden he could see the kitchen and the dining areas. Things like houses didn't usually impress Jonathan, but here he was really bewildered. Mary had built the most impressive home he had ever seen. Andy and Margaret found him standing in silent wonder. When he realized they were staring at him, he became all business.

He told them all about Doctor Bates and Doctor Wilson. He was particularly concerned about the need for them to close Mary's previous office. The main problem was that Mary was to have surgery tomorrow at 7:00 a.m. He wanted them to be at the hospital at 6:00 a.m. He said, "You will be able to see Mary rolled to the surgical wing, but you are to make no effort to greet her. While she is in surgery, I will be with you, and we will stay in the surgical waiting room until the surgery is over. Dr Wilson said that periodically he will send his nurse out to advise us of the surgical progress. When the surgery is over, Doctor Wilson will come and discuss what has happened, and tell us his expectations." He continued saying, "Mary will be in the recovery room for about 2 hours, and I can only see her when she is completely conscious." Jonathan indicated that during this time, they must go to Mary's former company and begin removing her things. He wanted them to stay at her office as long as it took to remove her belongings and bring them to her house. He left wanting to be with Mary as much as he possibly could. Andy and Margaret sat down to their first meal together.

When Jonathan left Mary, she found herself going over all the events that had happened. Jonathan's firm hand steadied her. She realized that she was becoming dependent on Jonathan. It troubled her to have any dependency. Now she, not only needed Jonathan, but also she was hopelessly dependent on him. It surprised her that she felt no anxiety. She buzzed for her nurse, and when she came, she asked her to help with her applying makeup. She said, "My boy friend has, for several weeks, seen me in bandages. Now, I want to look pretty for him." The nurse smiled and went to her locker and got out her cosmetics bag. She brought everything she had and started working on her face. She brushed her hair and tried to give it a casual look. When she finished, she held the mirror so Mary could see her new appearance. Mary was pleased and settled back waiting for Jonathan.

When the time came for him to return, he was not there. She began feeling anxious. She told herself that she was being foolish, but the anxiety increased. She was just beginning to cry when Jonathan walked in. He saw her tears and rushed over to her and tried to comfort her. She found herself saying, "Oh, darn, I have messed up my makeup, and I don't look pretty for you." Jonathan said, "Mary, I know you are trying to look pretty for me. All through this time together, I have felt that I was so lucky to have a beautiful woman interested in me. Even with your bandages, I was always struck with your beauty." Mary laughingly said, "Oh, Jonathan, you are such a wonderful liar. I have been lying here realizing how dependent I have become upon you. When you weren't back, I thought you weren't coming, and I started crying. This dependency is new for me, and I am somewhat frightened by it."

Jonathan thought he would test her memory and asked if she was thinking about Tom Carlson. She suddenly gasped. This was the first time that she had recognized a name in her past. She quickly tried to go further with this memory, but all she remembered was that Tom Carlson had abandoned her. Jonathan remembered Doctor Jones' admonition not to probe any flash memory. He encouraged her to relax and not push herself. She slowly relaxed, and the nurse came with medication that Doctor Wilson had ordered. He wanted her to have a good night sleep, and he had ordered the sleeping medicine that he felt would do the job. They brought a liquid diet that night, and they drank their supper. Mary laughed at Jonathan's insistence on having the same diet as she did. She was really pleased that he wanted to share everything with her. She ended up saying, "You can't share my surgery." He replied, "Maybe not physically, but I surely can mentally."

She slowly drifted off to sleep, and Jonathan settled down for the night. She slept soundly until 5:00 o'clock. A new nurse came in and turned on all of the lights. She inserted a large needle in the wrist vein of her right arm. At the open end of the needle she inserted a small plastic tube that was connected to a "Y" shaped object. To one end of the "Y" she inserted a connection to a long tube that ran to a large plastic bag that contained fluid. She regulated its flow to a slow drip. From the other part of the "Y" she drew blood. When she finished drawing blood, she stopped its flow. It was only then that she explained to Mary what she was doing. She said the blood was for tests so as to have a preoperational base line. The plastic tubing in her arm was to keep her from having any further puncturing of her veins for blood or giving of fluids. Jonathan interrupted and said he had gone thru all of this in a naval hospital, and he would explain it to Mary. The nurse left, and he explained it all to Mary. At six o'clock another nurse came in and gave her a shot. She explained that this was a drug that would relax her but not put her to sleep. Mary discovered it did exactly that, and she felt relaxed and dreamily talked to Jonathan. At six forty-five they came in and rolled her bed into the hall. Jonathan walked by her on their way to the surgical wing. Just before entering the wing, Doctor Wilson met them and chatted with them, and then rolled Mary into the operating room leaving Jonathan standing facing closed doors.

Doctor Wilson was talking to Mary as she was rolled into the operating room. Rolling up to the operating table, she was carefully lifted onto the table, after the attendants had carefully unhooked her leg from its pulleys. The anesthetist began talking to her about what he was going to do. He said, "I am going to give you some medicine in your vein, and you will go immediately to sleep. The next time you are awake, you will be in the recovery room, and your relatives will be with you." Mary thought what relatives and then everything went blank.

Jonathan with a heavy heart walked slowly to the surgical waiting room. When he arrived, Andy and Margaret were waiting. For a while nothing was said. Andy started talking. He said, "I have something to say to both of you. I have been wondering why Mary doesn't recognize me. As I think back on our lives, I realize that Mary and I were never close. I know at one time she was very close to you, Margaret. When you accused me of having something to do with Nancy's death, I just reacted with anger. Over the years I have been haunted by that accusation. I have reviewed my life with Nancy many times. I have come to the conclusion that, Margaret, you were right. When Nancy and I married, we were very much in love. I was 24 years old, and I felt I could conquer the world. In one year, Mary came into our lives. We were short of money so I joined the National Guard as it seemed to be an easy way to get extra income. When December 7, 1941, came, I was immediately called up, and by July 9, 1943, I was in Sicily. I had left my wife and my three year old daughter alone. If it hadn't been for you, Margaret, I don't know how they would have survived. At that time, I was not grateful as I knew that you didn't like me, and I feared that you would get too much control of my family. I was too busy to think much about this as many things were happening to me in Italy. It was there that I was wounded and was shipped back to the United States. I know I am rambling, but you need to know the war changed me. I was no longer a nice guy. I was impatient and easily roused to anger. I didn't try to change this as I felt I deserved to be like I wanted to be because I had fought for my country and had suffered severe wounds. I left an orderly productive ranch, and I came back to an abandoned house with all of the pastures grown up and no cattle. Nancy realized that she was not capable of keeping the ranch going and lived with you, Margaret. I was already angry about what had happened to me and now coming home to nothing really burned me up. It seemed that all of my anger shifted to Nancy. I blamed her for not staying on the ranch and keeping it up for my return. Deep down, I knew that she would have kept it up, but Nancy was a city girl and just didn't have the learning to understand ranching. I got back to my family in the spring of 1945. Mary was five and didn't know me. For the next seven years, Nancy had a bad time with me. She became ill, and the doctors could not find anything wrong with her. I was not sympathetic and accused her of malingering. She just gave up, and one day when I returned home, I found her dead. Mary was sitting by her bed crying. When she saw me, she jumped up and said words I will never forget "YOU KILLED MY MOTHER." Suddenly, all of the love I had lost for Nancy flooded in, and I was overcome with grief. I thought of killing myself. I don't know why I didn't. I became withdrawn and went on automatic. Somehow Mary survived. When I could start being human again, I had a talk with Mary. I told her I was so sorry that I had been cruel to her and her mother. She listened to me and said, "When mother was dying, she begged me to stay with you. She said that you desperately needed love, and she was not able to give it to you. She didn't want you to be alone." Mary added, "You are no longer my father, and as soon as I can, I am leaving. I am sure that is why she was so interested in Tom Carlson. He was a way to get away from me. I know now this is why Mary rejects me. I now think that somewhere in her unconscious memory her hate lingers."

Margaret and Jonathan were stunned by what they had heard, and all they did was sit quietly. They did not look at him, and said nothing. Silence dominated the room. Each was in their own thoughts. Jonathan felt a surge of concern for Mary as he had no idea what she was experiencing when he knew her in high school.

Margaret was puzzled. She didn't know how to respond. When she came back from her thoughts, she told Andy, "Let's let bygones be bygone." His bringing up all of that miserable time and awakening all of her despair and anger troubled her. She said to herself, "I don't want to go through this again. I am not going to beat up on this poor man." She got up and did something she thought she would never do. She went over to Andy and pulled him up into a standing position and put her arms around him and said, "Andy, I forgive you. I'm sure Nancy did. I think your main problem now is forgiving yourself. I am determined to help Mary recover, and I think you're a very important part of that recovery." She finished this by giving him a firm hug, and they both sat down. Andy still was numb from telling all this and didn't know how he was going to go on with this process of working with Mary. He feared what it would be like when her memory returned, and she as an adult confronted him with all his bad behavior.

Jonathan aroused himself from this period of silence and said, "We've got to get back on track. There is much to do in regards to Mary's office. As you know, we are going to stay here until we hear from the doctor as to the outcome of her operation. We all know that we can't see Mary until she is out of the recovery room. Doctor Wilson told us before she went into surgery that her recovery period would be extra long, and he estimated it would be over two hours. I have the idea that this is how we should progress during that period. We will all hurry over to her company and go up to her office. There we will try to find the personnel that were close to her and hire them to help us remove her files and her personal belongings. The new management wants to occupy her space." After saying this, they settled down and waited.

An hour and a half later, Doctor Wilson's nurse came out and reported things were going well, and they should be through with surgery in another forty minutes. To Jonathan, those were the longest forty minutes of his life. Finally, Doctor Wilson appeared, and there was a broad smile on his face. He immediately told them that Mary had no trouble during the surgery, and he was able to get good alignment of her tibia bone. He said, "Of course, you remember my lecture on bone anatomy, and you know it is her leg bone I am talking about. I still predict that she will need the same amount of time in the recovery room as I have indicated. I would encourage you to use this time to take care of any business you need to do." They thanked him and immediately got up and left.

Mary's company was on the eastern side of Albuquerque and just off Interstate 40. Actually, it was the first exit to Albuquerque that led to her company's grounds. When they drove up to the company, they were astounded at the size of the complex. There were a number of buildings, and they were arranged in a half-wagon wheel form. The hub of the wagon wheel was the main administrative building. It was twelve stories high and had the influence of the Pueblo architecture in it. On the rim of the wagon wheel were located four modest buildings, each about four stories high. All buildings were connected by skyways. They parked in front of the main building and walked into the lobby. It was basically a huge corridor, which ran the width of the building, and they could see through the opposite doors the inner courtyard. As they walked down this wide corridor, they stopped at the reception desk indicating their purpose. They were told that they were expected and needed to go immediately to the twelfth floor. When they arrived on the twelfth floor, they were met by Mary's personal secretary, Canela Montesinos. She was very pleased to see them and immediately took them to the section that had been Mary's office. It was really a large suite, and Mary's office could have served as an apartment. Canela told them that many times Mary would spend the night there. She said, "My boss is a very determined woman, and it seemed like she never had time enough to do all she intended to do." With that, Jonathan outlined what they wanted to accomplish. He said, "I don't know how long we are going to have to be here, but some of us intend to stay here until the job is done. We are trying to reconstruct Mary's office in her home, and we are looking for someone to be her secretary in that location. Do you have any idea who that person might be?" Canela said, "I have been informed that I will be terminated tomorrow. I would be greatly honored to be Mary's secretary." Jonathan couldn't believe his good luck. He immediately hired her, and told her that after she finished working here, she should go out to Mary's house and help them start organizing the office there. He said, "I will pay you whatever your salary is with Mary. Is that going to be satisfactory?" She quickly said yes and was very grateful for the opportunity being offered to her. With that they all began to work. After an hour-and-a-half, Jonathan left and hurried back to the hospital.

When he arrived back at the hospital, he immediately went to the surgical waiting room and began to pace back and forth. He knew that Doctor Wilson was right in saying she was okay, but he still had to see it with his own eyes. Finally, a person came out and told him that he could now visit Mary. When he walked into Mary's recovery room, he could see that she was drowsy and somewhat uncomfortable. She didn't greet him, and he went over and sat beside her. He took her hand in his and bent over and kissed it gently. Even though Mary was still in discomfort, a slight smile appeared on her face. As she slowly awakened, she began talking to him. She said, "When I left you they rolled me into this very cold, white room and very carefully unhooked me from my apparatus. It was slightly painful, but they were gentle. I was moved to the operating table, and a person at my head told me I would go to sleep immediately, and I did. The surgery must have been nearly over, and they must have been lessening my anesthesia because I started to dream. It was a pleasant dream, and you and I were in a field of bluebells. We were a bunch of kids running and playing. It felt so good. Now, I feel like hell." At this point the nurse came in and told them that she must be moved to her room.

Getting back to her room was somewhat trying for Mary, but when she settled back in her own bed without all the paraphernalia, she felt much better. As they were lifting her into her bed, she felt the cast on her leg. She was shocked at how it came up to her mid thigh. She had wondered, "How am I going to take care of my bodily needs?" The nurse gave her a sedative, and she went to sleep.

When Canela Montesinos greeted Mary's family, she was impressed with how handsome Jonathan was. She didn't understand how Mary could have kept this man from the staff not knowing about him. All of the staff was convinced that Mary was going to be a bachelor woman because she showed no interest in any male as far as they knew. She wondered how he came into Mary's life.

She had always thought that her life was quite similar to Mary's. She didn't know about Mary's failed early romance, but that experience had happened to her. Her thoughts drifted back to that moment in time. The Montesinos family was a prominent family in New Mexico. Her ancestors came to New Mexico in the early 1600's and were driven out by the Indians only to return and reestablish themselves. Her father had inherited a large ranch outside of Santa Fe, New Mexico. His father had been a strong dominant person, but her father was never responsible. When he inherited the ranch, he let it bit by bit disappear as he gambled and drank and completely destroyed his inheritance. He was finally killed in a drunken brawl, and she and her mother were left with nothing. At an early age, she had met this young man who also came from a prominent family. She thought they had fallen in love, but when her father lost the remains of his estate, that young man lost any interest in her. Canela, at the age of twenty, had to support herself and her mother. She went to a local secretarial school in Santa Fe and worked herself up in proficiency so that she could demand a private secretary's salary. She said to herself, "They now call that a personal assistant." One day when she was working in one of Mary's supply companies, she heard that Mary was in search of a private secretary. She applied and was accepted by Mary and had been with her for five years. She had seen the company grow from a struggling concept to being very significant in the cosmetic industry. She had lost all hope of marriage and decided that her career would be the main focus of her life.

Chapter VIII

Jonathan felt torn by the demands that he felt existed. He needed to be with Mary for her sake and his, but he had problems with his own company and getting Mary's office established in her home was difficult for him. He knew that Margaret and Andy would work hard, but they didn't have the ability to organize an office. Canela would help in the future, but at this phase, he felt the total responsibility. When he left his company, he had told his ranch manager, Bill Williams, and David Fremont who was manager of his production company not to call him unless some emergency evolved.

When he got back from Mary's old office, he had received a call from David Fremont. He had some production problems he wanted to discuss with him, and he had thought it was important enough to place a call to him. He could not talk to him at that time and told him he would call back as soon as he could. When Mary went to sleep, he went out to the nurses' station and made a call to David Fremont.

When David picked up the phone and learned who was on the other end, he immediately launched into all the problems that were troubling him. To Jonathan, they were routine problems and he said, "There must be something else that is troubling you because you handle these problems well." David said, "Our producing wells are decreasing their production, and this is of concern to me. We need to investigate new areas of the State for oil exploration. As you know I have been pushing the Four Corners area, and you have been resistant to this. I think now we really need to decide something because pumping is decreasing." Jonathan replied saying, "I will be tied up in this area in Albuquerque for several months. I want you to come to Albuquerque and set up an auxiliary office. You are to start the process of searching for leases in the

Four Corners area. I remember your telling me that you knew a Navajo Indian who had become a petroleum engineer. Did he come from the Four Corners area?" David said, "I think he did, but I am not sure." Jonathan continued to say, "Check into this possibility as you will need help acquiring leases in this area." While they were talking, Fremont was going through his card index and found this Navajo's name. It was George Kayani, and he came from Teec Nos Pos, a town four miles south of Four Corners. With this information, they hung up.

Fremont immediately called George who was working for an oil company based in Houston. He related to George his desire to have him come and work for his company as they were beginning to explore leases in the Four Corners area. George was excited to have this job opportunity, particularly because it would place him near his old home. Fremont asked him to fly to Roswell, New Mexico, where their base office was, and they would talk about salary and conditions of his contract. It was late Friday afternoon when he made this call. George said he would be there Saturday morning on the first plane. Fremont met George Kayani at the airport and took him immediately to his office.

When they arrived at the office, he laid out maps of the Four Corners area. He said, "Our production in this area is decreasing, and we are looking to explore new areas. We have studied the geology of the Four Corners area, and we think there is oil to be had there. My boss, Jonathan McCandlish, asked me to contact you to see if you could help us in this search for leases and to study the geology of this area." This excited George, and he agreed to make the move immediately. Fremont asked what he expected to earn. George said, "At least as much as I am making now, and if there is any extra, I would appreciate that too." Fremont said, "Our company shares profits with its employees, particularly at a senior level. That means if you are successful in the Four Corners area, you can expect bonuses." They discussed things further, and a contract was drawn up. George signed it. Fremont informed him that he was moving the office to Albuquerque, and he and George would work out of it. He was in the process of developing a staff to help them in their work there.

David Fremont left immediately for Albuquerque and arrived late that afternoon. When Fremont called Jonathan, he told him he could live in his condo near the hospital, and Jonathan would call him the next morning. They would discuss the development of his office.

When Jonathan got through all of this complexity, he settled back in a lounge chair next to Mary's bed waiting for her to awake. Six o'clock came, and Mary's post-operative diet was brought in, but Mary was still asleep. Jonathan had deliberately ordered a separate diet for him as he knew he needed more food than Mary was going to get. He ate his supper, and still Mary slept. It wasn't until 9:00 p.m. that she awakened. She didn't want to talk, but she did say she was glad he was with her. She said the pain of the surgery was almost as severe as the pain of the accident. Jonathan asked, "Are you in pain now?" She said, "No, but I feel it is coming on." With that, Jonathan went to the nurses' station and asked for pain medication for Mary. It would be like this all through the night, and neither one got much sleep.

When morning arrived, Mary roused up and was surprised to feel much better. The anesthesia had worn off, and the pain in her leg was not so severe. She asked Jonathan to ask the nurse to come in and freshen her up. She said, "Jonathan, you know a woman always feels better when she feels she looks good." They didn't talk for a while, and she drifted off into sleep. Prior to her going to sleep, he told her he would be leaving for a couple of hours, and he would be back for her lunch period.

Andy, Margaret, and Canela worked all day transferring all of Mary's materials. They moved everything to a room in Mary's house, which they had decided would make a good office. This room connected to a smaller room, which would serve well as the secretary's office. They settled in for the night, and Canela left to go to her home. Margaret and Andy were alone again, and both were somewhat uncomfortable together. Both were remembering Andy's confession of his cruelty to Nancy. Both were wondering how they could reestablish what they had going for them prior to this confession. Finally, Margaret said, "Let's have some supper and not try to deal with this problem we have between ourselves until we are more comfortable." Andy was appreciative of, not only this statement, but also he remembered her coming over and embracing him when he was so despaired.

They quietly got up and worked together preparing the evening meal. They ate in silence and went into the TV room and listened to some of the programs that were on. They didn't try to talk any further about their conflict and went to bed.

The next morning Canela arrived, and they began organizing Mary's office. Jonathan had instructed Canela to have several telephone lines brought to the house as he expected to office there temporarily. He told her he intended to establish a permanent location for Fremont and his staff. As she was doing all this, in walked David Fremont. Jonathan had called him and given him this address and said this location was a temporary office as later they would get one established in downtown Albuquerque. Fortunately for them, the telephone lines were in place, and Fremont established himself in an adjoining room. This room opened into the small room where Canela was, and he asked her if she would be able to do some secretarial work for him. She said, "Mr. Fremont, I was hired by Mr. McCandlish, so I am sure if you work for him that he would not object to me helping you."

David Fremont always had problems working with women. He was rather brusque and demanding, and it was hard for him to keep a secretary. Canela had a lot of experience with men like that, and she knew just how to handle him. She was so skillful at this and was so efficient that David was taking second looks at her. He noticed that she was a very attractive woman, but he thought she was probably a Mexican. He wondered if he had a prejudice about this. That was just a fleeting thought because she brought in some papers, and they were done so well all he could think was that this was really a competent person.

At 10:00 o'clock George Kayani arrived, and he set up himself in the same room with Fremont. They spread out on a table which had been brought into the room and started looking at maps of the Four Corners area. When Canela came into the room, she saw these maps and saw that they were near Ship Rock. She said, "Oh, that's where my father had a huge ranch." Kayani looked up and said, "What was the name of your ranch?" She replied, "The Montesinos Ranch." George didn't say anything in front of Canela, but when she left the room, he said, "That ranch is a very large ranch, and I know the story about what happened." Fremont was immediately interested, and Kayani told him how her father had lost the ranch by his drunken gambling nature. Fremont was impressed about her heritage and was thinking more seriously about her as a person. This was very unusual for Fremont. He liked women, but he had an amazing ability to turn them off. He was gruff and insensitive, and he didn't know he was doing this. He was to find out later that although Canela was a very calm and pleasant person, if she felt she was being abused, she would let that person know immediately to stop their abuse.

Late that afternoon, Jonathan came out to Mary's house and talked to Fremont about what he had accomplished that day. He met Kayani and indicated that he wanted him to go with Fremont to the Four Corners area the next day and start exploring the area. He asked Fremont if he had explored the geology of that area so they wouldn't waste time looking for areas they wanted to lease. He told Kayani that he expected him to use his skills with the Navajo people so as to help him acquire any leases that might be on their lands. As they were talking about leases in the area of Ship Rock and Four Corners, Canela interrupted and said that she and her mother had mineral rights to all of her father's Ranch. This was a startling revelation to Jonathan, Kayani and Fremont. This would mean that they would be negotiating with Canela for a large part of that area. Canela went on to say that her mother realized that her father was destroying the ranch. She insisted that all mineral rights be transferred to her just prior to him losing the ranch. She divorced him, and part of the settlement was that he could make no claim on these mineral rights. They were all amazed at the forethought of Canela's mother. When all of this information sank into them, they were silent. Canela felt excited as maybe this would give her the means to recover her father's ranch.

Jonathan ended their conference saying that they should find the boundaries of the old Montesinos Ranch, and they should begin working there first. He said, "For the next week, I have no intention of working with you at all. I am going to spend all of that time with Mary as she will be starting physical therapy, and it is a very important time for her. If you have any message to communicate to me, you will use Andy and Margaret to pass them on to me."

Andy and Margaret had not talked about his confession. Margaret could see that he was troubled by it and knew that it was time for them to talk. She said, "Andy, we can't hide from the past. We need to talk about what happened to Nancy, Mary, you, and me. I had no idea that you had been in such terrible battles in World War II. Nancy did tell me that you had received several medals because of your bravery in action, but it made no impression on me. When you returned and were so hostile to Nancy, I could hardly contain myself. Nancy was my baby sister, and I loved her dearly. In all that time when you all were having so much trouble living together, Nancy would talk to me and say, 'I know that Andy is troubled and regardless of what he says or does, I still love him.' That word, love, still clings in my mind, and I am thinking that you must be something special to deserve such a loyal wife. I know I have been blind to whatever good qualities you had, but when you told this story honestly, I was impressed as to how sad and distraught you were. I said to myself that if Nancy could forgive you and love you then I should do the same thing. I don't want the word 'love' to confuse you. I just want you to know how powerful I think love is." Andy thought about what she had said. He didn't know how to respond to it. He had not expected her to have any compassion for him. He was prepared to receive all the scorn she might have for him without him protesting at all. Instead, here she was being very kind and conciliatory. After being quiet for a few minutes, he said, "Thank you, Margaret, for being kind. I have much to carry right now, and it is a great burden. My main fear now is how I will find my lost daughter."

Jonathan returned to the hospital and was determined to stay there until Mary was able to leave. He called his ranch foreman, Bill Williams, and told him to continue his purchasing of Black Angus cattle and not to bother him over the next week. He said that in the near future, some geologists would appear on the ranch, and they would be surveying the ranch. He would give him the name of this company when he signed the contract with them. With this out of his mind, he could be with Mary.

Chapter IX

As he sat there by the bed, Mary roused up from her afternoon nap, and they began talking. It was nothing serious. They were just chatting about their current lives. Mary was saying to Jonathan that she knew things would be different for her when she again had some control over her life. At the present time, her helplessness seemed to be the binding force between them. "I don't want to have a relationship based on dependency. I have no memory of what I was like before, but somehow I feel I was a capable person. It's hard for me to realize I don't know anything about thirty-five years of my life. Now that I have the feeling that I am going to get well, I want you to explore with me what you know about my previous life."

Jonathan responded by saying, "You remember when you had that flash memory of Tom Carlson?" She nodded, "Yes." He continued, "Why don't we use that name as a beginning point of what I know about your past." She hesitated about this idea. When he mentioned Tom Carlson, she felt an emptiness and fear. She said to Jonathan, "When you said Tom Carlson's name, I felt fear. Having that emotion seems important to me. Let's see what we can do with it." Jonathan said, "Well, let's start with this. Tom was a handsome young man and very popular in Socorro High School. You started dating Tom in your sophomore year, and all the girls were very envious of you. You were close to each other for two years, and then you suddenly broke off." He didn't go into the details of why. He just let that sink in to see what she could do about it. Mary was quiet for a few minutes, but nothing came to mind except a feeling of anger. Out loud she asked herself the question, "Why do I feel angry?" Jonathan didn't say a word. He remembered Doctor Jones telling him that when you try to recapture memories, you make the involved person do most of the work. Obviously, Mary was trying hard to make sense of this feeling. Suddenly, she said, "Now, I feel lonely. I seem to have two feelings now, anger and loneliness." She struggled, but nothing else came forth. As they sat there, they sort of drifted away from their work, and when they realized it, they smiled and she said, "Maybe it's time for us to relax and enjoy ourselves. Maybe later something will happen in my mind that will be more than just feelings." The evening meal came, and this time she could feed herself. To her, it was a great accomplishment, but Jonathan had different feelings. He enjoyed feeding her and always gave her a small kiss after she had finished. Mary was developing the ability to read Jonathan and she said, "Jonathan, just because I am feeding myself doesn't mean that you don't kiss me." They both laughed at the forwardness of her, but to Jonathan it was a thrilling statement. It told him that maybe Mary really cared for him. When they finished, she asked him to stay the night. She said, "I still have fears of the night, and I don't know if I will ever get rid of them."

Canela left her work that day, and as she was driving home, she had great news to tell her mother. Taking care of her mother had been a burden at times, and on several occasions, men who had been interested in her stopped their relationship when they discovered her mother was part of the deal. She thought of the happy times with her mother, and now the fact that her mother had been so forethoughtful, they had a chance to be financially secure. Usually when she came home, she was tired and exhausted. She would go to her room and just rest. Her mother usually had supper prepared, and when she came out, they would eat their meal in silence. After supper she would go into the TV room, pick some program and stay with it until she got sleepy. They wouldn't talk. They just existed together.

This time, however, she came in excited, and she ran up to her mother and gave her a big hug. Her mother was astounded, to say the least, but she knew from the expression on Canela's face something very good must have happened. Her first thought was that Canela had found a new boyfriend, but much to her surprise, Canela was talking about mineral rights on their old ranch. Canela related how she had been sitting in her new office, and she was working for two people. One was for Mary and one was for a man who worked for Mr. McCandlish. It was the second person, a man named Fremont that brought all of this into focus for her. He had set up his office next to her small office and constantly was calling on her to come in and help him. About ten o'clock that day, a young man who looked like a Navajo Indian came in, and they started looking at maps of the Four Corners area. One of those maps included Ship Rock. Canela said, "As you know, Mother, Ship Rock was right near our huge ranch. It seems that they were going to try to get leases in areas near the Four Corners area with the idea that there might be oil and gas in that area. They are starting geological surveys and are trying to find the ownership of property around that area. When I realized what they were doing, I told them about the Montesinos Ranch. The man that looked like a Navajo immediately knew of the ranch and said he knew what happened to it. That wasn't very important to them, but when I told them you owned the mineral rights to that land, they got very excited. The big question now, Mother, is whether the geological survey shows any possibility of oil under that old ranch of ours. I don't know why, but I just know that we do have oil there. So here I am spending a lot of money I don't have, and imagining a lot of things I haven't imagined before. Most of all, I am happier than I have been in a long time." They hugged each other and sat down and had a very unusual supper time. They were talking about the ranch, and the exciting times they had before her father had become an alcoholic. They were into the good times now for the first time in a long, long time.

When Fremont realized that Canela came from such an important family and had such a valuable asset, his whole attitude towards her changed. He had discredited her as being a Mexican when he first met her. When her skills became manifest, he began to admire her. Now he realized that she came from a very old and important Mexican family whose history with New Mexico dated back to the 1600's. All of this was exciting, and for the first time he allowed himself to think of the fact that she was a beautiful woman. David never thought of the beauty in anybody. He was factual about everything and put no aesthetic value on anything. Now he was beginning to think new thoughts. These new thoughts were a little unsettling. He had developed his life into routines, and these routines were so dominant and so necessary to him that he had no time to ruminate about anything. He caught himself day dreaming, and his whole routine was disrupted. For the first time in many years, he began to feel some anxiety. His well encapsulated world was being invaded, and he was unsure about it.

George Kayani was very excited about his new location. He was 34 years old and had never married. He had chosen early in his life to go to a school not connected to the reservation. He had separated from the reservation. He knew that he wanted to marry a Navajo woman, but his work never brought him around any of them that he could be attracted to. He rarely went home to the reservation because he had chosen a white man's life, and he wasn't really a part of his old community. This new business location gave him access to the Navajo reservation as they were going to explore the geology of the area he grew up in. Very likely he would be dealing with important chiefs of the clans in that area, and just possibly he might find a woman who had taken the same road he had. He knew that a reservation woman would never fit into the world he was in. She would have been bound to the tradition that he had given up, and she would be miserable in a white man's community. He was in a motel room when he was having all these thoughts, and usually, in this kind of circumstance, he would have turned on the TV and kept it on until he went to sleep. Instead, here he was daydreaming and trying to picture what this new Navajo woman would look like. His day dreams stirred him up sexually, and so for the first time in a long time, he felt the need to be with a woman. These thoughts made it hard for him to go to sleep, and he was awake until past midnight.

The next week was filled with activities connected with Mary's learning how to mobilize herself. The cast was quite cumbersome, and she had a hard time maneuvering with it. She started her physical therapy and was improving rapidly the use of her left arm. She was only making slow progress in her ability to walk. What she was doing was waddling. She would get very exasperated with herself and depended on Jonathan to encourage her as she could not give that to herself. They tried to reengage working with her memory, but they still just had Tom Carlson and the feelings of anger and loneliness. Because they were at a stalemate, Jonathan decided to introduce some factual information about her life.

He thought he would start with the experience in the Madison Square Garden when he won the National Championship, and she won $1.25 million. He said, "Mary, I want to tell you a true story about what happened between us. We were both 25, and I had done very little with my life except going around to rodeos. You had gone through advanced training in finance and were working in a firm in New York City. You made a big bet on me in the rodeo I was in, and I won. Your winning a 50 to 1 bet was going to change your life forever. Does this bring anything to your mind?" Mary said, "That is a wonderful story, Jonathan. Let me think about it for a few minutes. As you know, I seem to get into feelings and not conscious thoughts." Jonathan said, "Doctor Jones told me that in working with people who have a memory loss, you try to get them to meditate on whatever it is that is in their past memory. I tried to find out from him how to do this. All he could say was that in meditation, one tries to block out all external stimuli and let whatever is within yourself become manifest. I know this might sound strange to you, but this is the best way I can describe it. Since he told me this, I have been trying to meditate on a level that I am not aware of what's going on around me. I didn't have the deep meditation that he described, but it did give me some insight that I probably do have thoughts that are not completely conscious to me. Why don't you try that now? Get out of bed and sit in this reclining chair I am sitting in and let it fall back and just close your eyes. Try to block any conscious thought that might come to your mind and see if you can't disconnect yourself from your surroundings. I will put myself behind you so that there will be no distractions." He got up and closed the window blinds, and the room darkened. Mary did as he said and closed her eyes and every time a thought would come, she would start humming. She had taken yoga classes in the past, and they used the term *Ah hum* in a humming voice to block out thoughts. She did it for about twenty minutes with no progress and said, "Maybe if I try to do it later on, I will be more successful. Your presence is so powerful with me, I can't really think of anything except your presence."

Over the next two weeks, she improved remarkably, and she became very skilful using her crutches. The third week post op, Doctor Wilson changed her cast to one that just covered her leg and her foot. It was still a walking cast. He encouraged her to use mostly her crutches as he wanted to limit weight bearing on her leg. By the fifteenth of March, she was discharged. During this period of time, Jonathan had stopped spending the night and came mid-morning till noon. He didn't stay for lunch but came late in the afternoon, and they ate supper in the hospital cafeteria.

As her discharge date approached, Jonathan started preparing Andy and Margaret for her return. He felt that Margaret was the one person in Mary's life where she had good experiences. He felt that Margaret should be introduced to Mary. He told Margaret that he wanted her to go afternoons with him and see how Mary responded. With Mary, he started talking about her Aunt Margaret. This name didn't disturb her, and even though she didn't remember her, she wanted her to come.

Their first meeting was frightening for both. After the introductions, they all three sat down and tried to start a conversation. Margaret was a talker, but this time she was very quiet. Jonathan didn't want to interfere as he wanted them to find a way to talk with each other. Finally Mary said, "Jonathan tells me that you are my loving aunt." Margaret, with a deep sigh replied, "Yes, I am. You were very important to me for the first twelve years of your life. Actually, you and your mother lived with me until you were five years old." She paused and waited to see how Mary responded. Mary was thinking as Margaret was talking that her words meant nothing to her, but her voice was sincere and loving. Her tenderness and loving feelings came across strongly as she expressed her memories. Mary could sense her fear when she stopped talking, and it reminded her of when Jonathan first came into her room.

Mary responded, "Margaret, may I call you by your first name?" "Yes, please do," exclaimed Margaret. "Margaret, I have no memory of what you have said, but I do like you. I don't want you to be afraid to talk to me about anything you want to. Please don't expect me to recognize any memories you have about our previous relationship because all of my past is lost to me. It is frightening for me to have lost 35 years of my life. If you can be patient with me as I try to recapture my past, I know that we can get along famously. Jonathan has told me in the next week I will return to my home. I have no idea what he is talking about. I don't remember any home, or any of the things Jonathan has told me. If I didn't trust Jonathan, all of this information would have been very frightening to me. Can you understand this?" Margaret said a firm yes. Mary continued saying, "Jonathan has been working with me for over six weeks trying to educate me about memory loss." There was a silence and Margaret said, "It is hard for me not having you back as you were to me, but, yes, I can be patient. I dearly love you, Mary, and I will do anything to help you. I hope you will be able to be patient with me because I am in this new experience, and I feel very clumsy." Mary smiled and held out her hand to Margaret. Margaret jumped up and grabbed it with relief spread all over her face. There were tears in her eyes as she said, "Oh, Mary, thank you so much for letting me in your life." She turned her head away trying to stop the tears that just wouldn't stop.

They talked for a few more minutes, and Jonathan said he felt that he and Margaret should leave. Mary told them that she didn't need a week with Margaret to decide that she wanted Margaret to be the person to help her get reconnected to her home. As they left the room Jonathan said, "I will be back shortly." In the hospital waiting room Jonathan talked briefly with Margaret. He told her he was very pleased with their meeting, and one of their big problems had been solved. Mary had a friend. Margaret came over to Jonathan and hugged him and gave him a kiss on his cheek. She said. "Oh, Jonathan, you have given me hope that I can find Mary and be a part of her life. For 23 years I have longed to have Mary back in my life. How can I ever repay you?" "Your loving Mary is enough for me," said Jonathan. Before he left the hospital to take Margaret home, he went back to Mary. She was obviously happy. She immediately began exclaiming what a wonderful person Margaret was, and for the first time, she felt that she could cope with leaving the hospital and living in her home. She held out her arms for a goodbye kiss, and they parted.

The drive to Mary's house awakened the old Margaret. She talked constantly. It didn't matter if Jonathan was listening or not. She just had to express her joy and relief. Jonathan barely heard a word that she was saying. He knew that in a week he would be back working, and he wanted to find a place where he could have an office and a place to sleep that would be near Mary. When they arrived home, Margaret rushed in and immediately started telling Andy what had happened.

Jonathan knew that he had another hard task to perform. How was he going to tell Andy that he could not stay in Mary' house, when she returned. He had tried on several occasions to talk about Andy with Mary, and she would always get angry and refuse to have anything to do with him. He knew this would be very hard on Andy as he could see Margaret was accepted, and he wasn't.

As things settled down, Jonathan said, "We have some housekeeping to do. I have to locate a place to live and an office that is close to Mary. Andy, you will need to find a place to live. We have to keep to a minimum number of people in the house when Mary comes home. She will not tolerate any persons around her that she does not trust." With these words both Margaret and Jonathan looked at Andy. To their surprise, Andy had been thinking the same thing. He told them that he thought that he might have a solution for himself and for Jonathan. "Over the past few weeks, I have been exploring Mary's estate. Near the gate is a house. I don't know what Mary planned it for, but it really is a small home. It has three bedrooms with baths and a large living area with a small kitchen. I think that Jonathan and I could live there and possibly you, Jonathan, could have an office there." This possibility excited Jonathan, and he said, "Let's go see what we have got." He told Canela to come with them to see if she felt that she could set up an office there. They all liked the set up, and Jonathan told Canela to start immediately getting phone connections and a fax setup in place as he had a lot of business to catch up on.

A short time later Fremont and Kayani arrived and reported that they had found a place for Kayani to stay, and they would be ready to start full steam working on the geology of the Four Corners areas. Fremont was immediately aware that big changes were in progress, and he didn't like changes being made without his being consulted. Canela knew just how to handle this. She went over to Fremont and gave him some of his files and told him to follow her. Fremont was too shocked to say anything and took the files and followed Canela. They walked the 200 feet to the new location, and not a word was said. When they got there, she told him his desk was in the big room. He would have his own phone, and she would have a fax machine and a copier in her office. She would take his dictation either in her office or next to his desk. That would be for him to decide. Canela knew that it was disorder and confusion that was difficult for Fremont, and if things were somewhat orderly, he would be amenable to the change. Fremont was saying to himself, "I surely do like this lady. I am going to get Jonathan to hire her as my personal secretary."

Over the next week, a lot of work had to be done, so when the time came for Mary's return, everything was functioning well. Jonathan had told Mary that he would live in a small house located on her estate. Mary knew nothing about this house but was pleased he would be near. Jonathan and Andy knew that Andy's staying close to Mary would be conditional on whether Mary found him. As of now, Mary did not want to have any contact with him.

Chapter X

GEORGE KAYANI HAD BEEN BUSY doing other things than geology. While talking to the members of the council of the Navajo clans concerning leasing Navajo land, he casually mentioned he was looking for a Navajo wife. The members of the clans didn't think any Navajo woman would be interested in leaving the reservation. One member suggested that he might be interested in a Navajo school teacher. He said that she had gone to the University of New Mexico. Many Navajo men had approached her, but she was not interested in being a reservation wife. He said, "She is getting too old for Navajo men, and maybe you might like her." George was excited by this suggestion and immediately drove to her schoolhouse. It was a one room schoolhouse, and she had just let her students out. George introduced himself and told her that he was interested in finding a Navajo wife. He told her that he was interested in a Navajo woman that would leave the reservation and be his wife. Mary Hani was amused by his frankness and said, "You surely sweep a woman off her feet." They talked for a while, and he felt that she was a very attractive woman. He suggested that they have some time with each other and see if they liked each other. She told him she had the weekends free. So began a new relationship.

When Mary left the hospital, she was using only one crutch and her walking cast. Jonathon drove his car up to the front entrance and helped Mary get out of the wheel chair and into the car. Mary liked his Mercedes convertible. As they drove away, Mary wanted to go to the place where she had her accident. She also wanted to go to where they were keeping her wrecked car. Jonathan started to object, but stopped and said, "Mary, that seems like a morbid request. I have not wanted to go near those places." Mary responded, "Jonathan, I have a lot to do to understand about what has happened to me. I think that visiting the accident place, and my wrecked car will be a beginning point." He didn't argue and drove to the place where her wrecked car was stored. Jonathan had her car stored as he wanted to inspect it for any information he might get concerning Mary. As he thought about it, he decided going to the car could serve two purposes. One would be Mary discovering what a terrible accident she had experienced. The other would be Mary finding her personal effects in the car. He hoped that her finding these objects herself would have a greater meaning to her than his bringing them to her. Her car had been stored in a closed stall, and Jonathan had the key. Mary was shocked to see the damage that had been done to the car. The driver's side was crushed in as was the roof on the passenger's side. She could see where the Jaws of Life had cut her out. She said to Jonathan, "How did I ever survive that?" She wanted to see if any of her belongings were in the car. She found a purse, a shattered cosmetic case, sun glasses [not broken], papers scattered all over the front seat and a hat. There was dried blood all around the driver's area. She looked in the glove compartment and found a copy of a driver's license. The picture on it was her, and it clearly said Mary McGregor, age 35, brown hair, blue eyes, 120 lbs, and five feet six inches tall. Her address was Number One, Riverview road. There was no doubt that she was in the picture, and here was an official document saying Mary McGregor. She said, "Oh, Jonathan, I really must be Mary McGregor." She walked around the car one more time and without saying another word got into Jonathan's car and closed the door. Jonathan pulled down the sliding door and locked up and got into the car.

 Nothing was said for a few miles, and Jonathan wanted to know if she still wanted to go to the site of the car wreck. In a low voice, almost a whisper she said, "Yes." They got on Interstate 40 and drove to where the last entrance to 40 was as it left Albuquerque. Jonathan slowed down his car and turned on the emergency lights. As they passed the entrance, Mary studied it intensely. She could see marks on the concrete and asked if that was where the truck hit her. He said, "Yes." she turned to Jonathan and said, "I must have not even gotten onto the interstate." Jonathan said, "You were not on the interstate when the truck hit you." Mary exclaimed, "What a bizarre accident. I just happened to be in the wrong place at the wrong time." They drove a short distance and exited on Riverview

Road, and in a mile she was at the gate of her house. Jonathan opened the gate with a hand signal, and they drove up to this beautiful home. Mary gasped and was overwhelmed by what she saw. Margaret had been waiting for them and ran out to greet them. Off in the distance, Andy stood alone watching Mary's arrival with tears in his eyes.

From late January, Margaret and Andy had lived in Mary's home. During that time they had many conversations. When Andy tried to look more into his relationship with Nancy, he wanted Margaret to listen to him. Margaret told Andy that she loved Nancy dearly, and she wondered if she should be the one he talked to concerning his later behavior with Nancy. After all, she was the one at Nancy's funeral who was so angry and accusatory of him. Andy indicated that was exactly the reason why he wanted her to listen to his thoughts as she would not be sympathetic and would be more critical of what he might say.

Andy continued saying, "I want to get a better understanding of my behavior. When I married, I was an easy going fellow. I think I was kind and considerate of most people. I liked to have friends, and life was easy for me. I met Nancy in my junior year. I was an agricultural major, majoring in large animal management. When Nancy and I started to be serious with each other, I told her about my relationship with Clyde Carlson. I said that we had been childhood friends, and we intended to go together to New Mexico and start buying ranch land. We intended to be cattle ranchers. We had already drawn up partnership papers, and we had decided I would go to college and get academic knowledge of ranch management. Nancy told me that she was a city girl, and she didn't think she would fit in with those plans. This didn't stop our dating, and you know the outcome. After graduation, we moved to Socorro, New Mexico. Things went well for a while until Clyde and I fell out over some of his dealings. Some of my neighbors came to me telling me that Clyde had done illegal things, and he was going to be arrested. I didn't believe them, but Clyde was arrested, and he went to trial. During the trial some bad things came out about Clyde's behavior. To me, they were unethical, but it was the judgment of the jury that it didn't raise to the level of breaking the law. He was acquitted, but our relationship was damaged beyond repair. We divided our properties, and I needed Nancy to help me on the ranch. She was trying hard, and I was patient. When we broke up our partnership, I needed some steady cash. I thought that

Charles Samuel Betts

joining the National Guard would be the answer. Having a college degree qualified me to apply for officers training. At that time we would go to night classes and had two weeks training programs. In short, by 1940 I was made a second lieutenant in the Infantry. This was helpful, but as you know when war came, I was activated into the service on May 12, 1942. Mary was born in 1940 and was two years old. Nancy and I knew she could not manage the ranch. I decided to board up the house and hire my neighbor to check on the property until I got back. Nancy wanted to stay with you, and I was grateful to you for taking care of her. Up to that point things were working out.

By March, 1943, I was in North Africa. I had been promoted to Captain and was in charge of an infantry company. We were in the 45th infantry division headed to Sicily which we invaded on July 9, 1943. We had many hard battles in Sicily. I lost many men that I had trained. This continued in Italy all the way up to Anzio where I was wounded and returned to the states. When I look back on those days, I can see now how much I changed. I became a hard, impatient man. I lost all feeling of kindness. I had seen too many fine young men that I knew and loved killed. During all of this combat, I was awarded several medals, but they meant nothing to me. I began to hate. At first it was directed towards the Germans, and then I began to hate everything. I didn't know it then, but I think now I became psychotic. When I returned to the United States, I had very severe wounds in the chest and the abdomen. As I recovered from these, they recognized my mental problems, and I saw a nice doctor who helped me a lot, but he was not able to help me get back my feelings of love and tenderness. I came home an impatient, demanding, mean person. In other words, I was a complete bastard. This is what Nancy and Mary endured until she died. It was the shock of the loss of Nancy that broke this viciousness in me. This loss of hate made my grief unbearable. When you and Mary accused me of killing Nancy, I knew you were right. I was planning to commit suicide. When Mary told me that she was staying with me because Nancy asked her to, I decided I had to live and be a better father to Mary. I failed because I had severely damaged our relationship. I am thinking of leaving as I realize that I will only complicate Mary's recovery. I know I have told part of this before, but I can't stop going over it all of the time. All I keep saying is, "I am sorry, so sorry, but the people this belongs to are Nancy and Mary, and they are gone for me."

Margaret listened silently to what Andy said and said nothing. All through his story she had many feelings. They ranged from anger to compassion. She had already forgiven Andy, and she realized as she listened to him that she had fallen in love with him. She wondered what she could say to him. She didn't want him to leave. Without thinking she burst out saying, "How dare you think about leaving. You failed Mary once, are you going to do it again? Sure it is tough to love someone when they seem to hate you. Mary needs a father now more than ever, and here you are, a war hero who can only think about running away. You listen carefully to me. For the past six weeks, I have been with you day and most of the night worrying about Mary. I have seen how much you care for her, and now I realize how much you loved Nancy. In fact, I can see now why Nancy fell in love with you because I have fallen in love with you." This last remark startled Andy because he felt the same way. For a few moments, they sat looking at each other. Neither knew how to express what was now clearly stated and thought. They had spent many years with bitter feelings towards each other, and now they were thinking about their love for each other.

Andy was the first one to speak. "Margaret, these six weeks being together has been the happiest periods in my life. When I told you and Jonathan why I thought Mary hated me, I was afraid you would attack me. Instead you were very kind to me. Your action changed all of my feelings toward you. I found that I had grown very fond of you. In the last two weeks, I fell in love with you. My loving you and the hatred of Mary have become too difficult for me to handle. I knew I would have to leave Mary's home, and you and I could not face the reality of this." Margaret got up and came over to Andy. She hugged and kissed him firmly on his mouth and said, "Andy, if you have any idea of escaping me, forget it. When I love a man, I expect him to marry me. I am not going to let you go. I don't know how things are going to work out with Mary and me. I hope she will forgive us both, but if she doesn't, we have a second chance in life. When Edward died, I thought I was going to be alone the rest of my life. Now I have you, and I will never let go of you." "Oh, Margaret, oh, Margaret," whispered Andy into her ear. They sat on the couch holding each other feeling they had been lost, and now they had found love again.

Chapter XI

When Jonathan came to the guest house, he found Andy packing. Andy told him that it would not work for him to stay so close to Mary. There was always a chance that she would run across him. He said, "I have found a small condo near here, and I will stay there until things work out for Mary. I want to be the first to tell you Margaret and I are going to get married." Jonathan was not surprised. During the past six weeks he had noticed the change in the way Margaret and Andy related to each other. Both had obviously become more caring for each other. Jonathan was happy for both of them and asked when they planned to marry. Andy said, "It will be soon as we are both in our sixties, and we don't want to lose any time not being together." Jonathan couldn't help but think of Mary and him. He wished that he had the same bond with Mary. Mary and he were good friends, but for now she didn't want to have any romantic interests.

When they left the hospital and were driving to her home, Jonathan told Mary that he loved her and wanted to marry her. After a pause, Mary said, "Jonathan, I have no memory. I have known you only three months, and I know that you are a loving and caring person. I have been frightened, and you have comforted me. I have seen you defend me and help me in very intimate ways. If I had my memory, I know that I would say yes in a New York minute. I must find some way to regain my memory before I commit myself to you. I hope you can be patient with me because I know I care for you." They were silent the rest of the drive to her home.

David Fremont settled rapidly into his new location. Canela made it easy for him to get his work done. He marveled at how he was changing. He attributed it to getting out of the Roswell area and getting a new work project. For some reason he wanted to house in Albuquerque. He would get up early every morning and drive to the Montesinos Ranch. The new owner was a banker in Santa Fe and was interested in the possibility of oil on his property. David was surprised at his interest and willingness for them to explore his property. He got the impression that this Mr. Fernando Gonzalez thought he owned the mineral rights. Fremont didn't say anything, but he decided to go to the local courthouse and see who really owned those rights. The records showed that a Mrs. Carlos Montesinos received ownership in 1965. In 1974, these rights were transferred to a Miss Canela Montesinos. Fremont was surprised and wondered why Canela had not told them of her ownership. He finished his work early that day and rushed back to his office in Albuquerque. He wanted to talk to Canela. When he arrived, he found a warm cinnamon roll and a hot cup of coffee fixed the way he liked it resting on his desk.

Canela had a friend in the court house where her mineral rights were recorded. This friend called her saying that a Mr. Fremont was looking up her mineral rights. This didn't surprise her as she knew that he would eventually do this. What puzzled her was why so early in the exploration of the Montesinos ranch.

Fremont was completely overwhelmed by Canela's thoughtfulness. He sat down at his desk and didn't know what to say. He thought it had been many years since any one showed this kind of attention to him. The best he could do was to clear his throat and say, "Thank you, Miss Canela." Canela casually said "You're welcome," and went into her office to finish her day's work. Fremont was lost for words and just sat at his desk and ate his cinnamon roll. To his surprise, it was the best roll he had ever eaten. With much hesitation, he got up and went into Canela's office. He cleared his throat and said, "Miss Canela, I was in your old court house today, and while there, I looked up your mineral rights. I was surprised to find that you were the owner." Canela looked up with a stern look on her face and said, "Mr. Fremont, did you look up those rights because you did not trust me to tell the truth?" When he saw her apparent anger, he hastened to say absolutely not so. He then told her of his dealings with Mr. Gonzalez. "I got the impression that he felt he owned the mineral rights. I went there to clarify the issue as I felt if he really didn't own them, he would not let us explore his ranch. I felt that Jonathan and I should immediately get you to lease your rights to us so that he could not prevent us from surveying his property." Canela was silent. She finally said, "Mr. Fremont, I will have to see a lawyer before I sign anything." Fremont indicated this was the right way for her to handle it. He continued saying, "Miss Canela, Jonathan and I value your work very much, and we wouldn't do anything to hurt you." He cleared his throat again and continued, "I find it hard for us to converse with all this mister and miss business. Can we dispense with it and call ourselves Canela and Fremont?" Canela smiled and said, " Yes, Fremont." They didn't know it at this time, but they had crossed a boundary and things were to change for them.

When Mary arrived to her house, she was emotionally drained. Jonathan did not get out when he saw Margaret waiting for Mary. When Mary realized that Jonathan didn't intend to get out, she turned and said, "Jonathan, I know I have hurt you, but please come in the house with me." Jonathan tried to not show his pain and got slowly out of the car. As he came abreast to her, she turned and pulled him to her and gave him a warm kiss and said, "Please be patient with me, Jonathan." Margaret knew something must have happened but said nothing. They all walked into the house, and Margaret began showing Mary around her house. The main thing that impressed her was the room where her office was. It looked so professional, and on the walls were pictures of her receiving awards. She looked at the pictures of herself, and here again she was named Mary McGregor. The office pleased her very much, and she asked Margaret who fixed up her office like this. Margaret pointed to Jonathan. Mary looked at Jonathan, and there was a warm glow to her eyes. Nothing was said, and they completed the surveying of the whole house. Mary was amazed by what she saw. To some extent she was fearful. She said, "Oh, Jonathan, I thought I was over being afraid, and here in this huge house, I feel lost. I know I told you I wasn't going to be afraid, but I am. Would you just please stay for supper?" Jonathan said he would and reminded her that this experience had quite a lot of new things to absorb. They went into her office and sat down and talked. Mary found that just talking to Jonathan calmed her. Her new found courage returned, and she smiled saying, "I am so content being in this room with you."

Andy left as Mary was walking into her home. He drove slowly to his condo. He felt lonely and left out of the lives of the three most important persons in his life. When he got set up in his condo, he called Margaret. She had just finished showing the house to Mary. She told Andy that Mary was overwhelmed by all of the new things she was seeing. She was able to talk with Andy now because Mary was talking to Jonathan. Andy was telling Margaret how much he missed her. They both laughed over this, for they had been separated less than two hours. He said, "What I am really missing is knowing I will not be with you tonight." Margaret felt the same. She said, "I don't know if Mary would want me to stay very long as we have only been with each other for one week." They continued talking about what came to mind, for they didn't want to hang up as that meant they would be without each other for the rest of the night.

After supper Jonathan got up to leave. Mary said to herself, "I must trust me and not depend on Jonathan to deal with my night fears." She got up from the dining table and walked with Jonathan to the front door. She asked where he would sleep that night. He told her about what they had done with her guest house. That house was big enough so that he was able to have a bedroom, and also an office. Mary asked him to come by tomorrow for breakfast, and at that time she wanted to learn about his business. It pleased Jonathan that she wanted to know more about his work, and in some way this seemed to ease the pain of her rejecting his marriage proposal. They kissed good night, and he left. Both felt an emptiness.

Mary went back into the living room and started talking to Margaret. She started by saying, "I know that Jonathan thinks you are my Aunt. I want to know that, too. I have no idea how one recovers a lost memory, but I have been thinking one way might be by your telling the story of my life with you." Margaret thought it was a good idea and started off by talking about Nancy, Mary's mother. "Your life began with me when you were two years old. Your mother, Nancy Canaday and your father, Andy McGregor, had been married for two years when you came into their lives. When you were nearly three, your father went to war. Your mother and you couldn't stay on your ranch without your father, and you came to live with me and Edward Baker, my husband, in Waco, Texas. Your father was away until 1945 when you were five years old. So, for a little over three years we all lived together. For me, those days were some of the happiest days of my life. When your father came back from the war he was severely wounded and was in the hospital for three months. Your mother went to the army hospital where your father was and stayed with him until he could come home. During that time, I had you all to myself. You were the daughter I was not to have. We liked each other, and we went every place together. I was the one who took you to the first grade. We loved each other very much. It was in December when your mother and father came to Waco, and you left to go to your family's ranch. I was distraught and Nancy wrote and told me that you missed me very much. The next summer, you came to stay with me for the whole summer. You did this until you were twelve. That was the year your mother died. I acted badly at the funeral, and your father and you decided that I was a person you didn't want to be with." She paused in her story and brushed away a tear. Up to this point Mary was enthralled by this story, but seeing Margaret tearing up, she interrupted and asked, "Why did you behave badly?"

At this time, Margaret didn't want to go into details. She briefly said that Nancy was her only sister, and she was two years younger than her. "I was too protective of her, and I had not wanted her to marry your dad. When Nancy died, I was convinced that your father was partly the cause of her death. I said some bad things to your dad, and you heard them. You told me that you were going to stay with your dad, and since I had the bad feelings towards him, you said you would never see me again. I was devastated, and I was to have no contact with you until six weeks ago. That would be for 23 years. I know you will find this story hard to believe, but I have and still do love you very much."

Mary was a careful thinker, and she felt that she had not heard the complete reason for Margaret's outburst at her mother's funeral. Since she had no memory, she didn't know how to question her about details. She thought to herself that she would think further about this story, but for now she had enough to deal with. They went to their separate bed rooms and prepared for sleep. As Mary lay in bed, she went over Margaret's story, and it was 12 a.m. before she went to sleep. Just before she went to sleep, she thought, "Margaret is a kind person, and I believe she is telling the truth. Why can't I remember?" She slept soundly and waked the next morning refreshed.

When Jonathan left, he went to Mary's guest house and felt lonely. He had wanted Andy to stay and was disappointed that he had left. When he would feel lonely, he did what he had done all of his adult life. He got to work with a stack of papers that he had neglected. He worked until 2:00 a.m. and fell exhausted with his head on the table and didn't awake until Canela opened the front door. He roused up and after greeting Canela, he told her of all the work he had done and listed things he wanted her to do. He called Mary and said, "I am not coming to breakfast as I need to get more sleep." When he detected disappointment in her voice, he said he would come for lunch. Canela got immediately to work on his material, and he went to sleep hearing her typewriter clicking.

While Mary and Margaret were sitting around the breakfast table, Mary told Margaret that she appreciated her telling about her relationship with her. "As I was listening to you about my mother and dad, I started wondering about what my dad was like. Margaret, do you believe the man that claims to be my dad is in fact my dad?" Margaret responded that she, not only believed it, but also she knew that he was in fact her dad. Mary thought for a minute and said, "When I reviewed in my mind your story, I got the impression that I didn't like my father." Margaret indicated that was true as far as the story went. "In the past weeks, I have reconnected with your father, and now I have an entirely different feeling for him. In fact Mary, Andy and I are going to get married this Saturday. We both have felt that you had some hidden feelings about us, and that your rejections of us had nothing to do with your loss of memory." Mary responded, "I have never rejected you, Margaret, but that man who was trying to hug me was too much for me to take at the time." Margaret said, "Someday I would like to tell you about your dad." Mary didn't respond, and there was a long silence. With nothing else said, they both got up, and each went in separate directions. Mary went to her office and Margaret went to the kitchen to discuss today's activities with the cook.

Jonathan waked up just before lunch and rushed to the main house. They had a pleasant lunch and were casually talking when Mary said, "I had the strangest experience this morning while I was going over the papers in my office. I was reading about the sale of my company, and I had what I would call a déjà vou experience. I have no memory of these papers but I felt as if I had." Jonathan didn't know what this might mean, but he hoped that maybe some of her memory was returning. Mary went on to say, "I want to have a detailed mental evaluation. I am beginning to wonder how much of my memory loss is connected to brain injury. I am wondering if a severe injury can exacerbate a psychological problem that is manifested by memory loss."

Jonathan recalled Doctor Jones talking about this possibility. He remembered him talking about traumatic neurosis and in extreme cases, psychosis. When Jonathan asked further questions about these two conditions, Doctor Jones tried to explain it this way. "We all live in a hostile environment. We are preyed upon by diseases, disasters, losses and so forth. Most of us know that we have limited control over our lives, and we try to build psychological defenses to protect us from these adversities. We build; let us call them core defenses that take over when we are exposed to some severe injury, whether they are physical or psychological. These defenses help us stay in contact with reality. When the event is so severe that these defenses break down, then what do we do? It is under these situations that one evolves bizarre defenses, i.e. total memory loss or others. In order to escape the overwhelming trauma you wipe out anything that might bring that overwhelmed state back into consciousness. This is usually the last defense available to you that will prevent psychosis." Jonathan didn't tell her this information but instead encouraged her to see someone. She said, "Jonathan would you contact that memory doctor you saw and see if he would recommend someone in Albuquerque that could help me with my memory?" Jonathan said he would and a short time later left to go to the guest house. Mary walked with him to her guest house and met Canela. Canela told her that she had been her private secretary when she owned the cosmetic company. Mary said she had no memory of this and returned to the main house.

Chapter XII

Later on in the afternoon, Fremont arrived. Canela had prepared some Mexican sweet bread and placed a slice of the bread with warm butter and coffee on his desk. Jonathan had wondered what Canela was doing, but when he got to Fremont's desk, he knew. Fremont came in hoping that she had done something like this, and Jonathan noticed the happy smile on his face. Old, serious, grumpy Fremont was smiling. Jonathan pretended that he was not interested and continued to work. Fremont went immediately to Canela's office and thanked her. He showed his pleasure more in actions than in words. He sat down in a chair next to her and told her about his day.

He said, "You know Kayani don't you?" "Of course, Fremont, what happened?" He continued, "I was just about to leave to come here when in walked Kayani. He told me that he had been offered a job by the Navajo council to supervise their oil holdings." He said, 'Since I am going to be married this weekend and live near the reservation, I have decided to resign my position with your company.' I told him I had no idea that he was thinking of marriage, but congratulations. We parted feeling good. He continued by relating about old man Gonzalez. He came out to our geology group and talked for about an hour. It was obvious he still thought that he owned the mineral rights." Fremont then went to his own desk and started eating his Mexican sweet bread. It was then he noticed Jonathan. He blushed, but nothing was said. That afternoon, when the office closed, Fremont asked Canela if he could take her home. This was to become a daily event.

Before the office closed that day, Jonathan called Doctor Jones and requested a referral. Doctor Jones said, "I will contact a Doctor Joseph and make an appointment for Mary. Furthermore, I will give Doctor Joseph your number so you can relay it to Mary."

Margaret realized that Mary was very impressed by pictures of her doing various activities. She knew that Andy had many pictures of Nancy and Mary. The next morning she called Andy and asked him if he had any pictures of Mary and for him to bring them to her. He said, "I have lots of them in my house in Socorro, but I always carry a snapshot in my wallet of Mary and me. She is wearing her graduation gown." She told him that pictures of Mary doing things seemed to impress her. They didn't affect her memory, but it seemed to make her more amenable to accept her past. Andy brought over his snapshot to Jonathan's office, and Canela brought it to Margaret.

After lunch, Jonathan left. Mary and Margaret continued exploring Mary's belongings. Her office contained information about her business experience, but there was nothing about her personal life. They searched in closets and furniture with nothing being found. Margaret suggested that they look in the attic. They found many boxes there. Fortunately, the boxes were marked on the outside with a name or a description of the contents. After going thru about half of the boxes, they found a box that had one word on it -- Socorro. They quickly took it downstairs and into Mary's office. The first thing they saw was a picture of Nancy and Mary. Mary looked to be about ten or eleven. They were smiling at each other. They hastily spread out all of the contents of the box. At the very bottom was a picture of Andy and Mary. She was wearing a graduation gown and cap. Mary looked solemn, but Andy was smiling and obviously proud of Mary. Mary was stunned and exclaimed, "My God, that man is my father!" She slumped in a chair and was lost for words.

Margaret and Mary sat silently together, and for over an hour nothing was said. Margaret was frightened. She feared that she had pushed Mary too fast in establishing who she was. Mary did not feel threatened. She was wondering how in the world she was going to be able to engage this man when she still had strong feelings of repulsion towards him. She finally decided that she felt it was time for Margaret to tell her more about this man. When she considered this thought, a sense of dread consumed her. Inwardly she shook herself, and told Margaret her thoughts.

Margaret was surprised when she heard Mary's request. She

responded by saying, "I am very much in love with your father. It is for me and Andy a second chance to find happiness. You already know that our wedding is to be this Saturday. I have only recently learned about Andy. For a long time, I have been bitter towards him. I have felt he was cruel to my Nancy. My first knowledge of Andy began when Nancy brought him to our home in Waco. They were engaged, and they were so happy. I was upset by their engagement, and I didn't lose anytime telling them so. Because I was so upset, they left soon after the announcement. The wedding was to be after their graduation, and when that time came, I was more civil and reconciled to the marriage. My impression of Andy was not favorable.

Andy was easy going, but I felt that he was weak and let his partner, Clyde Carlson, take advantage of him. As I tell you more about your father you will see how wrong I was. What I am about to tell you now can only be told by what I have learned recently.

After their wedding they left for a small town about seventy-five miles south of Albuquerque--Socorro. There he joined Clyde, and they began to buy and develop ranch land. Andy and Nancy were married in 1938, and in two years they had acquired much land. At that time, the depression had bankrupted many landowners, and their property could be gotten by paying back taxes. They used Andy's resources to make these purchases.

In 1939, Clyde was criminally charged with fraud and brought to trial. He was found not guilty, but Andy had found out too many bad things about Clyde and insisted on breaking up the partnership. At this time, I didn't know all of the details, but I felt that Andy let Clyde cheat him out of his fair share. What I didn't know was that Andy made a very clever deal. He agreed to give surface rights to much of their land, and in return he received all of the mineral rights. At that time, the oil industry of New Mexico was in a slump, and the depression was still very severe.

Andy joined the New Mexico National Guard in 1938 in order to get extra cash. He became a Second Lieutenant, and in 1940 you were born. Joining the National Guard was as far as I was concerned a bad decision. The War came and in 1942, he was activated. In 1943 he was fighting in Sicily and ultimately all the way to Anzio. I know you probably don't know much about World War 11, but the Italian campaign was very brutal.

Andy was in many battles and was a hero of many engagements. He received two Bronze Stars and one Silver Star. He was badly wounded at Anzio and returned to the states. This is when the tragedy began in your family. Andy returned to you and your mother a bitter cruel man. He was so filled with hate he could not reestablish a loving relationship with your mother. He was cruel to her and indirectly to you. He never struck your mother, but he was just continually attacking her with criticism. He made fun of her inability to be a ranch hand. Your mother had lost her loving husband, and you had at best, a distant father.

When your mother died, he finally realized what he had done and almost committed suicide. It was then that he tried to change his relationship with you, but it was too late. You don't know it, but your father is a very rich man. His mineral rights have made him millions. I have been with him constantly since your accident, and I have learned to love him."

Mary was not able to talk for a few minutes. She was remembering that man rushing into her room and trying to hug her. His being a war hero and a millionaire was beyond her comprehension. Why am I repulsed by this man? Am I still reacting to my childhood? Her final thought was that Aunt Margaret and Andy McGregor are the only relatives that I am supposed to have. Maybe I need to try again to relate to them. Margaret will be easy but Andy - UGH. I must talk to Jonathan.

Chapter XIII

On December 15, 1975, when it was obvious that the sale would go thru, Elizabeth Horne came to Mary and said, "I am going to go away for four months. The first three months will be on a world cruise. The last month will be spent revisiting places I saw on the cruise that I wanted to have more time with. Don't try to get in touch with me as I want to rethink my life." When she came back to Albuquerque on April 1, 1976, she expected to find Mary at her home. Instead, she found a man at her gate, and he refused to let her into the grounds. She told the gateman that she was an old friend of Mary's, and she knew Mary would want to see her. He said, "I am allowed to give a telephone number to inquiring friends. I suggest that you call that number." Liz went to the nearest phone and called. Canela answered and immediately recognized Liz's voice. Liz was relieved and asked why all the security. Canela told her the whole story about what had happened to Mary. She emphasized her total loss of memory. She told Liz that Mary has a friend, who has her power of attorney, and his instructions are that no one is to see Mary unless he approves. Canela said, "I will tell him of your desire to see Mary and of your connection with Mary. Please give me your telephone number so that I or Jonathan McCandlish can get in touch with you." They hung up and Liz was to wait to hear from them. Countless thoughts ran thru Liz's mind when she hung up the phone. The main thought she was having was, "I should have been here to help Mary as I consider Mary my best and only friend."

When Jonathan arrived to the office, Canela was just preparing to leave. She had many messages for Jonathan, but she said the two most important ones were from Mary and Liz Horne. Canela said that Mary had called in the early afternoon and told her that Margaret had told her about her father, and she wanted to see him as soon as possible. About the Liz call she started to explain her connection with Mary, but Jonathan was in a hurry to get to Mary, and he interrupted saying, "I know about Liz and Mary, and I have reviewed her financial connections with Mary." As Jonathan was rushing to get to Mary, he picked up an album that Andy had brought to the office. He told Jonathan it had all of the information and pictures of Mary from her early childhood up to the sale of her company. It even had the newspaper report of her accident that he had gotten from the newspaper files.

When he arrived to the main house, he hurried in and called for Mary. When she heard his voice, she ran to him. She said, "Oh, Jonathan, I am so glad you are here. When Margaret told me about that man, at first, I just heard it as an interesting story, but as I listened further, I began to get those sensations of déjà vou. I felt that I had heard this before. This frightened me, and all I could think was I must talk to you." Jonathan put his arm around Mary's shoulders, and they walked to her office.

He asked how she was feeling now. Mary said the déjà vou feeling had left her, and she felt she could talk more rationally about it. With that, Jonathan took a large album from his brief case. He told Mary that yesterday that man, Andy, brought this to his office. I have only looked at it briefly, and it covers your life from childhood to the present. Mary told Jonathan to stop calling Andy that man as she was now convinced that he was her father. They sat down on a sofa together and began looking at the album. They saw all of the pictures of Mary from her birth to her graduation from Harvard business school. This was the first time that Mary knew she had graduated from Harvard. Then they discovered a newspaper clipping from the New York Times. It was dated December 20, 1966. The clipping was a picture of a young man and a young woman. He was dressed in cowboy attire, and the woman was dressed in a smart coat and skirt. The caption read "Jonathan McCandlish, our new rodeo champion, and Mary McGregor, a lucky gambler, are standing in front of the pay window at Madison Square Garden. Miss McGregor has just won 1.25 million dollars. Is this a beginning romance? See the sports section for further information." They both smiled when they read this. Mary looked at Jonathan and said, "It wasn't a beginning romance then, but it surely is now." Jonathan leaned over and gave her a passionate kiss. The kiss aroused Mary, and for the first time, she began to think of Jonathan not as a dear friend but as a lover. This disturbed her, and she got up and said, "Dinner is ready." This startled Jonathan, but he got up, and they went into the dining room. Margaret was waiting for them to come, and they had a relaxed dinner. Margaret brought up the subject of her coming marriage. She told them that she would not be staying nights with Mary after she got married. Mary understood Margaret's need to be with her husband. When Margaret made this announcement, she told her that she had been looking at her father's scrapbook with Jonathan. She said, "Margaret, I think it is foolish for me to deny that Andy is my father. I still have this uncomfortable feeling about him, but I know now that you and Andy are my sole surviving relatives. I know I am lonely, and in my inability to remember, I have feelings of helplessness and incompetence. I know now that I need your support, and I hope in the future I will feel the same about Andy. The bottom line is, will you and Andy stay here with me until I can regain my memory?" Margaret was surprised and very happy. She asked Mary if she could hug her. Mary didn't answer. She got up and went to Margaret and gave her a big hug.

When things settled down, Mary said that she wanted the wedding to be in her home. "I will still have some difficulty with too many people. Do you think it would be all right with Andy if you just had very close friends attending?" She said to Jonathan, "I want to meet Don Wright. Would you bring him and his wife to the wedding?" She turned back to Margaret and said, "Jonathan and I have decided that we have a budding romance, and I want to meet important people in his life." This was the first time that Jonathan had heard Mary say this, and he felt a flood of excitement. Jonathan jokingly said, "Does this mean that I can stay at the house too?" Mary smiled and said, "In time, Jonathan, in time."

The evening ended well for all of them. When Jonathan left, Margaret got on the phone and called Andy. She told him to get his things together and plan to stay in Mary's house with her. She related how his scrapbook convinced Mary that he was her father, and even though she still had mixed feelings about him, she was willing to try to change those feelings. Their conversation continued with them talking about their wedding. Andy said he had only one close friend and that was Jacob Wright. He would call him tonight, and he was sure that he would come. Margaret wanted her next door neighbor in Waco to come. They had been widowed about the same time, and they had been a great comfort to each other. Later on that night, she told Mary that there would be only four new people coming to the wedding. Mary was relieved.

The next morning during breakfast Jonathan told Mary about Doctor Joseph. He said that Doctor Jones had highly recommended him and that Doctor Jones and Doctor Joseph had trained at the Chicago Psychoanalytic Institute. They were recognized psychoanalysts. He went further saying that Doctor Joseph was a board certified neuro-psychiatrist. "You have an appointment Monday at 2:00 p.m." Mary said, "You must go with me. I am frightened by this, but I know it is necessary." Jonathan said, "Of course."

He left shortly, and went to his office. He was far behind in his work, but he was so happy he didn't mind. The night before he had told Canela that she was to tell Fremont to stay in town as he wanted to talk to him about the Montesinos project. Fremont was waiting for him, and they went into his office. Jonathan asked Canela to come in with them. He told Fremont he had been reading his preliminary geological reports on the Montesinos property. Speaking rather loudly he said, "Fremont, I feel that we should talk to Canela about us coming to some agreement about how to exploit her mineral rights. Do you agree?" Fremont immediately said, "Yes, I do." Jonathan turned to Canela and said, "I think it is time for you to talk to a lawyer who specializes in lease agreements." Canela was very excited to hear this, and at the same time bewildered as to how to go about finding a lawyer who specializes in this kind of law. "Canela," said Jonathan, "Fremont and I want you to have the best of advice. My best friend is a lawyer, and I can ask him to refer you to an excellent lawyer in this field." Canela thanked him, and he immediately called Don. Don had instructed his secretary that if ever Jonathan McCandlish called, he was to be interrupted immediately. When Don came to the phone, Jonathan said. "I have two requests to ask of you. One is my secretary, who has a need for legal advice regarding leasing of her mineral rights. Since I will be the Lessee, she wants a lawyer that has no connection with me. Will you make a recommendation for her, and if possible get her an appointment for this afternoon. The second request comes from Mary. She wants to meet my best friend and wants him and his wife to come to her Aunt Margaret's wedding to her father. This will be this Saturday at 5:00 p.m. at Mary's home." Don was excited by the second request and said yes to both requests. He would call back as soon as he could get an appointment. Before they ended their conversation, Don wanted to know if the second request meant what he thought it meant. Jonathan laughing happily said, "Yes."

Jonathan then turned his attention to Liz Horne. He told Canela to call Miss Horne and see if she could come to his office this afternoon at 2:00 p.m. A short time later Don called with an appointment at 11:30 a.m. at a Mr. William Jackson's office. He said Mr. Jackson was expensive, but he was the best lawyer in Albuquerque for lease agreements. Don said this guy was sharp, and you would need a good lawyer. Jonathan said, "I already have the best lawyer."

When he hung up, he turned to Fremont and Canela and said they should take the rest of the day off in order to get the leasing agreement settled. This was very exciting to Fremont as his interest in Canela had moved from her being a good secretary, to thinking of her as his woman. He had been intending to ask her for a date but had been shy about it. This gave him the opportunity to have lunch with her and talk about things that were different than his business. To his surprise, Canela was interested in talking about other things, too.

Canela was the first to start talking about her family. She started by saying, "On my father's side, the men were very adventurous and came to America in the 1600's. They were late comers to the area around Mexico City, so they decided to go into what was then northern Mexico. They established a large land holding in the area that is now identified as the Montesinos Ranch. They were driven out by the Pueblo revolt and returned as soon as the Indians were defeated. The Montesinos' part of my life has lived in that area close to 400 years. My mother's family, the Gonzalez, was bankers. They came to Santa Fe about the same time as the Montesinos came to their ranch. So, I am half adventure and half merchant. My father was the last of the line of the Montesinos. He was a proud man, but he did not have the ability of his ancestors. He tried hard but failed and chose drinking and gambling as a solution. My mother was a business woman and had no control over her husband. She tried desperately to save the ranch but realized it was impossible. It was at this time that she persuaded her husband to deed the mineral rights of the ranch to her. When he lost the ranch, my mother and I went from being upper class to near poverty. It was a great shock to us, and I was the first of both lines to become a common laborer. I did this because my mother could not give up her upper class orientation, and I had to make a living. My mother lives in a state of denial."

Fremont was intrigued by this history. His history was quite simple. His family had come over from Ireland during the potato famine around 1840. They had struggled at various jobs, and he was the first one with a college education. He wondered how she would feel about his insignificant heritage.

Canela wondered also about Fremont. Knowing about all of her ancestry, how would he react to her mother? She had men before that were interested in her, but as soon as she brought them home to introduce them to her mother, they realized, that to have her, also would be to have her mother. Her mother was a haughty aristocratic woman, and she put down all of her suitors. Canela knew that she could not abandon her mother and accepted the fact that she would probably be an old maid. She knew that she was interested in Fremont as a suitor, but she wanted to get this issue settled quickly because she couldn't allow herself to become attached to him only to have him leave. All of these thoughts and conversations occurred prior to coming to Jackson's office. They arrived on time and were immediately ushered into his office.

Mr. Jackson was a distinguished looking man, about 55 years old. He was very friendly. Canela took over immediately and said, "I am here to get advice about leasing my property for oil exploration. Mr. Fremont is a friend of mine as well as my employer. This may seem like a complicated situation, but I have the greatest trust in Mr. Fremont." Fremont was surprised by this last sentence, and he glowed inwardly. She continued saying, "I really like the company that wants to lease my property, but I come from a merchant family. I have been taught that if I am engaged in some business transaction that I have no knowledge about, I should seek expert advice. I have come to you for that advice." Mr. Jackson was impressed by this lady and said, "Leasing mineral rights is basically a bargaining situation. If you have rights that are desirable, then you are in a good position to bargain. If things are shaky, then you have to be careful not to discourage that person that is trying to buy them." Fremont interrupted at this point and said, "Her mineral rights are highly desirable to our company." This startled Mr. Jackson as usually the acquiring company was very secretive about its interest in the property. He said to Canela, "This is a very unusual situation. You are seeking how to maximize your return on your mineral rights and sitting next to you is a representative of that company. I am wondering why you even need me as it seems that they are as interested in your welfare as I would be." They talked in general terms after that and came to the point of how much royalty she should ask for. Mr. Jackson said that usually for highly valued property 3/16ths is requested. Fremont interrupted and said that Mr. McCandlish and he had talked about royalty rights, and they both had agreed that she should have 4/16ths. Mr. Jackson said, "This simplifies matters, and I should have the lease agreement ready for your signature and theirs in a day or so."

When they left the office, Fremont said to Canela, "Let's have lunch together." Canela said, "That's a good idea. May I suggest a place to go? When I was wealthy, we always went to fancy places in Albuquerque, and I feel rich today. I don't think I should burden you with the cost, so I am treating." Fremont was taken aback by this because he had strong feelings that when a man was on a date, he always paid for everything. This was going to be a test of wills, and interestingly enough Canela won. Since they had the afternoon off, they wandered about town window shopping and talking. As the day progressed, Canela was finding herself more and more attracted to Fremont, and she felt she had to get this mother thing of hers settled as she was becoming too attached.

Canela suddenly said to Fremont, "I want you to meet my mother. Let's go to my house and sort of chat with her for a while. If things go well, I think she might ask you to stay for supper." The idea of spending more time with Canela excited Fremont, and immediately he was agreeable. The drive to her place was somewhat surprising to Fremont. He had expected it to be a modest place, and it surely was that. Even though it was modest, the grounds were well kept, and the house was very neat. When they entered, Canela introduced Fremont to her mother as a dear friend. Fremont responded in perfect Castilian Spanish. Canela's mother was surprised and immediately thought that he must be an upper class person. It seemed to her that Canela always brought home common people. This was the first time she had high hopes for Canela. With Fremont she was quite a different person, and this surprised Canela. Fremont and her mother talked and talked and talked. As time progressed, it became time for dinner, and her mother asked Fremont to stay. This was the first time that this had ever happened. Canela was excited, and when Fremont was about to leave, she walked outside the house to his car. Before he got into the car, she gave him a light kiss on his lips. Both knew they had crossed into a different type of relationship.

Chapter XIV

AT 2:00 P.M., LIZ HORNE appeared at the gate of Mary's estate. This time the gateman told her to report to the guesthouse, which she could see from the gate. She drove to the house and was greeted warmly by Jonathan. Jonathan wanted to cut through formalities and said, "Liz, I am Jonathan, and I would like for us to be on a personal basis. When Mary asked me to be her power of attorney, I immediately began investigating her financial situation, and the people involved in her business. Your name appeared in many places, and I soon realized that you were a 10% owner of the company. I don't know if you know it or not, but Mary has no memory. She has no memory of you and your relationship to her. She has given me specific instructions to limit the number of people that she would have contact with. She feels a great disadvantage in having no past memory and doesn't want to experience people claiming to have known her for a long period of time. I don't agree with this as I have hopes that the stimulus of these people might help her recover her memory. When we talk about extending a contact with these people of the past, all she experiences is anxiety. Next Monday, Mary is going to see a psychiatrist, and we both hope this will help her overcome her memory loss and lessen her anxiety. I want her to have access to you as I feel like you must have been a close friend of hers. The only way I see an opportunity for you to have contact with her is to be at an event that is to occur this Saturday. Mary recently has accepted her aunt and her father as people she wants to work with. They are to be married this Saturday, and she has permitted them and me to invite a few of our friends to the wedding. The wedding will be at her home, and I would suggest that you attend as my guest." Liz was thrilled that he was so willing to let her come into Mary's life. She asked Jonathan what was his relationship with Mary as she had never heard of him as being a part of Mary's life. Jonathan wasn't too sure he wanted to talk too much about himself, but he thought that if he was open with her, then she would be open with him.

After much thought, Jonathan started talking about himself and his feelings toward Mary. He used the event that had occurred in Madison Square Garden as a starting point. I have a past history with Mary in high school, but my relationship with her really began at a rodeo in Madison Square Garden in 1966. Mary bet on me and won over a million dollars. Our relationship then was more of a business relationship. I was drafted a month or so later and was in the Vietnamese War. I came back from the war and eventually developed a company. When Mary had her accident, I realized that I always had loved her, and I came to the hospital to be with her. Over the past four months, we have developed a warm, trusting relationship. I love Mary, but she still has problems with any relationship as she has no memory. So, you might say my relationship with Mary is more my loving her than she loving me." Liz could sense his pain and felt warm feelings towards him.

Since Jonathan was so open with her, she decided to tell him about herself and her relationship with Mary. She started by saying she appreciated his openness with her, and she wanted to share her past with him. "I met Mary at the University of New Mexico. We were both out of high school, and we went through four years of college as roommates. Mary was a very determined person, and I was sort of a carefree and careless person. I just barely graduated whereas Mary was a 4.0 graduate. We parted ways, and Mary went on to Harvard. I tried to find a job. I felt my only asset was my ability to talk to people. I seemed to have a salesperson personality. I moved to Dallas and got a job in a public relations firm. I progressed in that firm to some extent, but it became obvious I was not going to be upper management. About the time I realized this, Mary called me and told me that she had started a new company and needed a person to manage promotions and sales. She said, 'Liz, I can't give you the salary you are making now, but I can give you 10% of the company. Initially, we will have very little capital, and we will just get by. As you can see, it was a wise decision I made coming to Mary as I am now a multi-millionaire.

I realized when I had all this money that I had neglected developing warm relationships. I had always wanted to have a family, but I always sought out casual relationships. I wondered if I had the ability to attract people who were interested in having a permanent relation. Mary and I have talked about families and both of us decided we needed a family in our lives. Now we were successful, but we had no loving relationships. Two days before Mary's accident, I told her that I was going to leave on a long cruise to work with myself and try to see if I could be a person that could have serious relationships.

The cruise I went on was a three months around-the-world cruise. I hoped that having that period of time with the same group of people would give me some insight to my ability to establish a permanent relationship. I found that people taking this trip were not just going to be going around the world, but they too wanted to take a look at themselves. I had many interesting exchanges. I did meet one man who excited me, and we both developed a mutual interest in each other. We are now trying to see if we can be more to each other than just friends. My friend is a rancher outside of Amarillo, Texas. Oil has been discovered on his land, and he is well off. He has devoted much of his life to the ranching business and taking care of his parents. He has had very little experience with dating or being with women of his own age. His shyness attracted me, and his steadiness reassured me. I was more aggressive with him than he was with me. I think he is really interested in me, but we parted without any commitment to each other. I have hopes that he will contact me. I have given him my home address, my radio phone number and my line phone number. I have yet to hear from him." After she finished telling her story to Jonathan, he commented, "Liz, you and I love our partners more than they us. We have a kinship." She smiled, and said, "I will be at the wedding."

Chapter XV

THE NEXT TWO DAYS WERE filled with activities of the coming wedding. Jonathan assumed the responsibility of catering the wedding. He contacted the most expensive caterer in Albuquerque and insisted she arrange her best wedding feast. Andy and Margaret were busy getting their license and whatever was required by the State of New Mexico to become legally husband and wife. It was obvious they were in love with each other.

Mary was somewhat overwhelmed by all of this activity and stayed most of the time in her home office. She instructed her housekeeper to help Margaret with decorating the house, but she didn't feel she could participate with this. She got herself involved deeply in her ex-business, and she read all of the documents connected with its development, its success, and its sale. She found that even though none of this was in her memory, she somehow understood it. She wondered about this. She knew that her memory did not connect with the data she was reading, but her intuition seemed to understand all about it. She began to wonder if her conscious memory was somehow in one part of her brain, and her intuitive memory was elsewhere. As she thought about this possibility, she asked the question, "How could only her conscious memory be destroyed and not her intuitive memory?" She had already questioned whether she had organic brain damage or whether she had an emotional amnesia. This further suggested to her that she had a serious emotional problem. She knew on Monday she would be seeing her psychiatrist, but the anxiety of this self questioning troubled her. Whenever she was troubled and frightened, she always thought of Jonathan. She knew she had been keeping Jonathan at a distance. The fact that she always thought of him when she had some anxiety reassured her that she was beginning or was in love with him. She asked herself the question, "Why do I fight this?" The only answer that came was, "I am a person without memory. I am an incomplete person."

The wedding day finally came. From 9:00 that morning to 4:30 that afternoon, there was constant activity. The caterer arrived at 12:00 noon and began preparing the food in Mary's kitchen. The aroma of cooking foods filled the house and made everyone aware that this was really going to be a feast. Margaret and Andy were actively involved in this process. They would run around doing this and that and then suddenly stop and hug each other. The joy of their relationship was evident to everyone around them. At 4:30 p.m. everything stopped and people started dressing for the wedding that was to take place at 6:00 p.m.

The guests started arriving at 5:30 p.m. Don Wright and his wife, Virginia, were the first to come. Don was perfectly at home because he knew Jonathan would be there. Virginia knew Jonathan, and they were close friends, but the relationship of Jonathan with Mary was completely new to her. She knew that Mary had requested specifically that she come with Don, and she felt that Mary was trying to establish relationships with Jonathan's friends. She wondered why she was being anxious. Certainly being a friend is a nice thing. What came to mind was that Mary was a very successful and rich woman. For some reason she felt that she was inferior to her. She wondered how she was going to deal with this because she felt that a feeling of inferiority would damage any relationship. When she talked to Don about this problem, he said, "Jonathan is worth a billion dollars. Do you feel inferior with him?" She said, "No, but he's a man. Mary is a powerful and rich woman; that is a different situation for me." When she did meet Mary, she was immediately reassured because Mary was very warm and generous with her. She didn't know it, but the C.E.O. in Mary no longer existed. The Mary she was seeing today was a frightened, reclusive woman who felt incomplete and unable to live her life. Virginia and Mary broke away and talked for several minutes before the wedding began, and both seemed to want to continue knowing each other.

Jonathan had rented a large organ and hired a renowned organist from Albuquerque. All were called to attention by the impressive sound of the wedding march. There was no marching of the bride. They both simply came in front of the minster. There was no altar, and they stood holding hands as the minister read the service. The service was brief, and at the conclusion, they hugged and kissed. Since there was no walking down the aisle to exit, all the people who were there gathered around them and congratulated them. Jonathan was the only one who kissed Margaret.

Jonathan had been responsible for the seating arrangement of the people at the wedding table, and he deliberately placed Liz next to Mary. Mary began the conversation with Liz by asking what was her connection with the wedding. Liz said, "You." This startled Mary, and she asked, "How am I connected to you?" Liz started off by saying, "Mary, I have known you for almost fifteen years. We went to college together, and I have always considered you my best and only friend." The people in the past who had confronted Mary like this, tended to create anxiety in her. With Liz she felt no anxiety. She wondered about this. Was her intuitive self accepting Liz? She said to Liz, "I don't remember you, yet I feel that somehow you are important to me. When my father confronted me with his knowledge of me, I was angry and frightened. When you confronted me, I didn't feel anything. May I call you Liz?" "Of course, Mary, even though you do not recognize me as your close and dear friend, I am and always will be." Mary said, "I am frightened over my loss of memory. I am going to see a psychiatrist Monday, and I am hoping he will change things for me. I don't know if he can help me or not, but I feel like I would like for you to visit me and perhaps you could help me recover my memory." Liz replied, "Oh, Mary, I love you. Of course, I will come to visit you as much as you will permit." Mary could not feel the same intensity as Liz was expressing, but she was grateful for Liz's intensity.

Jonathan had asked Canela to be his assistant as he prepared for this wedding, and she was in attendance at the wedding feast. She had told Jonathan that she and Fremont were dating, and she would like for him to be there also. This was certainly agreeable with Jonathan as he wanted Fremont to be happy, and this dating could be a great comfort for him. Both Fremont and Canela were greatly impressed by the wedding, and both were fantasizing about the possibility they might have their wedding. The feast lasted until about 10:30 p.m. All left and Andy and Margaret went to a local hotel to celebrate their wedding night. The wedding had a great impact on Jonathan. Mostly, he felt sad as he could not see any future for him or Mary.

Chapter XVI

MONDAY CAME QUITE QUICKLY, AND everyone was back with their activities. Jonathan had his usual breakfast with Mary; only this time, it included Andy and Margaret. It looked like they might become a family. When Jonathan was leaving, Mary reminded him that he was going with her to her doctor's appointment. He reassured her and said, "Of course, I will remember because it is just as important to me as it is to you."

Doctor Jones had explained to Doctor Joseph Mary's condition. They both commented on the fact that a total amnesia was a very rare event. They wondered together how this therapy could begin as most therapist depended upon memory. Mary would be unable to give a history of her life. All she would be able to talk about was her memory from the accident forward. This would give a very limited clue as to the cause for her memory loss. They both decided it would be best for Doctor Joseph to get a test for organic brain damage. If this examination proved negative as they both felt it would, then they must consider this as a serious emotional problem. The fact that it was a total amnesia was of great concern to them because it might be covering up an impending psychotic episode. So Doctor Joseph felt a great amount of caution as he awaited Mary's arrival.

Mary and Jonathan arrived at 2:00 p.m., and they were immediately ushered into Doctor Joseph's office. Doctor Joseph was not the typical psychoanalyst. Many psychoanalysts at that period of time were very withdrawn with their patients as they feared contaminating the patient's personality by their own personalities. They tried to keep themselves at a distant from their patient so that the patient would only experience what was theirs and not what was a connection between them and their analysts. In other words, psychoanalysts at that time were concerned about their patients' development of a transference. They wanted the transferences that developed to be a product of the patient and not of themselves. They considered this as a therapeutic tool, but to a troubled patient with a limited grasp of reality, this could be very unsettling and could be damaging. Doctor Joseph had abandoned this position and participated wholeheartedly with all of his patients. He didn't care if he was a part of their transference. In other words, he was a very warm humanistic person and tended to instill confidence in his patients almost immediately. This sense of trust was immediately felt by both Mary and Jonathan. Usually, a new patient was brought in alone for their first session. Since Mary had no memory, Doctor Joseph felt that Jonathan would be an asset in getting the initial contact going. He explained to both of them that the first session would be very short as he wanted to outline his treatment program with them.

"The first thing I want to do is to make you an appointment to see a psychologist who will do a series of tests to see if there is any organic brain damage. While you are going through this process, I want to start interviewing, for information only, significant people who have information of your past life." Turning to Mary, he said, "I want you to choose those people as I don't want to create any conflict with you about my interviewing them. Can you tell me which people you would feel comfortable for me to interview?" Mary immediately turned and looked at Jonathan and said, "Jonathan first." Doctor Joseph noted the relief that she expressed when she said that. He realized that this man was very important to her. After this sudden burst of information, there was a silence. He knew she was struggling with the choices that were to be made. The next person she gave surprised Jonathan for it was Liz Horne. There was another long pause, and she finally said, "Margaret and Andy." He inquired of her why she had all these silences. Mary said, "With Margaret, I had no trouble. She recently married my father. My father came into my now life shortly after my accident while I was in the hospital. I totally rejected him then. I have grown fond of Margaret. When she announced she was going to marry my father, I knew I had to do something about my repulsion of him. I know my father has the greatest amount of information about me. It was his bringing of his scrapbook to Jonathan, and my reading it with Jonathan that told me I had to do something about this repulsion of him. I want to have a loving father, but as of now, to me he is just a tolerated stranger." Doctor Joseph knew this was going to be an important part of her therapy. This ended the interview, and an appointment was set up for the next week at the same time.

When Jonathan and Mary left Doctor Joseph's office, they both felt a great deal of relief. Mary was saying, "I really like that guy." Jonathan had the same feelings. They decided to celebrate. It was only 3:00 in the afternoon, and they decided to go to a local bar and have a drink. Mary didn't do things like this and was surprised at her inclination at this time to seek that form of relief. She thought being with Jonathan certainly was changing her life. When they were seated in this semi-dark room, and both were drinking wine, they discussed their experience with Doctor Joseph. Mary said, "I think now I know one of my fears about seeing him. I had been wondering about whether I had a serious emotional problem. Margaret had told me that my father had a near psychotic episode when he was wounded in World War II. I wondered if I was inheriting this tendency. I don't want a psychiatrist to treat me like an elephant in a china closet. I want one that will be careful and guide me slowly into whatever problems I have. I want to be able to master my problems and not be overwhelmed by them." Jonathan was amazed at how clear Mary was thinking. Of one thing he was sure, now he had a chance to have a whole Mary, and this meant they would be married.

Over the next few days, Doctor Joseph set up interviews of all the people that Mary had indicated she was willing for him to interview. He started first with Liz. He recognized immediately that this was a lady of the 60's. She had a flippant, casual way about her, and he felt that she had a limited ability for intimate relationships. As he talked with her, he realized that this casualness was not true with Mary. It was obvious that Liz had a deep affection for Mary and had permitted a deep relationship.

Liz said, "I met Mary at the University of New Mexico. We had come to college directly out of high school. Mary seemed to come with strong intentions of studying and had a no nonsense attitude toward other activities. I was the direct opposite. I didn't study. I made poor grades and just barely graduated. Mary was an "A" student and graduated with honors. I dated, and Mary did not. Mary left after undergraduate school and went to Harvard business school. I got a job in Dallas with a publicity firm. It was obvious that Mary was going somewhere, and I was going nowhere. We kept in contact, and when Mary needed a promotional person, she called on me. You probably have heard of the McGregor Cosmetic Firm. Mary founded that from scratch and developed that into a first class company. Have you seen the campus she has created?" Doctor Joseph acknowledged that he knew about the campus. "When Mary sold the company, I became a millionaire and also a person at loose ends. I was away when Mary had her accident, so I have no more information regarding that." Doctor Joseph asked a few questions to elaborate on some of the things she had brought up and concluded the interview thanking her and indicated that he might call on her in the future as information comes out in the sessions with Mary. When he was analyzing what he had heard, he was aware of how lonely Liz was. He said to himself, "This young lady, if Mary does well, will be a patient of mine."

The next person he called was Margaret McGregor. Margaret was a 60 year old attractive woman, and he found it easy to relate to her. She was able to talk quite frankly with him about her life with Mary and presented this picture of her understanding of Mary. She said, "Mary was three years old when she came to live with me. Her father was inducted into the Army in 1942 and sent overseas in 1943. It was in 1943 after he left the States that my sister, Nancy, and Mary moved in with me. He was overseas from 1943 to 1945. Those years that Mary and her mother were with me were happy ones. When Andy McGregor returned from war, he was wounded and had severe emotional problems. He recovered somewhat from both but came home a bitter, angry man. For the next 7 years, he made life miserable for himself, Nancy, and Mary. In fact, it was so miserable for Nancy that when she developed an illness, she had no desire to recover.

I think I need to tell you something I feel is very important, and I want to tell it in more detail than what I have said before. Toward the end of Nancy's life, Mary spent many hours with her as she feared the loss of her mother. She would run home from school, and she told me later, fearing that she would find her mother dead. Actually, the last day of Nancy's life, was a time when Mary ran home after school. She found Nancy very ill. Her mother, realizing that she was dying, talked very

Lost and Found

seriously to Mary about her father and what had happened between them. These are Mary's words as I remember them, "My mother said, 'I know your experience with your father has been one of fear and anger.' His anger is very frightening, and he is very critical of both of us. Your anger is justified because he is very cruel to both of us. I want you to know about another person that your father was. I met your father in college. He was a sweet, happy-go-lucky fellow. I fell in love with him immediately. We came from different backgrounds. I was a city girl, and he was from a cattle ranch. We knew that we had different backgrounds, and it would be hard for us to adjust to one another. We were determined to be married. We were so happy for the first three years, and you were a joy to us when you came into our lives. You were three years old when your father left us and went to war. He didn't talk to me much about his war experiences, but I learned from other people that he was a war hero. He had been in many battles. He came back to us from war a crippled bitter man. I know he still loves me, but he just can't get passed his despair and anger. I know when I die, he will be devastated. Mary, I want you to stay with him regardless of your feelings. Promise me you will do this. I know it is a hard thing I am asking. I love you and your father very much. My lasting regret is that I was not able to reach him and find him the way he was when we married.' It was a few minutes later that Nancy died. Mary just sat by her mother 3 hours as her father did not come home until 7:00 p.m. that night. During all of that waiting with her dead mother, Mary made a secret promise that she would stay with her father until she was able to take care of herself. When that time came, she would move away from her father and never see him again. I tell you this long story because I feel it is very important concerning her now relationship with her father.

Now, I want to talk about my behavior in regards to Mary. I was very destructive towards Nancy and Andy's marriage. I regret that. When Nancy died, I accused in violent terms that Andy had killed Nancy by an angry neglect. Then Mary did the same. I know my outbursts caused Mary to break her promise to her mother. When Mary realized what she had done, she turned to me and said, 'I am going to stay with my father and since you feel this way about him, I will never see you again.' So, I lost Nancy and Mary at the same time. It was 23 years before I saw her again. When she had her accident, I rushed to Albuquerque and have been here ever since trying to make contact and be a part of Mary's life. I feel like I have made progress because Mary does trust me. She has started trying to work with her father."

Doctor Joseph felt that she offered a lot of information about Mary, and he was beginning to see the severe trauma that Mary must have experienced in her relationship with her father, and the despair she must have felt in the loss of her loving mother. He saw a lot of emotional strength in Mary, because in spite of these two relationships, she was able to be, not only independent, but also aggressively successful in a very complex and competitive industry. He thought Mary had a lot of strong ego qualities, and he was very encouraged about her ability to recover. He thought he would use Margaret, not as information for more data, but as a support person for he expected Mary to go through some very trying times. He thanked Margaret for coming and indicated that he was glad to have her as an emotional support for Mary. Margaret left feeling good about Doctor Joseph, and she told Andy when she got home, she was so thankful that Mary was seeing a wonderful person.

Doctor Joseph saw Andy next. Andy was very concerned about seeing Doctor Joseph. He knew he had to talk about a period of his life that he was ashamed of and had still many guilt laden memories. He hated to open that book of despair and anger. When he walked into the room with Doctor Joseph, it was obvious he had a great reluctance about being there. Doctor Joseph sensed his difficulty and tried to relieve his anxiety by leading the conversation. He started off saying that he knew it was difficult for him to come as Margaret had told him about his difficulty with Nancy and Mary. "I hope you will be able to be open with me about it. I am not here to Judge you; I am here just to get information about Mary, and her life with you. I feel that your information is going to be very important in my working with Mary. Whatever you are able to tell me, I will use to help Mary get well. My therapy of Mary will not be designed to make anyone a scapegoat of her problems. My whole goal in any therapeutic situation is to restore the ability of the patient to love again, not only others, but also themselves."

After hearing all of this, Andy was silent for a few minutes. He didn't want to apologize for his behavior, and he didn't want to make himself sound like a hero who had suffered in battle and lost his family as a result of it. He thought the best way to handle it was to relax and let it come in whatever direction it would go. He began, "I loved Nancy, and I will always. I can never forget the first day that I saw her. It was my third year of college and we were in a cafeteria line. She was as cute as she could be. I wasn't the only fellow in the line looking at her. As the line progressed, I became aware that she was quite intelligent. On every occasion I had a chance to speak to her, I did. Finally one day I said, 'Would you have a cup of coffee with me, Nancy?' To my surprise, she said yes. That started a long relationship. It didn't take us long to realize that we had something serious going on between us. By the middle of our senior year, we were engaged, and I had met her angry sister. Her sister, Margaret, to whom I am now married, was very angry about our relationship and tried to keep it from progressing. She pointed out to both of us that I was a country boy and Nancy was a city girl. When I indicated I was returning to the country, it only made this argument more attractive to Margaret. Margaret was so aggressive with us that Nancy stopped going home, and we had a simple wedding. This didn't seem to bother us. We were just happy kids trying to make a way in the world.

We had cash problems, and in 1938 I joined the New Mexico National Guard. This was a terrible mistake. It was this action that put me in a war that really destroyed me. We had Mary in 1940, and we thought we were on top of the world. My ranch business was doing well and my partnership, which had a good beginning, had ended. We were feeling as if nothing could cause us any problems any more. Of course, you know December 7 occurred, and in May of 1942, I was activated. I was overseas in Sicily on July 27, 1943. I was a company commander of an infantry unit connected to the 45th infantry division. We fought many battles, and I lost many friends. I was severely wounded at Anzio, and by that time, I think I was psychotic. I hated everybody and everything. This is what I brought back to my family. I didn't recover from this hate until Nancy died. It was her death that made me realize what I had lost. I was suicidal. If Mary had not stayed with me, I would have committed suicide. I tried hard to overcome Mary's bitterness of me, and I constantly hear those words she said to me the day her mother died, 'You killed my mother. Mary was 12 at the time of her mother's death, and I was in touch with her from the age of 12 to 24. At 24 she had finished her MBA at Harvard and had a good job with a Wall Street firm. She wrote me a short letter stating that she thanked me for supporting her during the past 12 years, but she could no longer have anything to do with me. She stated, 'Your treatment of my mother, I can never forgive. You have taught me how to hate, and I can never forgive you for that, signed, Mary.' He was silent for several minutes. Doctor Joseph said, "I know this has been hard for you to talk about, but I need to know how you recovered from all this." "Actually, Doctor, I have never gotten over this. I will carry the guilt and shame of my behavior towards Mary and her mother until the day I die. I was fortunate to have one friend, Jacob Wright.

Jacob was with me all during my combat days. He was my first sergeant. He came out of the war without any hate, and I asked him how he escaped anger and hate. He said, 'You were in command and made decisions that involved life and death. You felt that responsibility and blamed yourself if any of us were killed or hurt. We knew you loved us, and we thanked God that you were our commander. You never forgave yourself over the loss of your men. You always felt you could have done better. Your guilt and despair lead you to anger and hate and it dominated you until Nancy's death.'

After I received Mary's letter, I don't know what I would have done without him. All of my efforts that I made during my early life with Nancy became very successful after Nancy died. Now I find myself a millionaire with a daughter who hates me. My only redeeming grace is that I found a woman who truly loves me in spite of knowing who I was. She has given me hope to be a person worthy of her love and hopefully Mary's, if she ever gives me a chance."

Doctor Joseph thanked him for coming. He thought this was a very sad story. He had seen so many people destroyed by World War II. He wondered why governments did such horrible things to their citizens. They take young men and throw them into horrible situations. On the one hand, they say to them, love your neighbor as yourself and then on the other hand, to kill them as they are your enemies. Where did love go? He didn't usually let himself be affected by a story like this, but somehow when it was all over, he felt depressed. He knew that depression was caused when people had severe conflicting feelings and refused to do anything about it. What had this story activated in him that produced this kind of situation? He felt you can't treat a person if you indulge in the same kind of despair that they are in. He said to himself, "I am going to have to look at myself because this has really stirred up something inside of me."

Lost and Found

The last person he was to see before starting his treatment with Mary was Jonathan. When Jonathan walked in the room, he saw a very capable man who was very sure of himself. He didn't have to start the interview as Jonathan had already made up his mind what he was going to talk about.

Jonathan started by saying, "Doctor, I am so glad that you are going to help Mary. You may think that I am jumping the gun on this, but I have felt for a long time that Mary's problem was not brain damage but was strictly emotional. The amount of anxiety she has expressed with me has caused me deep concern. I have done considerable reading about anxiety and the meanings of it in psychiatric terms. I feel that Mary is severely emotionally ill. This causes me great concern because I love Mary, and I want her to be okay. With this preamble, I want to talk about how I met Mary and what has happened over the years in my relationship with her.

I first became aware of Mary when I was just 16 years old. Mary came from a fairly prosperous family. My father and I lived on a very small ranch about 35 miles west of Socorro, New Mexico. We had very little money and just barely got by. Mary was a very attractive girl in high school, and I fell secretly in love with her. She had no interest in anybody except a guy named Tom Carlson. This relationship broke up because his father objected to it, and I know it was a very painful experience for Mary. I lost contact with Mary and didn't see her again until 1966 about 9 years late. After high school, I had become a rodeo tramp. I went from one rodeo to the other. I was really very capable, but I didn't care whether I won or lost. I was in New York City back in December 1966. I had been one of the few people who had been invited for the National Rodeo Championship. No one expected me to win; I just had enough points to be there. At this point I didn't know it, but Mary was desperate, and I was just having fun. She had just recently received a bonus of $25,000 and was wondering how she was going to accomplish what she wanted to do in her life. She read about the rodeo and decided to attend. When she saw my name on it with 50 to 1 odds, she put her $25,000 bonus on me to win all the events. I heard of this bet. I didn't know who did it, but somehow it changed something in me, and I really tried to win. I did win and that led me to meeting Mary. As I went to the pay out windows to see who had bet on me, there was Mary. I still loved her. It was sort of a casual meeting, but she did help me with the management of my winnings.

In January of 1967, I was drafted and inducted into the Marines. By November of 1967, I was in Vietnam. I was severely wounded in the Battle of Hui. All this changed my attitude, and I became a very aggressive, determined person. The outcome of this was that by 1975 I owned my own company, and I was worth over a billion dollars.

It was on December 17, 1975, that Mary had that terrible accident. I was on my ranch outside of Socorro, and when I picked up the Wall Street Journal the following Monday, there was a big article showing Mary. It stated the C.E.O. of the McGregor Cosmetic Company had been seriously injured in a severe automobile accident in Albuquerque, New Mexico. I knew when I read this article that I still loved Mary, and I rushed to the hospital determined to do whatever I could to help her survive.

It took me three weeks to get into Mary's room, and probably another two weeks to have her trust me enough for her to want me to have her Power of Attorney. I helped her through all that period. By the end of March, she was able to walk and was discharged from the hospital. From January to the present time, I have been her Power of Attorney and have managed all her finances. I have helped her to rehabilitate herself and now she lives in her own home. I have my office and my quarters in a guest house on her estate.

I deeply love Mary, and I have proposed marriage on many occasions. I know Mary loves me, but she tells me that until she is a complete woman, she will not marry anybody. She means by a complete woman that she has recovered her memory. I am a very impatient man about this problem. I want to be with Mary. We have talked about marriage, and we have talked about having a family. Both of us want to have children, and we realize the biological time of Mary is decreasing as the time goes by. So, Doctor, I am really saying this to you very forcibly, do the best you can to get her well as quickly as possible. I don't want to lose having a family with Mary."

Doctor Joseph was amused by this last statement, but at the same time, he admired the frankness of Jonathan. Apparently, he was a no nonsense fellow. He felt that he would be a real asset in helping Mary with the anxiety problems that he was undoubtedly going to uncover with her. They departed very cordially.

Chapter XVII

ALL DURING THIS WEEK, MARY had many thoughts. She was busy reviewing her experiences at the wedding. The one contact that interested her the most was Don Wright. She knew that he was a very close friend of Jonathan's, and she wanted to know more about their history. In fact, she found she wanted to know everything she could about Jonathan.

She was finally admitting to herself that she really loved this guy. Right after the wedding dinner, she cornered Don and asked him to come into her office. When they sat down, she immediately got to the point. She said, "Don, I am in love with Jonathan. I have only known him in my conscious mind since January of this year. As you know, my memory is gone, and I suspect that all my past memories of Jonathan have been quite limited. I want to know all about him. Would you tell me about your experiences with Jonathan?"

Don was very pleased to find that Mary loved Jonathan as he knew Jonathan was madly in love with her. He started off by saying, "I have known Jonathan since we were kids in grade school. We were small kids, and the big guys always picked on us. We found if we stuck together, and if we isolated them one against us two, we could convince them to leave us alone. This fighting together was a bond that was to last us all our life. After high school, I went to college, and Jonathan tried to go to college but only lasted for two years. He had gone to Texas A & M, and I had chosen to go to the University of New Mexico. We sort of rocked along until January of 1967.

I had finished law school and was just beginning my practice, and Jonathan had just earned $150,000. We both got a draft notice, and we were inducted into the Marine Corp. By November 1967, we were in

Vietnam and ended up with a group of Marines in a detachment that was to protect the MACV headquarters of the United States government in the ancient city named Hui. On February 3, 1968, Jonathan and I were on patrol around our headquarters. At 3:30 a.m. in the morning there was an explosion of artillery shells and rockets all around us. The Tet offensive began. The North Vietnamese army overwhelmed the American forces north of the Perfume River, and Jonathan and I and a group of soldiers established a defensive line on the southern shore of the river. The North Vietnamese immediately tried to cross the river as they wanted to capture the MACV headquarters. Large numbers of troops were advancing across the river in every kind of boat. It looked like we were going to be overwhelmed, and suddenly, I was severely wounded. Most of the troops were pulling back, but not Jonathan. He wasn't going to leave me there. The American soldiers had abandoned a machine gun nest, and Jonathan pulled me into the nest with him and started firing at the North Vietnamese who were landing on the shore. He, not only destroyed the landing forces, but also destroyed the boats in the water that were trying to land. He completely stopped the offensive from getting on the south shore. I give him credit for saving the headquarters and my life. In the process of doing this, he was severely wounded. When the other troops returned to see what had happened, they found two severely wounded unconscious Marines. Jonathan was lying across the top of his machine gun. All around the gun were dead North Vietnamese soldiers. We were flown to Saigon and ultimately to the United States. We ended up in the U. S. Naval Hospital at Bethesda, Maryland. Because of Jonathan's heroic actions, he was written up for the Congressional Medal of Honor, but he didn't receive it for some reason. He did receive the Navy Cross. Because of the severity of our injuries, we were retired from the service.

    After he was discharged from the hospital, he was a man on fire. He was determined to make something of himself. You had been investing his winnings, and at the time of his discharge, it was valued at $200,000. He went back to school and, in less than a year and a half, he finished two years, and he graduated. During his period at school, he had started buying oil leases in southeastern New Mexico. They were peripheral leases as the more important ones had been acquired years before. He also bought leases in the Albuquerque Basin. There had been many drillings in this basin, and they were all basically poor producers or dry holes. He had done some geology in that area, and thought he had a good chance to get a good well in one place. In 1972 he made a wild cat well in that area. He drilled a well over a slight dome of oil, and it produced 50,000 barrels a day. I don't know how many feet of gas. In other words, he was an instant millionaire. Over the next three years, he continued to have phenomenal success in the southeast area of New Mexico, mainly in Eddy County. He now is a very successful businessman, but more importantly to me, Mary, he is my blood brother. I would do anything for Jonathan as he would do for me."

Mary had no idea how brave Jonathan had been. The devotion that Don expressed towards Jonathan impressed her deeply. Her expanding knowledge and admiration of Jonathan warmed her heart. She ended these thoughts as she returned to the guests with one final thought. I have two heroes in my life. One I dearly love, and one to whom I am still struggling to relate.

Since there was a small number of guests, each had the opportunity to meet and talk. Jonathan had chosen this small group as he hoped that it would become a nucleus for Mary. He felt that Mary, not only needed to regain her memory, but she also needed to have a social life. She had isolated herself from people and spent all of her efforts in building her business. When Mary was in high school, she was one of the friendliest persons in the whole school. Jonathan was just beginning to realize how Tom Carlson's rejection was so damaging to her. She had been trying to escape a father who she could not forgive and find someone to love her. He could hardly imagine that night when she lay alone in her bed trying to deal with disappointment and despair. The loss of a person whom she felt would change her life had devastated her.

Jonathan was the last person to leave. By now Mary knew that he was the only man she could ever love. She walked him to the door and gave him a kiss good night. It was a different kiss. It was a kiss that seemed to express possession. Jonathan wanted a more passionate kiss, but this kiss was more reassuring.

Each departing guest had their own thoughts. Each had been deeply affected by the happiness of the wedding. It seemed all of this group of people had touched each other in some meaningful way.

Canela and Fremont left early in the evening. As they were driving to

Canela's home, she turned to Fremont saying, "It is too early to end this evening. I want us to drive around and just be with us. I am surprised how intimate my conversations were with the people at this wedding party. It has been a long time since I have been around socially successful people. I found them open and friendly. I was amazed at how smart and modest they were. I found myself being open with them and talking about thoughts which I had only recently been talking to you. I feel that there are big changes occurring in my life, and I hope you will be able to accept them. I don't want to lose you with these changes." Fremont was confused by what she was saying, but her saying 'I don't want to lose you' was reassuring.

They were silent, and as they approached the Rio Grande River; they exited on the Santa Fe highway. Soon they were headed to Santa Fe. Fremont started talking. He, too, had been affected by the wedding party, and he also had talked more openly about himself. Others had responded likewise. He didn't feel that any great change had occurred in him, but he was interested to find out what Canela meant. He said, "Canela, I haven't the slightest idea of what changes you are having, but I have fallen in love with you, and I would do everything to keep you in my life." Canela thought for a minute as she tried to figure a way to tell Fremont of her changes.

She started off by saying, "Do you remember my telling you of my family history. I told you about my conquistador father's family and my merchant mother's family. I was a well formed adult when my father lost our ranch, and my mother and I became poverty stricken. For a long time, I was ashamed and lost. I think it was my early pioneer Montesinos genes that took over me and enabled me to get the training I needed so that I could earn a living. I am a good secretary, but I am also an aristocrat. Fremont, I loved the life I had on the ranch. I loved the splendor of my father as he pranced around. Those memories are shallow, but the exposure to exciting successful people and feeling that you could be and were their equal, was bred in me. My mother hangs onto the past by sequestering herself and not letting reality be a part of her life. You and Jonathan have made the possibility of my becoming wealthy again. It has given me hopes that I can again be an authentic aristocrat. I can never be like my mother denying and living in a make believe world. I like the real world, and I want to live as a real aristocrat. If you and Jonathan do find oil on the Montesinos ranch, I intend to buy back my ranch and establish it as it was. If I do this, will I lose you?"

Fremont had no problem responding to Canela. He said, "Canela, when I fall in love and have a woman that loves me, whatever she wants her life to be is just fine with me. I have never told you about my financial position, but I am a ten percent owner of Jonathan's company. Even if there is no oil on the Montesinos ranch, I can still make your dream come true." Canela reached over and grasped his arm. Fremont stopped the car, and they had their first passionate kiss.

When they looked around, they realized they were near Santa Fe. They drove around and Canela pointed out the many places where significant events had occurred. It was dawn when they arrived back to Canela' home. Her mother was up all night worried and wondering about where was Canela. When she saw who Canela was with, she went to bed and slept with a smile on her face.

Liz Horne left the party soon after Canela and Fremont. She left not because she wasn't having a good time; it was because the way people were talking to her was so authentic and sincere that she found herself feeling very anxious. She knew they deserved her authentic self, but she didn't know what that was. This startled her. She realized that she had lived her life as an as-if person. She was like a chameleon. She could be what she sensed the other person wanted, and she could become that. She was a pretend person. She had only been real with one person, Mary, and she didn't even know her.

As she drove home, she began to realize that her being unreal was probably why she had not heard from Henry Feldhaus. How could he become involved with her if he could not find out who she was? Her next thought startled her. Mary and I are emotionally sick. I need to get an appointment with Doctor Joseph, too.

Andy and Margaret had a wonderful time at the wedding dinner and enjoyed being with all of the people that were there. His dear friend, Jacob Wright, came from Arizona, and he and Margaret spent a lot of time talking to each other. Jacob said, "Margaret, Andy and I have comforted each other over the years as we both had suffered many losses. We are friends and will always be friends. When we both retired to Arizona, we left Socorro because it was a place of bitter memories. We thought that we were tired of talking about our despair, and if we got away from

Socorro, we might have a new life. We just might find a new love. We were terribly lonely. When Andy came back to Albuquerque, I had no idea that he would find you. I don't want to be envious, but I want to find a woman like you. I don't want to spend the rest of my life being lonely and waste whatever years I have left." Margaret said, "Are you asking me to find you a woman?" Jacob said, "You hit it right on the head. I haven't met a single woman in that retirement community that interests me. All of them are wealthy and are more interested in protecting their wealth than taking the risk of a new love. If you think of any one that might be in the same boat I am in, call me, and I will be on the next plane."

When Margaret and Andy were leaving, Jacob kissed her and said, "I meant every word I said to you." As they were driving away, Andy asked, "What did Jacob mean when he said I meant every word I said." Margaret smiled and said, "He wants me to find him a woman."

Don Wright, Virginia, and Jacob were the next to last to leave. Mary and Jonathan had sat with them, and they had a meaningful sharing of thoughts and feelings. Don and Jonathan already had strong bonds but as the evening progressed, all felt that they had found some real friends.

The next day was Sunday and all slept late. Fremont waked around noon and could hardly wait to call Canela. He said to himself, "I will give her eight hours of sleep, and I will call." Just as he was having these thoughts, the phone rang. It was Canela, and she said with affection, "Why haven't you called me?" Fremont replied, "I was going to give you eight hours of sleep and then call you." They laughed and made arrangements to be with each other all that day.

Chapter XVIII

MONDAY CAME AND ALL WERE back to their routines. Jonathan had breakfast with Mary, and they both had much to talk about. Jonathan was saying, "Mary, I know that if I stay near you I will make too much sexual pressure on you. I have decided to go back to my ranch office near Socorro. I will work there during the week and return on the weekend." Mary knew the wisdom of this as she did not want to be sexual with Jonathan until she had recovered her memory. Mary said, "My news is that I slept well last night, and I feel I am less fearful." They kissed goodbye and said they would talk frequently with each other on the phone.

When Jonathan arrived to his office, he found that Fremont had not gone to the Montesinos ranch. He was talking to Canela, and Jonathan knew something new had happened. Fremont told Jonathan that he and Canela were engaged, and they wanted him to be the first to know. Jonathan went over and hugged both of them. He then told them he was going to go back to his ranch office, and he wanted to maintain this office. He told Fremont that he was to have an office here as long as the geology part of the Montesinos project was in that phase of development. He turned to Canela and told her she was Fremont's personal secretary. With this exchange Jonathan packed his belongings and left for Socorro. Fremont and Canela wondered what had happened.

Mary went to her appointment with Doctor Joseph. He told her that the tests for brain damage were negative. He didn't tell her about the other tests. The Rorschach showed a deeply disturbed person. This test revealed a severely depressed person who had a tenuous grasp of reality. Apparently the accident precipitated a near psychotic episode, and her memory loss was her last defense from a complete break with reality.

Mary started talking about Jonathan and his need for sex with her. She said, "I dearly love Jonathan, but I feel if I do have sex with Jonathan something terrible will happen. After I lost Tom," she gasped and said, "I talked as if I knew Tom, and he was in my memory." Doctor Joseph didn't say anything. She was silent for a long time and started talking again. It seemed to Doctor Joseph that she had repressed that slip as she took up talking about her problem of having sex with Jonathan. She related that she didn't feel that she had ever had sex. I know I am not afraid of sex as sex, and I know I love Jonathan. It puzzles me that I fear having sex with the man I love. Time was up and she left. As Doctor Joseph reviewed his notes, he reminded himself that he must keep the ending of her sessions open. He must not permit either him, or her to have a closure.

As Mary was leaving Doctor Joseph's office, she ran into Liz. Mary was surprised and asked what she was doing here. Liz was in a hurry for her appointment but said she decided to get psychiatric help and she liked Doctor Joseph. "I will call you later."

After Margaret and Andy got settled back in Mary's house, Margaret got a call from Jacob. He told her that he was very serious about finding a new life, and that meant finding a woman with whom he could find love. Margaret responded that she knew he was serious, and she had given it some serious thought. She said, "The only person that I could suggest would be my ex-next door neighbor, Lillian Blake. Lillian lost her husband two years ago, and she was a great comfort to me when I lost my first husband. I could invite her to come and visit me. You would be able to meet her while she visits Andy and me." Jacob was very excited and hoped she would do it this very day. Margaret indicated that she would call as soon as she hung up.

Margaret had invited Lillian to her wedding, but Lillian had other plans and couldn't come. When she received Margaret's call, she quickly said yes, and Margaret should expect her next Saturday. Margaret called back Jacob and said he was invited to dinner on Saturday and Lillian Blake would be there. He said, "I will be there."

Liz entered Doctor Joseph's office with some fear. She had never been serious about herself as she had felt that self analysis was silly. She had felt that one must live for the day as the past was gone, and the future was not there. She was reassured by Doctor Joseph's warm greeting. He started the session by saying that he wanted some psychological testing done, and he had ordered them. His secretary would give her the appointment as she left her session. He then said gently to her, "Would you tell me about yourself, but first, let us talk about why you wanted to see me at this time." The first two inquires frightened her, and Doctor Joseph could sense her anxiety. They were silent for a few minutes. In those minutes, Liz was saying to herself, "You want to get married, and you have found the man you want to marry so you must talk." She said, "Doctor Joseph, I have never been honest with myself or others except for Mary. From early in my life I felt that complaining or being self aware was futile. Doctor Joseph, I find it so hard to talk about myself. If I hadn't found a man I wanted to marry, I wouldn't be here. He doesn't feel that he can get close to me, and he is right. When I should be getting more trusting of him, I find myself drawing away. He senses this, and he is angry. He felt that I was leading him on without any intention of having a close relationship. I would plead with him to be patient with me, but by the end of our cruise, he told me that he loved me, and he felt that I was a wonderful person. He said, however, he didn't think I could ever let him be close. He said, 'You pretend to be close, but when I try to be close you withdraw. I can't accept this torture any more. Let's stop seeing each other.' He left, and it has broken my heart." Doctor Joseph asked, "Is his complaint of you true?" Liz answered, "Yes, and I feel so helpless to change." She burst out crying. It was a wailing cry like one would hear when a child was lost from her mother and is wandering around. Doctor Joseph came around and sat beside her. He put his arm on her shoulders and said nothing. When she stopped crying, he went back to his seat and Liz said, "That is the first time I have let anyone comfort me. I don't know why I let you comfort me, but it gave me hope that maybe I can change." Liz was silent for a while, and Doctor Joseph said, "Futile complaining is very painful for you." She answered, "Yes. I have been thinking about that. The first thought was about my mother. My mother was a very beautiful woman. She nurtured her beauty and used it as a way of manipulating people, especially men. Mother came from an old family of Albuquerque. That family is all dead now, and you probably never heard of them. Anyway, Mother's father was not very successful, at least not as successful as my mother wanted him to be. She always managed to be with important people. My mother marketed her beauty and married my father who was a very successful bond salesman.

She had the financial backing she had always wanted, and my father had a trophy wife. This was a good decision for what each wanted. Neither one intended to have children, and I was a mistake. My whole childhood was filled with various nannies. Neither of my parents made any time for me. Most of my nannies were cold and efficient. From as early as I can remember up to my sixth year, I was a shy child. I was always very afraid of the night and had to have a bright light on for me to go to sleep. I have no memories of either parent saying good night, much less kissing me good night. When I started to school, I met other children my age, and they would tell me of how their parents treated them. I became angry and started rebelling. I did things that I knew would upset my parents. I desperately wanted parents like other children. My rebelling did not work as all my parents did was to send me to experts to find out what was wrong with me. I have no idea what they were told, but for the first time, I had a nanny who really loved me. She was an older Navaho lady who was widowed and needed work in order to support her children. When my parents were out of town, she would bring her children to my house, and we would play with each other. She would bake cookies for me, and I loved her. I stopped rebelling, and I was happy. When I was thirteen, for some reason, they fired her, and I was really alone. I rebelled with a vengeance, and I made it so bad for my parents that I was shipped to Switzerland. It was about as far away from them as I could get. It was then that I started being flippant and not caring. I decided that I would not expect anything and give nothing. I was like my Mother, but I didn't recognize it. By being like Mother, I meant I was cold and indifferent to warm feelings. I was this way with everybody but Mary who had serious problems with her father, and I felt a kinship with her. With others, I would pretend what I thought they wanted, but I was never close. I can't say I was happy, but I got along. I was thirty-five when I realized I wanted to have a family. I found a man I could love, and I felt I was in love with him. He recognized quite early that when we got too close, I would withdraw. He has told me he was through trying to be close with me, and from his stand point our relationship was over. Doctor Joseph, I love this man. Can you help me?"

Doctor Joseph told Liz that she had given one of the best histories he had ever received. "What is a mystery to both of us is why, as conditions have changed, you still hang onto this withdrawal from closeness when you so desperately cry for it. Liz, I don't label my patients with a diagnosis. Generally, when they come to me, they are fed up with their past and want to change and haven't found a way to break away. I see you as a person who has been a survivor. I see you have a strong motive to change. I think we have a good chance of getting you to where you want to be. If you agree with what I have said, I think that we should talk about treatment plans. Liz, I am a psychoanalyst. I try to explore your inner and external experiences. I am not so much interested in changing your personality as I am interested in finding a way for you to be happy and to be able to love yourself and others. Our world is very frightening and to experience it without loving and being loved is a formula for disaster. To accomplish this goal, I think we should talk with each other three times a week. I have one requirement of you, and that is you must be on time and not skip any sessions. If you do skip sessions, you will be charged as if you were here. Now Liz, you have told me that money is not a problem with you, so in your case, if you miss more than two sessions, I will regretfully discharge you. It has been in my experience with people who have intimacy problems that they tend to avoid their sessions when they most need to be there. How do you feel about these conditions?"

Liz responded, "Doctor Joseph, I am desperate. I need this man. I am lost without him. I am so tired of being lost and never finding myself or others." Doctor Joseph closed the session saying they would meet Monday, Wednesday, and Friday at 3:00 p.m.

Chapter XIX

For Jacob Wright, Saturday would never come. He was staying at his son's home, and the only person to talk to was Virginia. Jacob talked about how lonely he had been since his wife died. "Kate and I would do a lot of pillow talking. We would share our activities of the day, and many times we would go to sleep holding each other. When Kate developed breast cancer, we thought that we had caught it early, but the disease progressed. We knew we were losing our fight. Being together was so important to us at this time. Towards the end, we prayed for a miracle but none came. During the last days of Kate's life, she told me I was still young, and I must find a new companion. She told me that if I was the one dying, and if she were left alone, she would find a new companion. I knew she wouldn't have, and she was saying this so I wouldn't feel guilty when my loneliness became unbearable." "Virginia," Jacob asked, "Can you imagine how lonely it is to have the love of your life gone forever?" Both were silent and Virginia didn't try to answer.

Jacob finally got up and walked to his room. That night when Virginia and Don were talking, she told him about her afternoon conversation with his father. Don told her that he knew they were very close. "Mother worshiped my father. They had been childhood sweethearts. As far as I know, they were only apart during the time Dad was in the army. Dad was overseas in Italy, and Mom told me she worried all of the time. When he came home after the war, Mom insisted they get married and never let him out of her sight." Don said, "I know it is very hard on Dad to be without Mom, and I have hopes that Margaret's friend will work for him." They both looked at each other, and thought they were so glad that their time for this to happen was hopefully far in the future.

Jacob woke up early Saturday. He was restless and decided to go for a walk. He walked for about an hour, but this didn't relieve his tension. After walking back and forth in his room, he decided to call Margaret. When Margaret answered the phone, Jacob asked if Lillian was there. She said she arrived last night, and they were having a late coffee. She asked, "Would you like to come over and meet my guest?" Margaret knew why Jacob had called, and she knew his answer before he said it. Jacob borrowed Virginia's car and rushed over to Mary's house. Margaret answered the door and led Jacob to the kitchen. She hadn't told Lillian about Jacob as she wanted them to discover each other themselves.

After the introductions, they sat and talked about many things. Margaret told Lillian that Jacob was a close friend of Andy's. Jacob had come to the wedding and had stayed a few days in order to visit with Andy and his son's family. Jacob was grateful for Margaret's introduction as he didn't want to scare Lillian away by his need for a partner. As the conversation became more relaxed, Jacob began looking carefully at Lillian. He saw a very attractive sixty year old woman. There were a few wrinkles in her face, but they were attractive to him. She had a slim figure and walked and sat without a hump in her back. She was gray headed with light blue eyes. He really liked her looks. Jacob lingered on until it was lunch time. Andy came home, and Andy asked him to stay for lunch. During lunch, Andy asked Lillian if she had ever been in Albuquerque. She said, "No, I have only been all over Texas." Andy turned to Jacob and said, "Why don't you take Lillian to see the town." Andy wanted Jacob to have some private time with Lillian. Lillian thought this was a good idea and asked Jacob if he would do this. They left shortly, and they spent most of the afternoon together.

Lillian found that she liked to talk to Jacob, but she did no evaluation of him as Jacob had done of her. Lillian was not lonely. She had a busy life in Waco and had not considered a new marriage. She was aware of how happy Margaret was, and she felt some slight envy. She decided to talk to Margaret about her new marriage. She wanted to know if it was hard to go to bed with a new person. About four o'clock, Jacob took Lillian back to Mary' home as they both needed to dress for dinner.

Jonathan was in town that weekend and he, Mary, and the four others had a good time with each other. As the evening closed Mary walked to the door with Jonathan and said, "Wait for a while as I want to talk about my visits with Doctor Joseph." Lillian walked Jacob to the door and was slightly surprised that Jacob asked her to go to a local event in which he felt she might be interested. Lillian paused, she had felt Jacob's growing interest in her, and she didn't know if she wanted to encourage it. In that short pause, she thought, "Why have I walked Jacob to the door? Am I really happy being alone? Margaret is really happy, and Andy is a very nice fellow." In her meditation she was not aware of Jacob waiting. Jacob interrupted her thoughts by asking her if she was all right. Lillian told Jacob that it had been a long time since she had been asked for a date. Jacob replied that it had been a long time since he had a person with whom he wanted to have a date. Lillian, with that, laughed and said, "Yes, I would like to go with you, particularly because you and I are such long time people."

They had many dates over the next two weeks and both enjoyed each other. Jacob had made up his mind that Lillian was the woman for him. Lillian liked Jacob, but she wasn't so sure that she wanted to start another marriage. When Lillian left for Waco, Jacob told her he was very seriously attracted to her. Lillian said, "Jacob, I have never intended to marry again. I have my home, my friends, and activities. I am not lonely like you are. If I were, I would be right with you considering marriage. I need to be away from you for awhile. I need to know if knowing you makes me less content."

When Lillian left, Jacob had the same intense feeling of loss he felt when he lost his wife. He came to Andy and told him of his despair. Andy said, "If I were you, I wouldn't worry so much. I think that Lillian is really considering you. Let's talk to Margaret about this." Andy called in Margaret and said that Jacob was very upset with losing Lillian. Margaret responded by saying, "What gave you that idea, Jacob?" He related Lillian's parting comment. Margaret didn't want to tell Lillian's private talk with her about Jacob. How could she help Jacob? She knew that Lillian was concerned about the intimacies connected with marriage. She had told Lillian that when she fell in love with Andy there never was a problem with sex. Margaret asked if she had intimacy problems with her first husband. Lillian said, "No." Margaret pointed out she loved James and that made a difference. She ended by saying you must not be in love with Jacob. After considering all of this, she told Jacob she knew that Lillian was seriously considering their relationship. She concluded by saying be patient.

Mary was anxious to talk about her session with Doctor Joseph. She told Jonathan it was so easy to talk with him. She particularly liked the fact that Doctor Joseph didn't push her for information. He let her find her own way. She didn't talk about her memory flashes as she had repressed them without any anxiety. They talked about how much they missed each other. This time, it was Jonathan who gave a possessive kiss.

Liz had a hard time the first week in therapy. She would not let herself talk casually. The more she suppressed this, the more she was anxious. She asked Doctor Joseph about this, and he said nothing. This troubled Liz and she complained to him about his not answering. Doctor Joseph knew that when Liz had complained in the past no one was interested or listened. He told Liz, "I will answer your questions when I think it will help you." This puzzled Liz, but it surprised her that that reply was reassuring to her.

The geology work on the Montesinos ranch was completed. The most promising part of her ranch was the part that was located in the Utah part of the four corners area. Plans were made to immediately start drilling. McCandlish asked Fremont if Canela had signed a leasing agreement. He told Jonathan that they were to meet today with her attorney, and he felt all would be settled. When they met with Mr. Jackson, Canela said that Fremont was her fiancé, and she wanted him involved in all of her affairs. The lease was written as they had agreed. Mr. Jackson said that the only thing they had to decide on was how much should she request per acre for this lease. Canela turned to Fremont and asked him to advise her. Without hesitation, he said his company would not want to pay for the entire 100,000 acres. They had talked about cherry picking the part that they thought would produce. If they paid for 20,000 acres at $20.00 an acre, it would amount to $400,000. He turned to Canela and said, "I thought it would be better for you if our company had all 100,000 acres. I asked Jonathan if he would pay one million dollars for the whole ranch." He said that Jonathan didn't think that the rest of the ranch was desirable for oil exploration, but if Canela agreed to that sum, so would he. Mr. Jackson told Canela that he felt that it was a generous offer as she was getting 4/16 royalty. Canela couldn't believe her ears, one million dollars! Her father never made that much money. She turned to Fremont saying, "We can now have the wedding I want."

She signed the papers, and Fremont gave her a cashier's check for $1 Million. They went to her bank and deposited the check and drove immediately to her mother's. They were going to get married, and they were rich. The only thing her mother heard was that Canela was marrying that wonderful Irishman. They all sat around talking in Spanish and began planning their wedding. While all of this excitement was going on, Fremont forgot he was to call Jonathan immediately when the papers were signed. He called and Jonathan immediately ordered the drilling to begin.

As they continued, Canela said she wanted to be married in the Conquistador Chapel of the Saint Francis Cathedral in Santa Fe. She recalled she had told Fremont that she was an aristocrat and wanted to repeat the life she had before her father lost their ranch. For her wedding, she wanted it to be attended by only her real friends. They were Jonathan, Mary, Margaret, Andy and Don Wright and his family. These people accepted me in my poverty when my aristocratic friends ignored me. My marriage is too important to be contaminated by insincere people. Consuela Gonzalez Montesinos, Canela's mother, interrupted and said, "The arrangement of the wedding was her right. Canela, you know that a Spanish mother has the right to direct her daughter's wedding." Canela replied, "Mother, it is now the first of May. David and I will be married on the second of September, 1976; if you can meet these requirements, I will let you direct it."

Jonathan ordered the drilling crew to move onto the spot that he and Fremont felt contained the most oil. The drilling crew was instructed to drill first to the 3,000 foot level. If they did not discover oil, they would reevaluate the core specimens and decide if they would go deeper. They did find some oil at the 3,000 foot level, but Jonathan felt the real large quantity was at the 6,500 foot level. When they hit that level, they hit a gusher. It was estimated they had a well that would produce over 50,000 barrels of oil a day with large quantities of gas. Jonathan was at the site when the well came in. He called Mary, Canela, and Fremont and said he would be back in Albuquerque later that afternoon, and they would celebrate. It was a gusher was all he told them.

Jonathan felt a great relief as it assured the stability of his company for the foreseeable future. All of the time that Jonathan was away, Mary continued her visits with Doctor Joseph. She continued to report daily activities and was having more flash memories. She would almost immediately repress them and did not ever remember or acknowledge them. It was late June of 1968, that she retained one of the flash memories.

It had to do with Liz. She was remembering their being in college. She was sitting in their dormitory room putting away her things when Elizabeth walked in. She said to Doctor Joseph, "Liz was nothing then like she is now. Now she is my loving friend." She stopped and gasped, "I remember Liz." She was very excited as she felt for the first time she was beginning to recover her memory. Doctor Joseph said nothing, and Mary tried to get in touch with as many memories of Liz as she could. Try as she may, very little new memories came out. She left her session both pleased and frustrated. She met Liz in the hall and said, "I remember you." They hugged.

Liz was Doctor Joseph's next patient. She was excited about Mary's memory and talked about it for a few minutes. She settled down and started by saying she was having a hard time coming to her sessions. She finds when it is time for her to come to her sessions with Doctor Joseph, she starts having anxiety, and she doesn't want to come. "I feel like I want to run and hide. I force myself to think about my last session. I think it was about Henry Feldhaus. I know we have talked about Henry as he is the main reason for me coming." Doctor Joseph listened carefully to what she was saying. They weren't talking about Henry at all. They were talking about her mother. He didn't say anything and continued to listening. She didn't continue talking about Henry and drifted off into random thoughts. Doctor Joseph thought that this was the way Liz handled painful experiences, she just drifted off. He didn't say anything to Liz as he felt she was having a hard enough time just hanging on to her sessions. Before the session ended he reminded Liz that at the beginning of her sessions, he had warned her that there would come a time she would not want to come to her sessions. He said, "This usually means some memories are coming to your conscious mind that you do not want to consider." She left without saying another word.

When Lillian left, Jacob was terribly lonely. He told Don that he must go back to his condo in Arizona and think about what had happened to him and to find a way to deal with it. On the flight back to Phoenix, all he could think of was Lillian. Arriving to his condo was a miserable experience. All he could do was to make himself eat and to go to bed. He realized he was depressed, and he started making himself go to the gym and walk at least two miles a day. This helped with his depression, but he continued to grieve over what he thought was the loss of Lillian.

Lillian returned home and felt if she could just get back into her old routines, she would get over her experiences with Jacob, and life would be the same again. When she said 'again', she wondered was life really the same. She knew that since her husband's death she had not really been happy, but she had managed to at least accept her life and fill it with activities that kept her from thinking how she really felt.

As the days passed, the memory of Jacob did not lessen. She found herself day dreaming of their adventures, and wondering if Jacob ever thought of her. She remembered Margaret's comment about when you loved again, sex was not a problem. She remembered when she was dating Jacob the idea of having sex with him was repulsive. Now she was finding this idea was not repulsive.

After two months, she found herself restless. She no longer liked her activities and was generally dissatisfied with her life. One morning after she had a miserable night, she called Margaret. When Margaret answered she had a hard time telling her why she called. She finally blurted out to Margaret, "I am terribly lonely. I can't sleep, and I keep thinking of Jacob. I told him to not call me. I wanted to think over my feelings for Jacob as I was content and didn't think I wanted another marriage. I am now miserable, and all I can think of is Jacob. What can I do?"

Margaret told her the simplest answer was to call Jacob and tell him how she felt. "I know that you have thought of this, and for some reason you haven't called him." Lillian replied, "It is hard for me at this time to admit that I need another person. When James died, I grieved for two years, and I told myself I would never again allow myself to become attached to any person. To lose them a second time would be impossible to bear." Margaret was silent for a long time, and Lillian found herself saying, "Hello, are you still there?" Margaret said, "Yes, I am just thinking if I ever had those feelings. My finding Andy was under very trying times. I had discovered my dearest niece was seriously ill, and Andy and I had not seen each other for 23 years. I expected Andy to reject me, but instead he told me to let bygones be gone, and he was very kind to me. He let me be involved in Mary's life, and the gratitude I had for him changed to love. When he told me, he had the same feeling. I knew I could not live without him. Lillian, you are really telling me that you cannot live without Jacob. Why are you so resistant to acknowledging this?" She heard Lillian starting to cry and heard her say, "You are right, and I am so frightened to step out and say to Jacob I want you." After a while, she stopped crying and thanked Margaret. She ended the conversation with saying, "I know what I must do."

When Margaret hung up, she called out to Andy asking him what was Jacob's number. He called back the number, and she immediately called. Jacob answered the phone. He sounded depressed and seemed irritated to hear from Margaret. Margaret, in her commanding voice, said, "Snap out of it. I have some important news for you. Lillian just called me and said that she thought of you constantly and was trying to decide how she could get in touch with you. I have only one message for you. Get off you seat and catch the next plane to Waco! Her address is 608 Main Street." She hung up before he could say anything.

Chapter XX

Mary and Liz were in their third month of therapy. Mary had recovered much of her memory. Her giving up her repressive defense made her more anxiety laden. She was beginning to explore her past relationships. She chose to talk about Tom Carlson. She talked about their dating in her junior and senior years of high school. "I didn't know it then, but as I look at it now, I realize he was a very immature boy. He acted like an important man about campus, but underneath he was dependent upon his father's strength. He felt that he would inherit a large ranch, and all he had to do was sit back, and it would take care of him for all of his life. I wonder now why was I so drawn to him." She puzzled over this for two sessions.

At the end of the second week of struggling with this, she started reporting that for some reason she always seemed irritable when she was around her father. His least kindness or thoughtfulness towards her angered her. At first, she would just walk away, but recently she was expressing irritation towards him for no real reason. She wondered what was happening to her. Doctor Joseph was concerned about this turn of events. He knew what she was struggling with, and he didn't think she had enough emotional strength to deal with it at this time. He cautiously listened and was prepared to interfere at any indication of a severe depression.

In the fourth week of this struggle, Mary continued with this increasing anger and disgust of her father, Andy. Her memory loss was disappearing in many areas. She remembered all about Jonathan. From that curly headed kid in high school, to the happy go lucky rodeo rider, the soldier, and finally the oil man. She was especially pleased to connect all of Jonathan in her memory. When that day happened, she came home from her session and immediately called Jonathan saying, "Jonathan, I know you." He was equally excited. They talked for a few moments, and he reminded her that she was supposed to be in Santa Fe at 5:30 p.m. as they were attending the Montesinos-Fremont wedding.

It was September 2, 1968, and the wedding was to take place at the Conquistador Chapel in St Francis Cathedral. Jonathan was in his office in Socorro, and he told Mary he would pick her up. They would go together. The wedding was elegant and was very private.

By September, 1976, Canela was a very wealthy woman. Her old friends were constantly soliciting her for their activities. She didn't respond to any of their invitations. She was changing her attitude as to what it meant to be an aristocrat. Her old view was that of her father. He felt that an aristocrat was proud and haughty. He felt one associated only with one's class. When Canela looked at her father's class, she realized that she wanted no part of them. She liked the solid honest way that Fremont and Jonathan lived and worked. Both were very wealthy, but they lived modestly and had loyal friends. That night, Canela told Fremont about her changing attitude. He said, "Canela, anything you want to be or where you want to live is fine with me. All I want is to love and be loved by you." They went to bed and consummated their marriage.

Liz, over the next few weeks, began to have erratic behavior. She would alternate between impulsive and depressive behavior. Doctor Joseph was suspecting that she was developing a manic-depressive pattern of behavior. He had not given up his idea that she had 'as if' personality disorder, but these changing behaviors troubled him. He was beginning to think that he was going to have to find more supporting people for Liz if he was to continue with her treatment.

On the day that Mary remembered Jonathan, Doctor Joseph was talking to Liz about having someone in her life that could help her if she became more depressed. Liz laughed nervously and said, "Mary would help me if she was okay, but the only person I want is Henry Feldhaus. He doesn't like the way I am."

Doctor Joseph asked about her parents. Liz responded, "Oh, Daddy would give you all of the money you want, but he would not have time for me. He was never affectionate with me." The use of the affectionate word alerted Doctor Joseph, and he asked, if he could talk with her parents.

Liz thought for a moment and said, "I will agree on one condition -- that you tell me what your thoughts are about them after their interview with you." Doctor Joseph said, "Our interviews belong to us, and so will theirs belong to them. I will use their information in order to help you. Liz, every person sees events in their lives from their perspective, and many times different perspectives have added truth value. In other words, people have prejudices and blind spots." Liz said, "I don't want Henry to know what I am doing, so I guess it is okay to talk to my father." The session ended with Doctor Joseph increasing her sessions to five times a week and gave Liz his home phone number.

When Doctor Joseph called William Horne, he had difficulty getting thru to him. He was only able to get the secretary to call Mr. Horne to the phone when he said, "His daughter requested him to call Mr. Horne." William Horne was surprised and immediately picked up the phone. He answered the phone asking, "What kind of doctor are you?" Doctor Joseph answered, "My name is Ben Joseph, and I am a psychiatrist. I am treating your daughter, and she has agreed for me to interview you." "What kind of trouble is she into now?" asked Mr. Horne. With the emphasis, "what trouble now", Doctor Joseph felt anger. He replied, "Mr. Horne, I know from Elizabeth's accounts that you and she have problems relating with each other. I am calling you now because I am deeply concerned about Elizabeth's welfare. She has been seeing me for over six months, and I am concerned about her continuing with me without any loving person being available for her." Mr. Horne's response was to the effect that he was surprised that she had stayed with him that long. Doctor Joseph responded with some anger and said, "Mr. Horne, I called you because I am concerned about your daughter's life. I can see by your reactions that you do not give a damn for your daughter. I regret that I bothered to call you." He hung up.

William Horne was not used to anyone talking to him like that and immediately told his secretary to call that doctor back. Doctor Joseph's secretary refused to call Doctor Joseph to the phone, and Horne grabbed the phone and demanded to speak to Doctor Joseph. There was a click and a busy signal. He slammed down the phone and yelled, "Get me my car and the address of that damn psychiatrist." He left cussing. It was the worst tantrum his secretary had ever experienced.

He continued being angry all the way to Doctor Joseph's office. He burst into the office and demanded to speak to Doctor Joseph. Doctor Joseph's secretary told him Doctor Joseph was busy and would see no other patients that day. Horne raged that he was not a patient, and he was going to see him this minute. Doctor Joseph's secretary calmly picked up the phone and called the police. She said to the answering officer, "I have in my office an abusive man that is threatening" -- Horne put his hand on the phone and cut off the call. He said, "I will wait, and I won't threaten you."

Doctor Joseph had called Horne during his lunch period. He had a full case load that afternoon. Horne sat and waited. He saw five patients pass thru Doctor Joseph's door. At five o'clock, his secretary left and didn't say a word. At six o'clock the last patient left. Doctor Joseph completed his notes, put on his coat, and walked into the waiting room. Mr. Horne got up and asked if he could talk with him. Doctor Joseph said, "Mr. Horne, I don't think we have anything to talk about. I am only interested in people that love Liz, and it is obvious that you are not one." Horne felt anger rising in him and knew if he didn't control it he would have no chance with this abrupt doctor. Instead of answering angrily he said, "Doctor, I wonder how you can draw such an idea of me from my outburst of anger. You have no idea of the pain Elizabeth has caused me. You called me out of the blue and told me my daughter is in danger and then when I don't respond like you felt I should, you became hostile and hung up on me." As he was talking, Doctor Joseph was walking to the door. He had no intention of wasting any time with this man. As he was ushering Horne out of his office, Horne said, "If waiting for four hours doesn't mean I care for Elizabeth, then you tell me what it means. When you called, I had my most important client waiting for me. I left him standing. If this doesn't mean something to you, it is I who is wasting my time." With that, Doctor Joseph paused and said, "I will talk with you for a few minutes." They went into his office.

When they sat down, Horne started talking. He said, "This isn't the first time I have talked to a psychiatrist about Elizabeth. We have been to Child Psychiatrists and probably ones like you. I don't know what brand of thought that you practice under, but I am sure I have had some experience with it. If you sense I am bitter about your profession, you would be only partially right. I just want my daughter to be happy, and none of your profession has helped Elizabeth." Doctor Joseph was silent and let him talk. "All of that is past, and I want you to know that I love Liz. I would do anything to help her."

Doctor Joseph was impressed and told Horne that Liz was in a bad position. She wanted to change her way of relating to people and was having a hard time facing her problems. I told her that I would have to hospitalize her if she didn't have someone to respond to her if she became desperate. In other words, I feel that Liz is potentially suicidal. I asked Liz if she had anyone who could help her with this danger. She thought of several, but felt you were probably the only one that would help. She gave me permission to talk to you. Horne sat quietly and tears began to run down his cheeks. He took out his handkerchief and blew his nose and didn't say anything. Finally he said, "What must I do?" Doctor Joseph said, "Can you come in tomorrow at nine o'clock?" He said a simple yes.

At 8:30 a.m. the next day, Doctor Joseph's secretary arrived and found William Horne waiting. They didn't exchange words. He simply walked in and sat down. A few minutes until 9:00, Doctor Joseph arrived, and he and William Horne went into his office. Horne said, "I know that I am to start talking, and you will respond when you feel it is appropriate. I want to start with my early life. I was a prodigy child. My father was a barber, and my mother was a school teacher. We were middle, middle class. It soon became obvious to my mother that I quickly grasped information, and she pushed me. I responded quickly, and by age 14, I had graduated from college. By 18 years old, I had two graduate degrees. I had a PhD. in economics and a PhD. in finance. I started my company when I was 18 1/2 years old, and in two years, I was amazingly successful. I was mainly a financial advisor for large companies and wealthy individuals. I was 20 years old at this time, and for the first time, I became interested in women. I was very inadequate in my attempts to date. I was invited one night to a large party. There were many different age groups there, but I was particularly attracted to a young woman whom I later discovered was only 18 years old. We were drinking heavily, and we had sex. As it turned out, it was my first experience as well as hers. I didn't hear from her for three months, when suddenly, I got a call, and she identified herself as Suzanne Thompson. I didn't know the name Thompson, and I asked who was she and what was our connection. She recalled her sexual experience with me and told me that she was pregnant. She said,

'I am calling you because I want to meet with you and see what we can decide to do about this problem. My parents are insisting that they be involved in the decision making of this problem.' She requested that I come to her home as soon as possible, so I immediately left the office and went to her place of residence. I want to describe to you about my feelings when I entered that house. I was suspicious that I was not the father and felt I was about to be taken. On top of that, if she really was pregnant by me, I was scared of her parents. It was very awkward being with these people, and we had a difficult time starting to talk. I opened the conversation saying, ' I have serious doubts that I am the father of this child. Suzanne, can you tell me anything to indicate to me that I am the father?' Suzanne responded, 'You are asking a very awkward question because my parents are here, but I feel it is necessary that I be frank. If you will remember, we were very awkward in our sexual experience. You had difficulty asserting yourself, and I had difficulty responding to it. We were rank amateurs. If this doesn't indicate to you that I was a virgin, I don't know what other way I could do it. My parents can tell you that I have not dated since that night. I have been depressed and troubled. I was just about recovering from all this when I missed two periods, and I went to my doctor to see what the problem was. He told me I was 3 months pregnant. I was mortified, and it took me two days to tell my parents about it. If this doesn't convince you that you are the father, I have no other evidence for you.' I was struck by this and knew then that I was the father of this child. I felt bewildered and asked them what they thought we should do. I was referring to the parents and Suzanne. The father immediately said, 'Suzanne is a child of a strict Catholic family. There will be no question of an abortion. Suzanne must carry this child to maturity. The problem now is what kind of role do you want to play in this? Since both of you were drunk when this happened, I think both of you are mutually responsible. You have the right to choose whatever course of action you want. We have told Suzanne that we think she should get married to the man who is the father of this child. Hopefully, they could work out a relationship with each other and have a successful marriage. Suzanne is undecided about this.'

I knew it was my time to talk. I didn't know this woman, and I certainly wasn't intending to get married at 20. My mind was going in a rush of thoughts. I don't know how long I was silent, but I heard myself saying, 'I was raised in a Christian family, and I was taught that one was responsible for their actions. I will marry Suzanne if she is willing, and I will try to be a good husband and father.' Her father then said, 'I want you and Suzanne to see her family Priest. Would you be willing to do that?' I agreed, and we met with Father McCarty. Father McCarty was an old Irish Priest and was a classical Catholic priest. By that, I mean he had rigid ideas. He said, 'Man must pay for his sins, and I agree that you both should be married. Since you are not a Catholic, I don't feel responsible for your religious health, but I would advise you to see your own minister.' He told Suzanne that he wanted her to have a confession, and as she was leaving the confession booth, I heard the Priest say, 'Say 40 Hail Mary's.'

I am not a religious person, so I didn't see anybody. We set the wedding date as early as possible as she was already three months pregnant. So in May of 1940, we were married, and Liz was born in November, 1940. During her pregnancy, Suzanne stayed with her parents and well into 1941, she was living with them. When Liz was one year old, we moved together and were actually only together one month before December 7, 1941.

I had gained a reputation of being a problem solver. Many of my clients were high up in the political circles of our country, and when they were trying to establish a brain center for the purpose of developing skills in code breaking, my name was brought up. I was immediately inducted into the Army and assigned to a code breaking unit. They gave me one week before my incarceration in order to settle up my business affairs. I placed all of my accounts in the hand of my second in command, and he was able to maintain it throughout the war. I did only the basic things to take care of Suzanne and my daughter. I use the term incarceration deliberately because that's what really happened to me. We were sequestered in a remote area outside of Washington, D.C. and were not allowed to leave the premises or have any visitors. We communicated with our families through another post office, and the implication was that we were overseas. So, Suzanne and I had no contact from January of 1942 until August of 1945. I was in the group that was trying to break the Japanese Naval Code, and we were successful in doing this. This gave me some prestige in our organization, and I was involved in many code breaking efforts. The sequestering of these 'brains' led to complications as some became depressed, and on one occasion, one committed suicide. The Army was greatly concerned about this and drafted a psychoanalyst from New York to be available to any of the code breakers that might have emotional problems. The name of this psychoanalyst was Doctor Samuel Goldstein." Doctor Joseph recognized this name and knew him to be a classical Freudian Psychoanalyst. Horne continued, "For some reason, Doctor Goldstein and I became friends, and he introduced me to many of the concepts of psychoanalysis. I mention this because in my efforts to control my daughter's distress, I used that knowledge in pursuing help for her distress.

When I arrived back from my incarceration, I found that Liz had been mothered by her grandmother. Suzanne did not like the fact that she had a child by a man she didn't know or love. She wasn't cruel in her rejection of Liz but was bitter over the changes in her body. She was only 18 and had striae on her abdomen, and her breasts were no longer erect and firm. They were now somewhat enlarged and were hanging. In other words, she felt that I had robbed her of her youthful look and made her a middle aged woman. So when I returned, I had a daughter whose mother was her grandmother. Her real mother had rejected her child and me.

We were not going to reengage our relationship and were thinking seriously of divorce when suddenly Mrs. Thompson died. This was a disaster for Liz, Suzanne, and me. We were forced to become parents because there was no one to take care of Liz. This was very difficult for Liz because she had lost a very loving person and was now dealing with two angry adults. Fortunately for me, I had some time with Liz before her grandmother died, and I admired her spunk and energy. In a way, I was very proud of her. I was determined that I was going to be a good father to her. I don't know what happened, but whatever it was, I was not satisfactory to Liz. At first, she was grief stricken and depressed over her grandmother's death and then violently angry. We could hardly deal with her. I say 'we' but, actually, I was mainly the one dealing with it. Suzanne just walked away emotionally and physically.

I want you to understand one thing, Doctor, I am not being critical of Suzanne. I think she was doing the only thing she could do at that time. Anyway from age 5 to 7 was living hell for Liz and me. Child psychiatrists were just becoming available at that time, and she saw several during that period without much help to Liz. As you know in those days, the parents were seen as much as the child, and I was the only parent who attended those meetings. My wife still lived in the apartment with us but did not participate with Liz on any level. It wasn't until she was 7 years old that I found a nanny for Liz that seemed to show her the love that she needed so desperately. This nanny was a middle-aged Navajo Indian woman. She had a large family that she needed to support and was very grateful to get the job. From 7 until 13, things went fairly well with Liz. At age 13, I discovered that this nanny was stealing from me by taking expensive antiques from the house and selling them. I talked to Liz before I fired this woman, and she was enraged that I would even consider firing her even though she was stealing significant items from our family. I decided to fire her anyway, and all hell broke loose with Liz. Things became so desperate, I sought help from anywhere I could get it.

My wealthier clients talked to me about how they had handled their rebellious teenagers. They had not used the psychiatric route as I had. By this time, I was pretty discouraged about its effectiveness for Liz. They told me about a private girls' school in Switzerland that treated and educated troubled teenagers. I sent Liz there, and she was there for four years. I visited her several times a year and got monthly reports as to her progress. The school's position was that the child was from a failed family, and they would be the family as well as the educator of the child. They discouraged any parental involvement during that four year period of time. Liz came home from Switzerland a total stranger to me. She was more an European than an American girl. In a very formal way, she told me, 'Father, (she addressed me as father, not dad or daddy), I have decided that what's best for you and me is for me to get a college education and then go my way.' I can hear that accent even now. She continued saying, 'I want to go to the University of New Mexico.' She was there for four years being an average student. At graduation, I received a letter from her which was as follows, 'Dear Dad, (notice she changed it from father to dad), I appreciate all the help you have given me in getting my college degree and making it possible for me to be an independent person. I know that I have been a problem for you, but I feel that we have nothing to offer each other. I feel that it would be best now if we parted company. You go your way, and I will go mine.' She ended the letter by saying good-bye and a brief thanks.

I was not able to let her go that way, so I hired a private investigator to follow her on a daily basis and report to me once a week as to what was happening to her. In 1970, he reported that she had left Dallas and had joined a person by the name of Mary McGregor. They were starting a start-up company in cosmetics. Since this company was placed in Albuquerque where I had my office, I assumed the responsibility of following Liz' career. I was very proud of her, and when 5 years later, I read her company had been sold, and she was a 10% owner, it didn't take much to figure out how much my daughter was worth. I knew she had gone on a cruise, and I had no contact with her until you called me.

Now, Doctor, I think I need to bring you up to date about what happened between me and my wife. For some reason, we never got a divorce. She went her way and had her own apartment, and I went my way and had my apartment. I gave her a generous allowance that was automatically applied to her account every month, and we had no reason to have any association with each other. I went about the business of my life. My business was stable and productive, but my personal life was chaotic. I had numerous affairs. I used women sexually and developed no loving relations with any of them. Suzanne had the same experience.

In 1970, I was 50 years old and Suzanne was 48. We got together one day, for some reason I don't remember why and talked about getting divorced. We both at that point in our lives were discouraged about how we had lived our personal lives. I started telling her of my utter disregard for anything that approached a normal, loving experience. I told her I was very lonely, and I was determined to find someone that I could love. She talked to me in a way that I had never experienced. With almost tears in her voice, she said, 'I am also intensely lonely. I have never had a successful relationship with any man. The only man I ever loved was my father, and he has been dead now for 10 years.' When I was listening to her describe her despair, a thought came to my mind. Maybe we should try to see what we could do with each other. I looked at Suzanne and saw a very attractive middle-aged woman. She was intelligent and certainly would be an asset to anyone. I didn't say anything immediately about my thoughts, but I suggested that we continue to talk. She agreed. It surprised me that I found her interesting and before long, we were talking regularly.

I told her that I would like to start dating her and see if we could develop any kind of a relationship. And we did. At first, it was twice a week. It was usually a dinner in some quiet place where we could talk. We both began to like each other and wanted to see each other more frequently than twice a week. After doing this for several months, we decided we would move in together and see if we could get along with a more intimate relationship. As I look at it now, even though we were experienced sexually with other people, our first contact together was just as amateurish as our first. When it was over, we looked at each other and said, 'We certainly have not improved our sexual ability.' We both laughed. From that point on, we grew to love each other, and now we are a dedicated husband and wife. When I got home last night, I told Suzanne all that happened in my talk with you. She wants to do everything she can to help Liz. She says, 'I have absolutely no relationship with Liz, and I know I cannot be of any help to her. I would like to say I love her, but I have no feeling for her. I want you to help Liz, and I will do anything to help you do that.' So, Doctor, in conclusion, that is the situation between Suzanne and me, and what I perceive as my relationship with Liz."

There was a long period of silence, and Doctor Joseph felt that Mr. Horne was not going to say anything else. He usually would end a session in silence, but he felt like this was not a therapeutic session. He started talking to him about being a caring person for a very disturbed person. He said to Mr. Horne, "Thank you for coming. You have been very helpful in your information. I think I need to tell you something about how Liz perceives this. She doesn't have the memory that you are reporting. She thinks that you were much older when you married her mother, and you had been seeking a trophy wife. She thought her mother was seeking a rich man. I don't know yet how she got into this perception as it is so contradictory to what you have told me. I do know that probably that the period of time between ages 7 to 13 was a time that Liz established a good relationship with you, at least a relationship, she now wants to depend upon. I don't know how much of an emergency Liz is going to present to us, but if it is as severe as I suspect, you will be required to spend a lot of time with her. Mainly you will be protecting her from herself. This is a duty that you cannot put on anybody else. You will very likely be required to be with her 24 hours a day. If you can't do this or are not willing to do this, tell me now because when that time occurs, I do not want to have a person that won't be committed to her care. I think she will need this care to survive."

After a long silence, Mr. Horne started talking. He said to Doctor Joseph, "My silence had nothing to do with my reluctance to assume this responsibility. I was really trying to inventory myself and see what strengths I have that would be beneficial to Liz if this demand becomes reality. I think the only resource I have is a love I have developed with my present wife. I know how to love now. When I said that to myself, I felt reassured, and I can say positively to you, **yes I will be available**. I know I can be loving and I do love Liz." This ended their session. No future appointments were made.

Chapter XXI

AFTER CANELA AND FREMONT'S WEDDING, Mary and Jonathan drove back to Albuquerque. She was telling him in more detail about the difficulty she was having with her father living in her house. She said, "I still don't remember him as being my father. I have become increasingly irritable with having him constantly around the house, and I have asked Margaret to move with him into the guest house, at least during the night. I know that I am increasingly depressed, and it troubles me that I am dealing with this problem in this way. I don't want to be a burden to you as I have already imposed on you a lot during this period of time. I have been seeing Doctor Joseph since March. Jonathan, how have you endured all this? I have shown you that I love you, but I haven't been willing to commit myself to you."

Jonathan was reluctant to get into this kind of conversation. He didn't want his feelings to complicate whatever feelings she was dealing with. He had been having second thoughts about their relationship. Even though Mary had regained much of her memory, he was losing hope about the future of their relationship. It had been almost a year since he came into that hospital desperately trying to find a way to relate to her. In many ways, he was still up against a stone wall. He was silent as he had all these thoughts and didn't try to get any answers. He just drew her closer to him in the car and said nothing.

When they arrived back at Mary's house and said good night, he drove all the way to his house in Socorro, New Mexico. He would later think that this drive to Socorro rather than his apartment in Albuquerque was the desire to break away from this unhappy relationship with Mary.

Over the next month, Mary's sessions with Doctor Joseph became more and more disturbed. She was struggling hard to work with the memory connected with her father while at the same time fighting to keep her loss memory of him. She was having strong conflicting feelings with the result being she was becoming deeply depressed. It was on October 25, 1976, during one of her sessions, she abruptly shouted out, "I know that bastard is my father." The rest of the session was filled with rage and in many ways appeared to Doctor Joseph to be psychotic.

At the end of the session, she became a retarded depressed patient. She sat frozen in her chair and had a blank depressed expression and didn't utter a single word. He knew he had a serious problem on his hands. The question was whether to try to treat her at her home or in an institution. At that time, Albuquerque had no really good psychiatric facilities. They generally warehoused people there and nothing constructive was done with their problems.

He immediately called Jonathan. He told him that in lay terms, Mary has had a nervous breakdown. He said, "She is severely depressed, and if I admit her to a local institution, the only treatment I can perform there would be shock treatment. I do not like that treatment. Many times it damages the brain, and the consequences of it are more damaging to a patient's future life than trying to work through it psychologically. What I'm telling you, Jonathan, is I need you to come here and be a significant caretaker of Mary as I try to work her through this episode. I will try to use some medication to help her, but I want to depend heavily upon your supporting relationship. You will have to spend 24 hours a day with her. I would not trust her with any less care. As we work through this retarded depression, the main problem we get into is the agitated state that usually evolves from it. The mobility of the agitated state increases the risk of suicide. In other words, as she becomes an agitated depressive person, suicide becomes an increased possibility. I lay out all this to you, Jonathan, because it is going to be trying on both you and me. If we are successful in this, you will have a wonderful person in your life."

Jonathan was quiet for a long period of time. He said, "Doctor, I need to be honest with you. I still love Mary, but recently I have been withdrawing from her. I think I have been losing hope that she would ever be my wife. In my silence, I was trying to inventory myself. I was asking myself, 'Do I still love Mary enough to go through this crisis?' To my surprise, a resounding yes came into my mind. Yes, Doctor Joseph, I will be there immediately, and I will build whatever is necessary to

Lost and Found

modify in her home to facilitate the care of Mary. I will not fail you for I believe as you do; Mary is going to be a wonderful person with or without me." Doctor Joseph canceled all of his patients and called for an ambulance. He got in the ambulance with Mary and went with her to her home and stayed with her until Jonathan arrived, which was about an hour-and-a-half. They both went over the house and decided how they could best develop a care facility for Mary by remodeling the bedroom and the adjoining bathroom.

Jonathan called Margaret and told her that he needed her there immediately as he initially was going to be involved with changing the structure of Mary's house. When she arrived, Doctor Joseph talked to her and explained what she was facing. He said, "Jonathan is the primary caretaker of Mary, and you are the caretaker of Jonathan. Neither one of you realizes the task that you are now attempting to undertake, and I am just as concerned about Jonathan as I am about Mary." Margaret didn't understand all that was being told her, but she did understand one thing. Her niece was severely ill and was in a crisis. She had no problem being a caretaker of Jonathan and had begun to love him. She was deeply impressed about his caring for Mary.

For the next two weeks things were very chaotic. Mary would lay in the bed curled up in a fetal position and had regressed in all manner of ways. She did not control her personal hygiene and the care of this fell all on Jonathan. When she had bowel movements, a female aide and Jonathan cleaned her. He fed her, and he tended to her constantly. After two weeks of this regressed behavior, she slowly began to recognize Jonathan. Even though she didn't appear to know what was happening, there was an inner awareness of what she was doing to herself and Jonathan. This awareness aroused her to break loose from this terrible reaction to her rage towards her father. She abandoned her fetal position and became agitated and started talking to Jonathan in a slurred voice. It was almost a muttering. She regained use of her personal hygiene and started eating by herself.

By the fourth week she was talking to Jonathan and some of their previous relationship was becoming a part of their life together. Her muted stage with Doctor Joseph stopped, and she started trying to deal with her rage towards her now recognized father. Slowly, she rebuilt her defense systems and abandoned her psychotic behavior. She began raging in every session she had with Doctor Joseph about her feelings towards her father. She described in detail to Doctor Joseph about how cruel he was when he returned from the Army. Her mother endured these cruelties 24 hours a day while she only was with him in the mornings and late afternoons. She reviewed with him the horror and sadness she felt while she was sitting with her dead mother who was lying on that bed with the waxen look of a dead person. As she was experiencing it now, she didn't know how she endured those three hours of being with her dead mother. When her father arrived, she was numb, and it wasn't until her mother's body was removed that all the rage that she felt towards him came out. She remembered trying to hit him with anything she could get her hands on. As she was looking at it now, she realized that her father was in shock, too, and she remembered him saying, "Oh, I'm so sorry, so sorry. I have killed the only person I have ever loved." That memory shocked her. She paused and said, "Doctor Joseph, my father really did love my mother." As they talked further in that session, she said, "I think I am ready to confront my father. I want to have a session with him where I tell him what he has done to my life. I am not sure whether I will have the strength to be nonviolent. I want Jonathan with me because I can trust him to be strong enough to protect me while I go through this process."

When Doctor Joseph approached Andy about coming to a session with Mary he said, "It could be violent." When Margaret heard the term violent, she immediately was very protective of Andy. She said to Doctor Joseph, "I don't want Andy to be involved in this. I know that Mary is my niece, and I love her, but I don't want to lose my husband to a psychotic niece." Doctor Joseph said, "Mary is not psychotic now. Margaret, I don't think she will be psychotic in this session. I have taken time to try to explain to Jonathan what we are trying to do, and he assures me he will protect Andy from Mary's rage."

It was a Wednesday afternoon on December 18, 1976, that this session occurred. Doctor Joseph, Mary, Jonathan, and Andy were seated in a circle in his office. Jonathan and Doctor Joseph were on either side of Mary, and Andy was opposite Mary. They were separated by about 8 feet.

Mary started talking. She said, "I know you are my father, and knowing this has brought into my awareness all the hate and despair

I feel for you." The more she talked about her rage towards him, the more agitated she became. She started shifting around in her chair and started moving her arms as if she was going to push herself up from the chair. Every time she did this, Jonathan put his hand on her shoulder and tried to reassure her. On one occasion she jumped up from her chair and started toward Andy. She obviously intended to harm him. Jonathan grabbed her and held her tightly in his arms, and she burst out crying. She was crying and shouting, "Oh, how can I ever get through this anger and despair? Will this never end?" She collapsed in his arms. It seemed that she had gone into a state of unconsciousness, and Jonathan laid her on the floor. Doctor Joseph immediately knelt down and felt her pulse and motioned for his secretary to bring in his blood pressure machine. Her pulse was 120 per minute, and her blood pressure was 170 over 110. He made a judgment that she would probably only maintain this seemingly unconscious state for a short period of time and suggested that they all sit near her and wait for this to clear up. Slowly, she came back into consciousness and looked at Jonathan. She held out her arms to Jonathan and said, "Oh, Jonathan, will this never end?" He said, "Yes, my darling, it is going to end, and we are going to go home and get some rest. You will feel better tomorrow."

With Doctor Joseph's permission, Jonathan took Mary home and put her to bed. Mary said, "Oh, Jonathan, don't leave me. Come to bed with me. I need to hold on to something sane and comforting. You are the only one I know that can give this to me." So, they went to bed together. Both were lying on their sides, and Mary was in a spoon position with Jonathan. Mary went sound asleep, but Jonathan was wide awake. There was no sexual feeling between them. It was 2:00 in the morning when Mary awakened and asked Jonathan if he would get some food for her. He said, "Mary, you will have to get up and go into the kitchen with me. I cannot leave you alone." So, at 2:00 a.m., Mary and Jonathan had their breakfast. In many ways Jonathan noticed that Mary was different. She didn't have that crazy look about her, and all the anger she had been expressing seemed to be out of her face and body. They had a quiet meal, and she said, "Jonathan, I think I have broken through all this despair. I think I am going to get well now. I know I still have a long way to go, but for the first time, I see real possibilities for us." Jonathan didn't say anything. All he felt was utter exhaustion. He said, "Mary, I haven't slept all night. Let's go back to bed and see if I can get some sleep." He somehow felt she was safe now, and for the first time in a long time, he slept deeply.

When Doctor Joseph arrived the following day, he saw a marked change in Mary. She was not depressed and was talking rationally. After the session, he met with Jonathan and told him that even though Mary seemed greatly improved, it was in his experience a dangerous period in her treatment. These miraculous changes do not portend good changes, for she may have actually decided to commit suicide. The relief is because suicide would solve her problems. He said, "I would feel better if she had continued with her rage and despair. I want you to hire another person to come in and assist you. Actually, I want you to hire three people to be here for three consecutive eight hour periods. Any time you have a possibility of being away from her, I want one of them to be in attendance. I am not going to lose Mary." Jonathan had a hard time understanding this position, but he believed in Doctor Joseph and became fearful.

Actually, Mary was thinking of suicide as a solution to this hate and had developed an intricate plan of seducing Jonathan to be willing to sleep when they went to bed. When he was sound asleep, she planned to kill herself. She was terribly frustrated by all these attendants, and the anger returned. She began to express anger more towards Doctor Joseph than Jonathan. She accused Doctor Joseph of thinking she was going to commit suicide, and how ridiculous could he be. She deliberately used contempt as a way of persuading him to abandon his anti-suicide position. After two weeks, she realized he was not going to do this, and she began to express her rage again towards him. She said, "Why didn't you get out of my way and let me commit suicide? You did everything to keep me from getting out of this terrible mess. You are supposed to be a kind doctor and look what a sadistic bastard you are." Doctor Joseph realized this was a transference problem and listened carefully. She had transferred all of her anger away from Andy to him and was going to try to work through it by raging with him. He was a person she knew she would not harm. This rage lasted for a month, and she slowly began to resolve the pain and agony of her death wish for her father. Slowly, she began to regain control of herself and began to think in terms of living rather than in dying. Doctor Joseph did not know whether this was real or not and was continuing his careful observation. By the middle of

February, 1977, he was convinced it was safe and told Jonathan he could be relieved, and he felt like that Margaret, with her daytime care, would be sufficient to maintain Mary. When he told Mary this, she agreed that she was no longer suicidal, but she said, "I need Jonathan to stay with me for another week." She wanted Jonathan to spend the nights with her. They didn't sleep in the same bed that week. Jonathan slept on a reclining chair by her bed. She continued to improve and told Jonathan that she felt now she could make it by herself. It was the first of March, 1977. She had been in intensive psychotherapy for about a year.

Chapter XXII

THE NEXT DAY AFTER HER father's session with Doctor Joseph, Liz came to her session anxiously expecting to learn about what her father had said to Doctor Joseph. Doctor Joseph reminded her that her father's session with him was private as well as her sessions with him were private. This was not satisfactory with Liz, and she was very angry during that session. In fact, the following session became more turbulent. She was no longer willing to be flippant and disconnected. She seemed to grab hold of her anger and the despair of her life with a vengeance. She started talking about her father's firing of her nanny. She said, "How could a father be so insensitive? I lost my real mother (my grandmother) and found someone that I loved, and my father got rid of her." She began to rage about him and it lasted over the next few weeks. Doctor Joseph became fearful that she would slip into a psychotic episode.

It seemed to Doctor Joseph that he was having another very disturbed patient like Mary. He knew he was going to have to develop the same kind of care for Liz as he had for Mary. Liz didn't have a Jonathan that he knew of, and certainly her father had not been intimately involved with her.

What was he going to do? He knew that she was interested in a Henry Feldhaus in Amarillo. He decided to try to locate him and talk to him. He paused with this and said to himself, "Maybe I ought to involve her father in this process." At the end of the session, he asked Liz to wait in his reception room. While she was waiting, he called Mr. Horne and related the change that was occurring in her treatment, and that he felt she was moving into a dangerous period. He said, "Liz does not have any place to go where she will be protected. I have only two alternatives with her. One is to admit her to the local psychiatric unit of a general hospital, which would just warehouse her. By that, I mean they would feed and clothe her but would do nothing to help her with her psychiatric problems. What I would prefer to do is for you to establish a place for her where she and you can live together. Hopefully, I can find another person. I am going to call and see if a Henry Feldhaus is at all interested in helping Liz. Liz has told me in her sessions that she dearly loves a man named Henry Feldhaus who lives in Amarillo. In fact, her love for this man is the reason for her being in treatment. If I am able to get this man to come and help us, assuming you are willing to do what I have proposed, I feel we have a chance to get a complete recovery for Liz and a better life."

Mr. Horne said, "Doctor, I thought it was very clear to you that my wife and I are dedicated to Liz. I will establish whatever you prescribe for her, and I will go to Amarillo and talk to this Henry Feldhaus. I will do it immediately." Doctor Joseph said, "I will tell Liz that I am suspicious that maybe something is wrong with her brain because of her changing behavior and that I want to admit her overnight to get some tests done. If she resists, I will insist on it, and I feel like I can get her to go to the hospital. I will keep her there for at least two days and in that period of time, I hope you will be able to establish a place where you can stay with Liz, or both you and Henry can stay with her for 24 hours a day."

Mr. Horne immediately left his office, and after procuring the address and telephone number of Henry Feldhaus drove to his private airport. He was on his plane when he called Henry Feldhaus. He directed the pilot to fly directly to Amarillo as fast as he could. He felt fortunate that this man, Henry Feldhaus, answered the phone.

He opened the conversation by saying, "Mr. Feldhaus, my name is William Horne. I am the father of Elizabeth Horne, and I am inquiring of you if you know this woman." There was a silence, and then in an anxious voice Henry said, "Has anything happened to Liz?" This response assured Mr. Horne that he was talking to the right person. He said, "Mr. Feldhaus, my daughter is in serious trouble, and I am now in my personal airplane flying to Amarillo to meet with you. Will you meet me at the airport? There is much I need to discuss with you." Henry interrupted and said, "What has happened to Liz? I know you don't know this, but I am madly in love with Liz. I wouldn't be sitting here in Amarillo if it weren't for the problems we have in relating to each other. Your calling me has given me the first hope I've had of reuniting with Liz. Yes, I will be at the airport waiting for you. What is your ETA?" Horne indicated that the flight to Amarillo was about an hour. He looked at his watch and said, "We are about twenty miles east of Albuquerque, and I should be in Amarillo in about forty-five minutes." They hung up, and Mr. Horne settled back in his seat and pondered what was happening to him.

Horne's plane pulled up to the private part of the Amarillo airport. He got off the plane and was wondering how he would identify Feldhaus. A tall slender man in a cowboy hat approached and asked if he was Mr. Horne. They shook hands, and Henry suggested that they go to the airport lounge where transits rested between flights. It was obvious to Horne that Henry was concerned as he asked immediately about Liz.

Horne said, "Let's cut out the formality. I am William, and you are Henry. Is that okay with you?" He answered yes, and the conversation began. William opened by saying he had recently talked to Liz's psychiatrist. He informed me that Liz had been in treatment with him for six months. When Henry heard six months, he realized that they had been separated for six months. He recalled their last conversation. They were both saying that they would not be able to work out their problems. Henry had suggested that they should seek psychiatric help. Liz had said, "I have been involved with those fellows since I was a child and never got any help." He remembered saying, "Being an adult and responsible is different than being a child. Children can't direct their lives like an adult can." Liz didn't respond.

William continued saying, "I have had a long interview with Liz's doctor. He tells me that Liz has come into treatment because she is in love with a young man. She is unable to allow him to be close to her. She knows that she loves him and should enjoy his closeness. Instead she becomes frightened and withdraws. Her young man feels the withdrawal as rejection and reacts. I don't want to go into the details of her problems with intimacy; I just want to tell you the problem that exists. For her to continue treatment, her doctor feels that she has two options. One is to be admitted to a psychiatric hospital and be managed there, or have a 24 hour care structure being set up in my home so that she can be protected during this treatment crisis. At this point she will only accept the latter. I have been a problem for my daughter all of her life. She has never had normal parents. My wife and I had to get married because she was pregnant with Liz. It was a bad decision for all three of us. At the age of fifty and 48, I and my wife have resolved our problems and now are happily married. Dr Joseph, her doctor, advises me that I am the person with whom she loves, and I would be the optimum caretaker for Liz during this critical time. The only other person is apparently you, since her other friend is unavailable."

Henry inquired about this other friend. Doctor Joseph said she was too ill to help. This information was frightening to Henry. He was just a rancher, and he felt that Liz needed a more professional person than he could ever be. Henry said, "I am not a professional. I am not qualified to help Liz." William replied, "I am just a failed father, but I love Liz. If her doctor feels that I can help my daughter, then if being a professional person is necessary, I will be one." Henry was impressed with this declaration. He was silent as he recalled the intense despair that he felt when he tried over and over again to be close to Liz. Finally he shook himself and said, "Liz has told me about her family. She has said that you stuck by her until she was thirteen and then fired a woman she loved. She told me that she hadn't seen or heard from you in 11 years. Frankly, William, you confuse me, but that aside, I, too, will do anything for Liz. When will this procedure begin?" William said, "I have already started construction in my house that will support this. My wife, Liz's mother, will stay in the house as a backup support. She will not be involved with Liz. Liz is now in the hospital and will be discharged tomorrow to my house. I am a wealthy man, and I will be able to manage any expense that is incurred." Henry took offence when he mentioned wealthy. He replied, "William, we need to get something straight from the very beginning. I am not a poor man. I have a large ranch and on that ranch I have 100 producing oil wells. Besides, I hold considerable real estate in Amarillo. I have a pineapple plantation in Costa Rico, and a large cattle ranch in Argentina. I just want you to know that I am on equal footing with you financially." "If I offended you, I apologize", said William. "All three of us have no financial problems. If you didn't know it, Liz is a multimillionaire." This banter seemed to clear the air, and Henry said, "In three hours I will be at your home in Albuquerque. You don't need to wait for me as I will use my own jet."

Liz didn't object to going into the hospital and having a physical evaluation. While she was in the hospital, Doctor Joseph told her about the way he was going to manage her during this period of having too much anxiety. He didn't tell her about his concern that she might attempt suicide. Liz said, "Thank you, Doctor, for caring for me. I have so much anxiety and depression. I have felt at times I would be better off if I just got out of this world." She had not talked about these thoughts in her sessions. This alerted him to be aware that she might pretend too well, and when everybody relaxed, kill herself. He told her that her father would be in constant attendance with her, and that Henry Feldhaus had agreed to assist him. When he mentioned Henry, she was obvious pleased that he was coming to help her.

Chapter XXIII

AFTER TALKING TO MARGARET, JACOB Immediately called Southwest Airlines to see when the next flight was to Dallas, Texas. He was told that the next flight to Dallas was at 4:00 p.m. He had three hours to get to the airport, and he could just make it. He landed in Dallas at 5:00 p.m., and after getting a rental car, he was soon on the highway to Waco. He arrived at her address about 6:30 p.m. and knocked loudly on the door. Lillian was cleaning up the kitchen and hastened to open the door. Opening the door and seeing him was too much for her. She gasped, and when she recovered, she found herself in Jacob' arms. She heard herself saying, "Oh, Jacob, how did you know I needed you?" Jacob said, "I have needed you for two months and when Margaret told me you might need me, I was on the next plane." Jacob said immediately, "Lillian, I am very much in love with you, and I don't ever want to be separated from you. I have been miserable not having you in my life." Lillian was pleased to hear this and said, "How long can you stay?" Jacob said, "Forever." Lillian said, "Jacob, I want to be with you a while before we commit our lives to each other. I am proposing that we live together and see if we can make the long haul." Jacob said, "You mean living as man and wife together without marriage." Lillian replied, "Yes, but I don't want to jump in bed with you. I want us to be together for a while without sex and see if we really like each other. In my first marriage, we were driven by sex and didn't really know each other. We had a hard time adjusting to each other when the pressure of sex was relieved. I don't want us to have that type of experience." Jacob said, "Lillian, I know that I love all of you and that means sexually, too. My thoughts and feelings for you during this time we were apart, have been about you as a real person, not simply sex. Don't get me wrong about this statement, because I do find you very desirable sexually, but it doesn't drive me. It is all of you that drive me to want to be with you forever." Lillian thought this man surely knows how to talk to a woman. She smiled and said, "Jacob, is there any Irish blarney in you? If you don't know it, what you just said to me was thrilling. It just almost made me want to jump in bed with you. But seriously, will you be patient and live with me for a while?" Jacob replied, "You know I will." So thus began a trial marriage.

It was on April 30, 1977, that Jonathan left Albuquerque to return to his ranch. The experience with Mary had been physically and emotionally draining. His weariness produced some disturbing thoughts. He had been involved with Mary for the last 14 months, and it seemed that it would take more time for Mary to be well enough for them to have a normal relationship. He was questioning whether he wanted to continue with her in this struggle. It troubled him that he was having these thoughts. He was wondering what was love. He knew his attraction to Mary as a teenager was more of a sexual attraction. As he grew older, he felt that he was thinking of her as a companion, and this was important when he felt lonely.

During those times when he had only known her casually, he could not have really known if she would make a good companion. He knew his rush to her when she had her accident was driven by a feeling of a loss of an idealized person. His contacts with Mary during the last 14 months had been with a very seriously ill person. He wondered if Mary's stated love for him was related to her dependency or was it real love. He had gone in a circle. He still had not discovered what he meant when he told Mary that he loved her. He told himself that he was too tired to think about this. I must get some real sleep. Some sleep where I don't have to keep one eye open.

He went to bed without taking off his clothes. The first few hours of his sleep were dreamless. The early morning sleep was filled with a confusion of dreams. One time, he dreams he is madly in love with Mary. Another dream was that he was tired of waiting for a normal Mary, and he wanted to break away. He was now 37 years old, and he needed to have a family. He didn't need a woman who had so much garbage to deal with. This dream awakened him. He said to himself, "Why am I dreaming all of these dreams now? The past few days Mary has made amazing progress, and it looks like very soon she will be thru with her therapy. She has dealt with anger and despair over her father and has recognized the qualities in him that her mother loved. She is willing to start over with her father and her life. In other words, she could now be a normal loving wife for me."

He was again puzzled. He wondered, "Maybe I should look at my own life." Had he ever had a loving relationship with anybody? The first thought was Don Wright. They had always been friends, and when they were both fighting for their lives at the battle of Hui, they both seemed to be looking out for the other. When Don was hit and seriously wounded, and they were ordered to retreat, he had no thought of leaving him to those murdering bastards. When he recalled this, he remembered thinking, "I can't live without my buddy." He felt he must have gone crazy at that moment as he had no awareness of what he was doing. He was just raging loudly, "You can't have my buddy." That feeling that Don was part of him, and he was defending their fusion of selves, startled him. He pondered, "Does love mean that you are so attached to another person that you would feel dead if you lost them?"

His thoughts shifted to his mother and his dad. He could hardly remember his mother, but he knew that his dad was really in love with his mother. His dad never talked about his mother, but he felt that his dad was never happy. His dad looked after him when he was a child, but he was always grim about everything. He wondered, "If I had not had the experience of my uncle's family, would I have thought that all fathers were grim. My uncle is my mother's brother, and he and my dad were close friends. In fact, my uncle said he introduced my mother to my dad." He recalled one time asking his uncle about his mother. His uncle got out a picture of his mother and showed it to him. She was to him a beautiful young lady. She was blond headed and had blue eyes. This picture startled him as she looked very much like Mary. He stopped thinking about his mother and asked himself, "Am I in love with Mary because she reminds me of my mother?" He knew that this was a common psychiatric speculation about young men finding their mother in their spouse. He never knew his mother, and his functioning mother was his uncle's wife. Elsa was an overweight black headed, brown-eyed woman. Jonathan thought, "She was very kind to me, and I was attached to her. I was very sad when she died while I was overseas in Vietnam. I also lost my Dad while I was in Vietnam."

The word attachment echoed in his mind. He asked himself the question, "Is love an attachment?" That word attachment didn't sound like love, but it allowed for him to pursue this love issue further.

He drifted back to Don. In that relationship, they would do anything for each other. They weren't concerned about how much each gave to the other. They just liked to share with each other. For lack of any word, they just had mutuality. He thought that was a strange word. So it seemed to him that love had attachment, selflessness, and mutuality. With these thoughts he put Mary in the picture. They were definitely attached. He did put Mary ahead of himself, and he did like to give without return with Mary. As far as he could tell, Mary was too sick to think of putting him ahead of herself. The same applied to mutuality. Mary had so much hate she could not love herself. He ended by thinking that when Mary is well they were going to have a talk about each other. He felt now he didn't need to be so involved with Mary, and probably was best if he distanced himself from her. He didn't call her that night or the next morning.

Chapter XXIV

DOCTOR JOSEPH WANTED TO INSPECT the structure that Horne had built in his house for the care of Liz. He was surprised at the level of security the structure had. In spite of this, it was a very comfortable suite of rooms. It had a bed area for Liz that was open to what might be considered a nursing station. Liz could not leave the facility without an alarm system being activated. She had no bathroom privacy. In other words it was a homey closed ward structure.

Before he released Liz, Doctor Joseph insisted on interviewing Suzanne and Henry. The first one to come to his office was Suzanne Thompson Horne. Suzanne had some concern talking to Doctor Joseph. She had done many things that now she was ashamed of. She felt that these events were behind her, and she didn't want to bring them up.

When she entered Doctor Joseph's office, she was tense and hostile. Joseph didn't have to wait for her to talk as she immediately said, "I don't see the need for these talks. It doesn't take a genius to know that I was a terrible mother for Liz. In fact I wasn't a mother at all. So I ask you, Doctor Joseph, why am I here at your request? " Doctor Joseph didn't respond immediately. He wanted to observer her body language as she recovered from her prepared speech. He felt that she was frightened and wanted to get control of the interview. It was evident that she was uncomfortable with the silence as she said, "Oh, I see you are one of those psychiatrists who try to make the patient responsible for the whole interview. Well, Doctor, I am not buying into that kind of interview. If you don't talk to me, I am leaving." With that she got up and left the office.

Doctor Joseph realized how fragile she was and wondered how he could handle this runaway defense she manifested. Prior to her interview he had insisted that Mr. Horne accompany her to her session, and if she left early, he was to stop her and if possible persuade her to return. After a few minutes there was a gentle knock on the door. He went the door and said, "I am glad that you were willing to return as it is important for me to know you. You will be important to Liz's recovery." She said, "Doctor, there is something about me you need to understand. If something is unpleasant or creating any anxiety, I am gone." Doctor Joseph responded, "Mrs. Horne, there is no way that in my interview with you that I will be able to avoid those two conditions. I want to assure you that I do not want to harm you or be critical of you. I just want to understand you so when issues come up in Liz's treatment that involves you, I will know your perspective of the event."

She said, "Okay Doctor, I will give you a chance to interview me." He knew by the use of the word 'chance' that her staying with him was conditional. He decided she could not tolerate silence so he said, "Let's start with your life about which you feel more comfortable to talk." She responded, "What you don't understand is that there is nothing in my life that is comfortable for me to discuss unless it is my discovery of William. In 1970, William and I met with the purpose of discussing how to go about getting a divorce. Both of us were lonely and had no successful relationships. As we discussed our options, we both discovered we were two lonely people. When we came to our meeting, we were unaware that our reason for wanting to get a divorce was the same. We had both been successful in earning a living, but we had failed to find a loving partner. As we talked further, we were surprised that we had a lot in common." She stopped suddenly and said, "I know you probably have heard from Liz and William how our relationship began. I want you to hear my perspective. I came from a strict Catholic family. My father was the undisputed ruler of my mother. I had two older brothers. I was born in 1922. I was just 18 in January, 1940. I had finished high school when I was seventeen. I was very popular in high school, and I could have had lots of dates if my father had not been so strict. Anyway I was beginning to rebel, and my father and I just weren't getting along. I moved out of the house, and I was living in an apartment with friends. I was an attractive girl, and I had a job modeling. One day my cousin called and said he needed an attractive date to go to a large party that would have many important people. It was going to be at a local country club, which had many rich people as its members. I was excited about going, and I was determined to make an impression on those rich people. I dressed well, and it was at this party I met William. He was a handsome young man, and I left my cousin and agreed to let him take me to my apartment. I was hoping to interest him in me and when he told me he wanted to show me his apartment, I readily agreed. We had sex, and it was a disaster for both of us. I started crying, and he didn't know how to deal with me. I don't remember how we parted, but both of us wanted never to see each other again. One month later, I didn't get my period, and I was fearful that I was pregnant. By the third month I had missed two more periods, and my clothes were tight. I went to my family doctor, and he told me my suspicions were correct. I was pregnant. I thought of everything I could do, and finally decided I wouldn't get an abortion. When I lost my job because of my body changes, the only option I had was to go to my parent's home. My father was enraged that I had exposed his family to such a terrible stigma. For the first time in my life, my mother told my father to shut up. She said, 'This is our daughter, and she has come home for us to help her. I will not tolerate you abusing her. What she needs now is our love, and not your talking about how she has disgraced her family. What is a family for if it doesn't take care of its members when they are in trouble?' My father was shocked that my mother would challenge him. They had a big fight, and my mother won. She told him in no uncertain terms she would leave if he didn't treat me with respect. When my brothers heard my mother say she would leave, they told their father if mother left, so would they. At this point, my brothers were an important part to his business. Anyway all settled down, and we began to try to figure what to do.

It was decided that I would contact the father of the child, and we would see what his position was concerning this pregnancy. I found his address from my cousin and went to his office. At first, the secretary wouldn't let me see him. I told her he had gotten me pregnant, and if he refused to see me, then he would deal with my lawyer. She could see that I was pregnant and immediately went into his office. He came out, and we went into his office. I explained the situation, and he agreed to come to my house and talk with my family.

The meeting we had was a disaster for me. First, he wanted me to prove he was the father. He implied that I was promiscuous because I had sex with him on our first date. This enraged my brothers, and they almost attacked him. My mother calmed things down. We finally agreed to have a private wedding. He also stated he didn't want to have anything to do with me and the baby. I didn't want a baby by this disgusting man so I rejected the baby. My mother said she would take care of the baby, and he agreed to support the baby. I told him I did not want anything from him, and when the baby came, I never wanted to see him again. God, I hate to go over this again. Is it really necessary for me to continue? Isn't it sufficient for you to know that I was terrible mother, and I didn't love my only child?" Doctor Joseph said, "It is hard to look at things like this, particularly with a stranger and not knowing what he is thinking while you are recalling a very sad and life changing event." She said, "Yes, Doctor, that one five minute event changed my life and led me down a road that did not give me a family, only despair. Anyway Doctor, it was William's implication that I was promiscuous, and his not wanting to have anything to do with the baby humiliated me so much that I hated him and wanted to hurt him in any way I could.

As the pregnancy advanced, and I saw my young body becoming ugly, my hate for him only grew. Doctor, can you imagine how I felt when those horrible striae appeared on my belly? My breasts became engorged, and after the baby came, they began to hang down. I had the appearance of a middle age woman when I was just eighteen. When the baby came, my mother was the only one to be with me. William was not there, and my father was to never forgive me. We lived in a small catholic community, and you can imagine the gossip I endured.

Now the big question, why didn't I divorce William and began anew? I have no answer for it. We didn't live together, and William gave me and the baby $70,000 a year. My mother raised Liz, and when my father died a year later, she and I rented a house, and for the next three years we lived together. These were the years that William, from our stand point, disappeared. As you know, he was in that code breaking outfit. Shortly after the war was over, Mother died and until William returned, I took care of Liz. I didn't love Liz, but I felt she was a little girl who had no one to love her. She was suffering because her nana had gone away. During those few days, I was looking for a nanny for Liz as I had formed my own business, and I didn't have time for her. Actually I didn't want to make time for her.

Lost and Found

When William finally showed up in 1945, I told him he would have to take his daughter as I wanted to be free of her. At first he refused, and I put her up for adoption. When he learned of this, he came and took Liz. I became very successful in my business, but my personal life was chaotic. I could not develop any relationship with any man. I didn't want to ever marry again, and my marriage with William was a convenient subterfuge. You will have to ask him why he hung onto any connection with me. I think he was too busy to think about it, and I didn't put any pressure on him. So he just forgot that I existed. It is interesting to me that we both wanted to get a divorce at the same time. My last comment to you, Doctor, is, as I look at Liz today, I see in her the same quality I had. We both fear intimacy."

Doctor Joseph was silent for a short time, and then thanked her for being willing to tell him her perspective of what had happened to Liz and her. Suzanne said, "Doctor, I regret terribly how I treated Liz. She has turned out to be a beautiful young lady, and I hate to realize that I contributed to her present condition. I don't see how I can be of any help with her care, but I will do anything you might feel would help her." They parted.

When she came out of his office, William asked how it went. She replied, "Well, at least he is different than those critical and all knowledgeable child psychiatrists that you found." William could sense that this interview had stirred up many memories, and he let it drop.

Henry Feldhaus was the next person that Doctor Joseph interviewed. Henry had some reservations about his being interviewed. He felt that his private life was his business, and didn't want to explore it. He talked to William and Susanne about his feelings. William said, "I have been interviewed so many times during the course of Liz's problems that it is just another event. When you discuss all of your failures, they become less emotionally charged, and for me, they reach the level of so what. I made a mistake, and I paid for it." Suzanne felt different. She said, "Henry, I haven't forgiven myself for how I rejected Liz. It was not her fault that she was born. I never considered her a human being. Most of her life, she had no one that unconditionally loved her. I hated the sight of her because I felt that she ruined my life. This, of course, was completely false. Liz was just a little girl searching for someone to love her. Every time I was interviewed, I shuttered when I related what I had done. My shame I projected onto the interviewer and felt my criticism coming back to me. How will I ever get over this terrible feeling?"

The part where she said, 'unconditional love' impacted Henry. He realized that he had never loved Liz unconditionally. He had expected more from her than she had the ability to give. How could he be so self centered that he never realized that? When he considered that, he felt his private life was insignificant, and he now wanted see Doctor Joseph. He intended that his interview was going to be a two way street.

When Henry walked into Doctor Joseph's office, he presented himself as a strong Texas rancher. Doctor Joseph had seen this type many times. He had learned that this usually meant that the person was unsure of what was going to happen and was going to be damn sure he was strong enough to meet the challenge. This analysis was confirmed by his competitive handshake.

Doctor Joseph wanted to lessen the tension, and he started the interview. He said, "Mr. Feldhaus, I want to thank you for coming in to see me. I am very concerned about Liz' welfare. She came to see me because she felt that her inability to allow closeness was causing her to lose the only man she had ever loved. I am sure that the Hornes have told you about her life with them. This background has caused Liz many problems. As she has been working with them, she has become hopeless, and I fear that she might commit suicide. She even told me that she was considering it." With this information, Henry's attitude changed remarkably. His defiance changed to a fearful concern.

He said, "Doctor Joseph, I have always been a quiet private man. I took care of my affairs and never sought help from anybody except my parents. I was the only child of my parents. My dad in the nineteen thirties bought a ranch south of Amarillo, Texas. We had a hard time making a living. My father was determined that I get a college education, and he just was able to send me to Texas Tech in Lubbock, Texas. I studied ranching and livestock management. My father insisted that I also major in business administration. I had five years of college. During that time, my mother and dad made many sacrifices for me. Soon after I came home from college, they both became chronically ill. They did the best they could to help me with the ranch, but in reality, it was all on my shoulders. We struggled for about five years and a miracle happened. They struck oil on our ranch, and over night we were millionaires. My parents enjoyed our wealth for only a few years. My father died first and then shortly thereafter, my mother died. It was a great loss for me as we were a team that struggled together for so long. I loved my parents very much.

All during those years, I worked all of the time. I didn't date and had very little experience in talking and being with women my own age. When my parents died, I realized how lonely I was, and I decided that I had to get away from Amarillo and try to find some woman with whom I could be comfortable. I decided that a long cruise would be a way to do this. It so happened that a world cruise was being offered that left from San Diego, California, and went around the world ending in New York City.

I took that cruise. One of the conditions of the cruise was that passengers were assigned their table for their evening meals. Singles were assigned to their tables and so forth. I was lucky because Liz was assigned to my table. We didn't talk to each other in the beginning. I finally managed to get seated next to her, and we got a conversation going. She told me a little bit about her life, and I talked about mine. After a couple of evenings, I asked if we could meet during the day as I wanted to get to know her. I think my frankness startled her. She told me that most of her life she had been around people who were not so frank. My frankness seemed to please her, and we became friends.

I began to feel that I wanted to be with her all of the time. She seemed reluctant at first but tried to be close with me. I realize now what was happening to her. She was into her fear of closeness. I tried harder to reach her, and she seemed to withdraw more from me. I began to think she was turned off by me, and I stopped seeing her. When I did this, she would become frantic and seek me out saying, 'Don't leave me.' At that time, I didn't realize what she was experiencing. Now I realize it was her problem with closeness. She would cling to me almost like a lost child. I would respond, and we would go through a period of some closeness. I would press for more than she could give, and the same thing would happen. Finally towards the end of the cruise, I told her I could not endure her on and off behavior. I was through with our relationship. I left with her crying, and I was very depressed. Doctor, I am a no-nonsense, impatient kind of guy, but I love Liz. She makes me feel and see things that I never considered. I know I need her. My knowing that she is trying to change for me---well, I would just do anything to get her well." Doctor Joseph realized he had two alpha males and a bitter female to deal with, but in spite of this, he felt good about his support team.

Chapter XXV

WHEN JONATHAN DIDN'T CALL AT noon, Mary was concerned. She walked down to the guest house and talked to Canela. Canela said, "I haven't talked to Jonathan today. I know he has a lot of problems to handle concerning his projects in the San Juan area. His eddy wells are decreasing in production. He is trying to get carbon dioxide injection for those wells." Mary decided to call Jonathan. He answered the phone.

He said, "Mary, I got home last night, and I slept in my clothes. The ordeal we both have been going through finally exhausted me. Now that you are doing well, I decided that I needed to get some rest and take on some problems in my business. I got to thinking about the last year-and-a-half and how hard it has been on both of us. I will come this weekend, and we will talk about it. You know we have never had any normal courtship. I haven't romanced you or done things with you. Your accident, your memory loss, and your struggle to get over your problems with your father have made our relationship at best limited. I know I love you, but I have for a long time. You haven't had this experience with me. I was just a person that you trusted and took on faith that I loved you. I know that we have a deep friendship, but as far as having a man and woman bonding, I am not sure."

Mary was initially shocked by his comments, but as she listened she knew he was right. She had treated him as a brother or father but not as a lover. For a long time, she knew to get in that position was impossible. She wondered if now she could. Jonathan continued saying, "I feel you don't need me in my old role. You don't need me to have your power of attorney. I have told Don that I felt that you could manage your estate, and when you are ready to cancel, it is my wish also. I am hoping that now we might have a more normal courtship. I think you need time to figure out what you want. The best way to do this is by my not spending as much time in Albuquerque with you. I would like for you to reserve your weekends for us." Mary felt a twang in her heart. A change was happening, and she was fearful as to what it meant. She had been comfortable with the old arrangement. In many ways, she had been like a child with Jonathan. "Could she be a woman and especially his woman?" She wondered. Mary ended the conversation with the request that they talk at least one time a day on the phone, and yes, she would reserve the weekends for him. After she hung up, she found herself feeling somewhat anxious, but it was the anxiety of facing something new. She had gotten rid of her hate for her dad. She didn't have any love for him, but she was glad that Margaret did. She could sit around with him with no bad feelings. She had shifted to her mother in her sessions. She loved her mother, but at the same time, she had no respect for her. She felt contempt for her mother for staying with her father. She didn't like having this feeling, but she was stuck with it. As she talked about it with her doctor, she wondered if this feeling she had for her mother was anyway affecting her ability to be the role of a wife and a mother. When she sold her business, she remembered saying, "I want to get married and have children." Now she was not so sure. She had thought she had wanted to marry Jonathan, but her talk with him had got her thinking.

She found herself talking to Doctor Joseph about her recent conversation with Jonathan. She said, "When he started telling me that he felt that we were moving into a new relationship which he described as a normal courtship, I thought maybe he was having second thoughts about us. I soon learned that he was really expecting more from me than he was getting. He didn't want his past help for me to interfere with my deciding about him as a lover. To put it in simple terms, did I want him as my man? When he asked this question, I knew I didn't have the answer. Doctor Joseph, when Tom Carlson chose his father over me, I changed. This was the second time I had a man to betray me. I was determined that I would never be vulnerable to a man again. I was not going to be like my mother. I was going to find my own way, and no man was to be in my life. I think I lost my femininity. Now with that thought, I suddenly felt lonely, and it is the same feeling I had with my black hole nightmares.

I had this nightmare dream just after I recovered consciousness with no memory. I could not sleep because I felt this nightmare would reoccur.

Jonathan came into my life at this time, and he told about his time in the hospital following his receiving battle wounds. He told me that the fellows on his open ward would stay beside the bed of a soldier who had nightmares. If they felt one was starting, they would gently awaken him or reassure him until the nightmares disappeared. He did this with me, and I lost my nightmares. So the black hole must have meant having no one." She ended her sessions with, "I have a lot to think about."

When Doctor Joseph told Liz that she would be staying with her father and Henry, she was relieved. She was especially concerned with Henry being there. She knew that she would be very sick over the next few months or maybe not recover at all. What would Henry think? She said, "Doctor Joseph, I am worried about Henry being here. He will see me, in what kind of shape? I am afraid I will really lose him." There was no answer, and she kept on talking. There was no real change in her thoughts and behavior for the next several sessions. The routine was established that Henry would be with her during the day, and the father would be with her in the night. They would periodically change with each other. Suzanne had no direct contact with Liz.

Soon Liz's thoughts began centering on the period of time when her father sent her to Switzerland. It was a girl's school for wealthy girls that had behavioral problems. Most of the girls there were or had been on drugs. Some were promiscuous, and some were like her. They had no one to love them, and they struck out in anger. She said, "It is a much worse place than being with a cold dad. With him, I had at least someone I could hope would change.

The school was in a narrow valley. The only way you could get to it was by train. There was a little village there, but at first, we could not go there. We had school, and a mentor assigned to each of us. I was assigned a middle aged woman who was a no nonsense person. If she had any tender feelings, I never found them. She was always on guard about my tendency to have episodes of violent behavior. My admission report read that I was admitted because I was unmanageable in my home. When I sneaked into the office in order to read it, I was surprised by the word unmanageable. I just wanted my nanny back. It was here that I developed the personality that you saw in our early sessions. I had let myself care for my grandmother, and she died. I cared for my nanny, and she got herself fired. It was too painful to love and need someone and have them leave you. I was determined not to be close to anyone. The problem with that was I was so terrible lonely."

When she said this to Doctor Joseph, he could see her face had that empty blank look of depression. She stopped talking and left the session silent. Henry was waiting for her. He could see how depressed she was and put his arm around her. She did not pull away. He tried to talk to her, but she didn't respond. Henry couldn't think of what to do that would show her he cared for her. He remembered the sad cowboy songs his mother used to sing to him when he felt bad. He started singing them to Liz. The gentleness and the longingness reached Liz, and she was able to talk. She said, "Oh, Henry, I am so lonely. It hurts so bad I can hardly breathe. I was thinking of that horrible place in Switzerland, and everything went black." Henry said, "Liz, I want so much to help you. I can feel your pain, and I am so helpless to help you." They held each other until Liz went to sleep.

Liz stayed with her Switzerland only a short time and returned to her father. All of the hate and despair returned, and she would have violent rages. Her father could not be around her during this period. She would only let Henry be around her. Doctor Joseph treated her like she was on an inpatient closed ward.

He thought about starting her on thorazine, but he wanted her to cathect her anger by allowing her to express her rage. Eventually, the rage changed to a wailing cry. She would wail over and over, "Why didn't they love me, why didn't they love me?" William and Suzanne heard this wailing, and for the first time, they felt how much she had longed to be loved.

It tore Henry apart. He never could stand to see an animal abused, but to realize the woman he loved had been so abused was hard to take. He confronted William and Suzanne with anger and was almost ready to attack them. William and Suzanne didn't defend themselves or say anything to Henry. He didn't see the horror in their faces, as they realized what they had done to their daughter.

Eventually, Liz was able to return to her sessions. Henry was the only person with her 24 hours a day. As Henry was experiencing this, he thought, "Liz is willing to go through all of this agony just to be close to me. Will my love be enough for her?" When she was able to have a more rational talk with Henry, he asked her that question. She said, "Henry,

I have longed for the love you gave me on the cruise. I would endure anything to have your love and not run away from it. Please, Henry, don't ever stop loving me. I would die if you did." They hugged each other, and there were tears in Henry's eyes.

Doctor Joseph knew that Liz must somehow resolve her feeling for her parents. It was obvious that when she needed them the most, they were not there. From 6 to 12 she had a better relationship with her father. He encouraged her to explore that period. In previous sessions, her father wasn't much in that period. She would talk about her nanny, and how much she loved her. She only recalled his firing of her nanny. When she worked with this period again, she was able to see her father had to do something, but she could not forgive him for not seeing how much she needed to have someone to love her.

Doctor Joseph felt that she had enough emotional control now so that they could begin having family sessions. Liz had only one condition, and that was Henry must be with her. She needed his love to support her. William was ready for this session, but Suzanne was so upset by Liz's wailing, she didn't see how she could face Liz. Her shame was almost unbearable. She was so condemning of herself that William was fearful for her safety. He insisted that she see Doctor Joseph. She didn't want to get into therapy, and Doctor Joseph medicated her, and she got some relief. Finally Suzanne agreed to the family sessions.

The first session started with Liz turning to Suzanne. She said, "May I call you mother. I say that because you have never accepted me as your child." Suzanne replied, "I don't deserve that honor." Liz continued, "I was a helpless baby, child, and now I am an adult. I have always wanted a mother. Why didn't you put me up for adoption? You just shifted me around and let chance determine my life. Did you hate me that much? Couldn't you see that I had nothing to do with my birth? I was the product of your mistake, and you treated me like a stray cat. I have often wondered why you didn't put me in a tow sack and throw me into the river." At this point William interrupted and said, "I was just as inhuman as Suzanne. I feel I was more of a criminal than Suzanne because I did nothing to protect her. She was pregnant and scorned by her father. She carried you in a moralistic catholic neighborhood, and received much moral abuse. I ignored her and felt that sending money was all I needed to do. I did the same with you." Liz listened and said, "I am not through with my biological mother. I want to hear answers to my questions." Suzanne responded, "May I call you Liz." Liz nodded her head. Suzanne continued, "I have insulated myself for years from taking responsibility of my actions. I don't want now to try to explain it. I don't want to give myself excuses. I was a horrible person. My regret doesn't help you. I was devastated when I heard you wail like a baby, and I wondered why, when you were a baby crying, I didn't respond to you. My only response is, I hated the world and most of all, I hated myself. I couldn't love anybody or anything. I know how it feels to be unloved as this was my experience all of my life. My mother who worshipped you was the only one who took up for me and showed me love. I think I felt the same pain you did when you lost your own real mother. "

Everyone was silent, and William started talking. He said, "Liz, I was not responsible for Suzanne. I was twenty years old, and the first time I got interested in sex, I got a virtual stranger pregnant. For almost twenty years, I had been admired by many people because of my mental ability. At twenty I was a very successful business man. I thought I was a superior person, and all this pregnancy stuff was irrelevant. To put it simply, I was a spoiled brat. I don't see how all of this 'mea culpa' helps you. Do you have any idea what we can do now?" Liz responded, "I have no idea." All were silent as they left the office.

Chapter XXVI

LILLIAN AND JACOB QUICKLY ADAPTED to living together. One of Lillian's first requests was to ask Jacob if his friends called him Jacob. He said, "No. When I went to grade school, my classmates thought I was connected with God. This was difficult enough, but when they started making fun of my name, I told my parents my name was Jake. Up to now, I am called Jake." They laughed. At first, they hesitated touching each other. The commitment to a trial marriage was going to take a little getting used to. The first night was awkward. They finally kissed good night, and each went to their own bedroom. It took a month for them to start sleeping together. Before they started this, Lillian said emphatically, "I don't want to start having sex." During the second month, they started their sexual adventure. After the first time, they became like young lovers. For a time, they could not get enough of each other. They were now busily planning their wedding. They wanted it to be in Albuquerque, and they wanted Margaret and Andy to be maid of honor and best man, respectively. The wedding was a quiet private affair, and only close friends were present. Lillian wanted to live near Margaret, and Jake wanted to be near Andy, so they moved to Albuquerque.

Mary didn't discuss with Dr Joseph her conversation with Jonathan. She wanted to wait until the weekend and find out more about what Jonathan was thinking. The idea that she had lost her femininity haunted her. She wanted to talk to a woman friend about femininity. Liz was her long time friend, but she always felt that she was in the same boat. She crossed out Margaret for she was too close to Andy. Only Canela and Virginia seemed good possibilities. Canela had known her as a C.E.O. of a large company. They needed each other and were never woman to woman with each other. She remembered her conversation with Virginia at Margaret's wedding. They seemed to be talking women talk. She called Virginia and asked her to come to her house for lunch.

Virginia was pleased to hear from her, and they planned to meet the next day. When Virginia came, Mary got right to the point. She said, "Virginia, I was a C.E.O. for ten years, and I was in a man's world. I learned to think and compete like a man. I lost all of my feminine qualities. Now, I am considering marriage, and I want it to be a man-woman marriage. I need women friends. I want to be a woman again. I don't know how to begin this process, but I thought of you." Virginia said, "Mary, I have always admired you for what you have accomplished. I never thought how this might have affected you. I have never thought about how to be a woman. I think I just followed my mother, copying what she did and experimented with little changes. Have you thought of this possibility?" "Virginia," Mary said, "I loved my mother, but she let my father abuse her and me. It is hard to love and not have any respect." Virginia said, "To love your mother tells me that you mother must have had some good qualities. You can't love someone who is a nothing. Have you ever sat down and listed the things about your mother that you admired. I know that this must seem simplistic, but this is what I do when I am confused."

Mary started thinking about her mother's good points. She was loving, caring, forgiving, unselfish, generous, never vengeful, she could go on and on about her good qualities. With all of this, why didn't she copy her mother? The answer was my mother let my father take advantage of her and me, and I could not forgive her for that.

When Jonathan came for the weekend, they both had issues to talk about. Mary wanted to talk about her wanting to have a man-woman relationship. Jonathan didn't understand what she meant. She said, "Jonathan, when Tom Carlson rejected me, I felt I was being like my mother. I was determined to never let a man hurt me again. I was determined to destroy any feminine qualities that I may have had and not let any return. In college, I didn't date, and I think many people felt I was a lesbian. I became competitive and chose to enter the financial world and compete with men. I don't like the product of the financial world. Stocks and bond are uninteresting to me. I chose a very competitive product, cosmetics. My gosh," she exclaimed, "I just realized I had chosen a feminine product. Maybe my subconscious was at work and was fighting for my femininity. Anyway, when I was a C.E.O., I fought for my company like I perceived a man would do. Jonathan, how do you perceive me? Am I too masculine like?"

Jonathan was all prepared to talk about his issue, and now Mary was asking him to think about something he had not even considered. He was silent for a while. He began, "Mary, for years I have loved you from afar. You were a beautiful girl, and I didn't think about your personality. In my idealizing you, you were the perfect woman, whatever that was. Our being together over the past year-and-a-half has been dominated by your memory problems, and the emotional problems connected with it. I haven't had a chance to explore your feminine abilities. I just feel that they are okay, and I expect to enjoy them to the fullest."

Mary laughed and felt a warm feeling towards him. She thought silently I have a real smart man in my life. I am so thankful to have him wanting to be with me during this entire struggle. This thought passed, and a question came to her mind. "Is that enough to support a marriage for a life time? Whatever love my mother had for my father was sufficient to support her marriage even in bitter times. Do I have my mother's strength?" For the first time, she was seeing her mother in a different light. Instead of seeing her as a long suffering woman, she was beginning to see her as a persevering woman that would not give up the man she loved even though he had returned a bitter and angry man.

This still didn't explain her mother letting her father abuse her. She was wondering now if her mother did protect her from his anger. As she pondered this, a faint memory intruded in her mind. She was recalling a night she awakened, and she heard loud voices in the next room. Her mother was shouting at her father. She was demanding that he stop being hateful towards their daughter. In no uncertain terms she was telling him to stop. He was yelling back cruel things, and she stood her ground. Finally, he left the house slamming the door. Things didn't get better, but now she knew that her mother did defend her.

Jonathan was aware that Mary was working with some thoughts and kept silent. When she said, "Let's go find my father", he knew she must have realized something. They found him outside on her patio. She went over to him and said, "I just had a memory, and I want you to tell me if it is true. While I was talking with Jonathan, he said something to me that set me to thinking. I remembered a scene of you and mother arguing, and you left angry and didn't come back for a week." Andy was taken aback. He remembered that fight very well. He had been very cruel to both of them that day and particularly to Mary. He had gone over this scene many times in his mind, and he always felt so ashamed of his actions. Mary could see the despair in his face as he began to talk.

"Mary, I don't know how complete your memory is, but your mother gave me a tongue lashing that night. I had never seen her so angry. She gave me an ultimatum that I was to stop attacking my child. She said, 'I will not tolerate you abusing her. She is a child, and she can't help it that we don't get along.' Andy continued saying, "I was surprised by her defiance and tried to overwhelm her until she told me to leave the house and not come back until I could behave better toward you. I taunted her and told her to try and make me leave. She picked up the phone and called the sheriff. I left immediately and didn't come back for a week." Andy told her that this wasn't the only time that her mother had defended her. I wish now I had really changed after that fight, but I soon relapsed into my old patterns. I never understood why your mother would defend you but not herself.

Mary was appalled hearing this. All these years she had maligned her mother. Why would she remember this now? Could she have been so fearful of having a similar marriage that she had to change a lot of memories in order to avoid marriage? Was she now trying to avoid marrying Jonathan? Had she started withdrawing and that was why he wanted to back off? She didn't have the answer, but she was going to find out what she was doing. She turned to Jonathan and said, "I have just found myself discovering many things about myself, and I think that it might be related to what you wanted to talk about."

Jonathan said, "Mary, I came today all fired up to talk about something that I felt was so important. Now I am not so sure, but I know it will be important, so here goes. Just a week has passed since we both realized you were nearly well. You are now an independent person who can take care of yourself, and no longer need my care. I felt so relieved, I decided to go home. After having a good night's sleep, I began to think of our relationship in a new way. I felt our experience together was not the kind that produces a marriage. You have been too sick to consider the kind of relationship that will support a marriage. I felt in a way we were really starting all over. I began to ask myself the question, what was love? I wasn't thinking of love taught in general psychology one. I was trying to find out what it meant to me. I came up with the idea that love was an attachment between two people. It wasn't simply an attachment, it had other commitments. It seemed to me that two people in love would feel that their loved one's self interest was as important as their own. I feel clumsy trying to explain this. In other words, when you were sick, I was more concerned about you than I was about me. Maybe I can do better with my last idea. I felt that both lovers would give more to the other without regrets. I called it mutuality. I then applied this to us. We have a dependent attachment. You were too sick to be involved with the other two."

Mary thought for a while and said, "I had been thinking that I was not enough of a woman to be married, and you were thinking I was too sick to love. In a way, we both thought that something was incomplete in our relationship. I know I get a deep feeling of closeness and comfort from you. Is that love? I could feel that with a dog or a horse. When I think of those animals, I know my feeling is different for you. I have been aware that I liked to kiss you, but I don't think that this feeling is the same feeling a woman would have if she were passionate for her man. Yes, Jonathan, we do need to think more about where we are going."

Now, Liz wasn't so concerned what her parents could do. She had exhausted her life trying to find someone to love her. This is what she wanted from her parents, but she realized that they were so handicapped that to keep trying to get love from them was impossible. She wondered why all these years she had never realized this. The old saying came to her mind, "you can't get blood from a turnip." She knew now where her love was located and would be given to her freely and uncomplicated by bad experiences. It was Henry's love. The next day in her session with Doctor Joseph she said, "Doctor Joseph, I feel I am better now. I have decided that I no longer want to have my parents' love. I feel that they are too traumatized to ever love me as I want to be loved. I am going to let go and find my peace and love elsewhere. I know now I am not afraid to be close to people. I don't feel that I will be hurt by whatever they might do intentionally or otherwise. Henry loves me, and I love him. I can walk out of this room now and marry Henry. I can be as close to others as I might want to be. I know that you have a deeper understanding of me than I have, but I feel strongly I should terminate my sessions in the near future."

Doctor Joseph was amazed by what he had heard. Just a few weeks ago Liz was raging and crying over her lack of love. Now she was talking quite maturely. Could she be planning suicide? How could he evaluate this? He thought that a directed inquiry would be helpful. He said, "Liz, I am quite impressed by what you have said, but you have changed so rapidly since we last talked in your family session. I am concerned that you might be trying to escape your confinement and commit suicide as you know you have had those feelings."

Liz was silent and didn't try to deny his inquiry. She seemed to be looking at her motivations. She finally said, "Doctor Joseph, in all my life, I have never been sneaky. If anything, I have been too demanding. I know I am not depressed, and I haven't had any suicidal thought since I learned in my family sessions how handicapped my parents are. In fact, I feel sorry for them. I don't want to punish them now by expecting them to be something I don't think is possible for them to be. I am grateful that they have found each other, and I don't need anything from them. When Henry and I drove back to my suite, we were talking about what we had heard from my parents. Henry said, 'For a long time, I was angry at your parents, but as I listened to them I realized that they were really people to be pitied, not despised. They had a miserable life, and in spite of their successes they really had nothing.' When Henry said this, a burden seemed to lift from me. I began to think and feel like I had never felt before. I no longer felt love hungry. I felt free for the first time in my life. I felt that I was somehow whole. I know that is not the right word, but maybe there is no word that describes how I felt. All I know is I was no longer a crying baby. I felt strong and adult like. I remembered moving over closer to Henry and told him to stop the car. As soon as he did, I put my arms around him, and he got the most passionate kiss he had ever had. We started laughing with joy, and all we could talk about was what we were going to do with our lives."

Doctor Joseph asked, "Liz, would you be willing for me to invite Henry into your sessions?" Liz immediately agreed. Henry came in, and Doctor Joseph immediately engaged him with inquiries. Henry answered all of them to his satisfaction. When Doctor Joseph stopped talking, Henry said, "Doctor Joseph, I appreciate your concern, and Liz and I are not going to do anything that you object to. We are perfectly willing to stay with the same arrangements for a reasonable time, but for us, we feel we are okay and plan to marry as soon as possible." Dr, Joseph said, "Let's continue for two more weeks with family sessions. If things go well for Liz, I will be willing to discharge you."

The next two weeks went well. Doctor Joseph was pleased how maturely Liz handled her parents. He heard her say to them that she now realized how painful their lives had been, and she didn't want to hurt them by any of her very immature outbursts or demands. She told them that she didn't know what kind of relationship they might have in the future, but she hoped that some kind of connection could be made. She ended by saying that she wanted her children to have grandparents, and that they were the only ones she wanted. She then went over and hugged them both. Both William and Suzanne broke down and cried, and there was Liz comforting them. Even Henry came over and hugged them. The whole event was very unusual for Doctor Joseph. He decided to end Liz's treatment. After the family session was over, all four went to William and Suzanne's home. After saying goodbye, Henry and Liz left.

They left for Mary's home. Liz had not heard about or from Mary for several months. They arrived at Mary's home during the celebration of Lillian and Jake's wedding. Liz at first thought it was Mary and Jonathan's. She was glad it wasn't them, because she wanted to be in Mary's Wedding.

Chapter XXVII

MARY WAS VERY EXCITED TO have Liz again. Liz introduced Mary to Henry saying, "Henry, until you came into my life, Mary was my only friend." She asked Mary, "Where is Jonathan? I want him to meet my Henry." Almost in the same breath, she wanted to know how she and Jonathan were getting along. Mary told her they were very close, but they have things to work out. Mary said, "Liz, you are fortunate that you met and fell in love before your treatment. My journey has been more tortuous. My injuries and my memory loss have complicated my relationship with Jonathan. We are still very close friends, but marriage is not in the near future." Liz was concerned and said, "Is it as bad as your words sound?" Mary said, "I want to talk to you alone as soon as possible. Will you and Henry be staying in Albuquerque for a while?" Liz said, "As long as it takes for you to help me with my wedding." At this point, Jonathan walked up and introductions were made. Henry and Jonathan hit it off well. Henry and Jonathan stayed together and talked while Mary and Liz wandered around with the other guests.

Jonathan left early and drove back to his ranch. His talk with Mary confirmed his feelings that they were not close to being married. For the first time, he began to wonder if they would ever be married. He knew that he needed to involve himself in other activities, and maybe he should consider dating other women. He had told himself that Mary was the only woman he wanted, but if this was not to be, he still wanted a family and children. He was approaching middle age. When he first had similar thoughts, he pushed them aside as if he was being disloyal to Mary. Now after their conversation, he wondered where their relationship was going. Actually, he felt free for the first time in almost two years. He realized that he had been pursuing an idealized Mary, and now he and she were discovering themselves in a more realistic light. She was trying to be a woman, and he just wanted a wife and a family.

As he was driving to Socorro, he thought for the time being, this new woman thing would be put on a back burner. He wanted to let things happen. In these last two years he had been involved with two things, his business and Mary. Now was the time to look at his life and see if there was anything he wanted to do that was just fun. An old desire came to his mind. He had this beautiful ranch along the Rio Grande River. The land sloped from mountains on either side of the river. It gave the appearance of a basin. He knew that no significant oil had been found on his ranch, but he felt that in lower strata there just might be a large gas field.

When he got home, he put in a call to Fremont. Canela answered the phone, and they talked for a minute. She was excited because her uncle was having financial problems and wanted to sell her father's old ranch. He had no mineral rights, and he was not a rancher so he found the thrill of ownership not appealing. Her uncle had always been a greedy man, and he was asking a ridiculous price for the ranch. Initially, she was going to pay it when Fremont asked her to let him do a little investigation.

Fremont got in touch with some real estate friends, and they knew all about this property. Apparently, Mr. Gonzalez had taken out a loan from his bank with the ranch as collateral. When a loan payment was due, Mr. Gonzalez couldn't make the payment. The investment he had made with that loan was a total loss, and his bank was in receivership. The bankrupt officials were in charge of this property and had been trying to sell it. There had been no offers, and this friend felt any offer would be acceptable.

Canela said, "If you are calling for Fremont, he is up in Santa Fe negotiating to buy my old ranch." Jonathan congratulated her and asked her to have Fremont call him at his ranch as soon as it was convenient.

When he couldn't reach Fremont, Jonathan pulled up the geology of his ranch. He spent the rest of the afternoon studying different strata. At 6,500 feet, the Pennsylvania strata looked promising. While he was studying, the phone rang and he picked it up thinking that it was Fremont. Instead, it was Mary. She noticed the immediate change in the tone of his voice after the hello and his recognizing it was her calling. At that time, she ignored it and asked why he had left without saying goodbye. He said, "Mary, I don't like weddings that aren't mine. You were so busy; I just wanted to leave without any fuss." Mary was silent for a while and asked, "Are you alright?" Jonathan answered, "Mary, I don't know why you are asking that question. We know that we are facing a change in our lives, and I don't like change and indecision. When I get into situations like this, all I want to do is to be by myself and either distract myself, or do some deep thinking. Right now I am trying to distract myself, and your calling me put me back into indecision." Mary said, "I can see that my call has irritated you so I will hang up." Jonathan didn't like how the call had ended, but from now on, he was going to let Mary experience him as he is and not cover up any feelings. He tried to go back to his work but was still too upset by the call and decided to go to bed early.

When Mary hung up, she had an uneasy feeling. This was the first time that Jonathan had been abrupt with her. She wondered what was going on with Jonathan. He had always been so aware of her needs, and she had gotten used to it. She was just beginning to realize that he was tired and impatient with her. She needed to talk to someone. Maybe, Margaret would be of some help. She would have to talk to her tomorrow.

At this point, Liz walked up, and they started talking about her wedding. Mary asked if she and Henry had a place to stay. Liz said, "No, I just wanted to get to you, and we didn't think of lodging." Mary said, "Why don't you and Henry stay here? I have six bedrooms with baths and a staff. It would give us time to talk about your upcoming wedding and catch up on what has happened to the both of us." Liz wanted to check with Henry. When she found him, she told him she would like to stay that night with Mary. He told her it was okay with him. He said, "I can go to a hotel." Liz said, "No, you won't. You are staying with me. Mary invited you, also." Henry grinned as it pleased him that Liz was so positive in wanting him.

It was 9:00 o'clock that night when Fremont called. The phone call awakened Jonathan, and they talked about his plans. Jonathan was planning to shift his main office to his ranch and close his Albuquerque office. He was going to build several small guest houses for Fremont and Canela and others when they were working at this new office. Fremont commented that there seemed to be big changes in the wind. Fremont told about his purchasing of Canela's Montesinos ranch. He related that the Bankruptcy Judge wanted him to ask Canela if she wanted to buy her uncle's bank. The Judge said, "An infusion of $5 Million would make the bank solvent. Should we be interested in this?" Jonathan said he would think about it. They ended with Fremont saying, "Canela and I will close down the office at Mary's guest house tomorrow."

Mary wanted to talk with Margaret and Andy. She had to clear up some ideas about her mother. She got up early the next day and had breakfast alone. She was getting used to that way of living, but she still had fond memories of Jonathan being there with her. She knew she had to clarify more about her mother and her father. A lot of her rage toward her father had lessened. She felt she would engage them individually at first and see if she would have a better understanding of her mother. She was convinced that her mother did take up for her, but she was having a hard time understanding her willingness to endure an abusive husband.

She decided the first person to talk to was Margaret. She told Margaret why she wanted to talk to her, and in particular, she wanted to know more about how she and her mother grew up. In other words, she wanted to know more about her mother's family. Margaret was interested in knowing why she was making this inquiry and asked her why now. Mary said, "Margaret, I have allowed myself to have bad memories of my mother when they were absolutely false. I told myself that my mother was a defenseless person and let my father abuse me. This bizarre way of handling reality troubles me. I have talked to my doctor about it, and we both feel I should know more about my mother's background."

Margaret started off by saying, "We lived in a small town named Waco, Texas. At least it was small when we were children. It isn't small anymore. My father was a successful business man, and we had the usual upper middle class kind of life. There was nothing really remarkable about how we grew up. Our parents were loving and caring. We had no difficulty in relating to them. I was your mother's big sister. I think I probably bossed her too much, but I really did love her and wanted to make sure everything was good for her. I was two years older than your mother, and she followed in my footsteps. We went to the same schools and were only separated from each other when I graduated two years ahead of her. I always thought your mother was too kind and let people take advantage of her, but when I left for school, and she was all alone, she was a different person. She met your father during those years, and she was very positive about the fact that she was going to marry him. She actually defied me and the whole family in regards to Andy. She showed us strengths that we didn't know existed. Your mother, at that time, would just make up her mind and act upon it."

Margaret continued by saying, "Mary, I think you need to understand one thing. Your mother was a city girl, and she went with her husband to raw ranch land. She stuck by him while they developed a ranch that was the envy of the county. She didn't understand ranching, but anything Andy told her to do, she did and did it well. If the war had not come, you would have had a different life."

This conversation had a profound effect on Mary. She needed to talk to Andy now and really get a clear idea of his and Nancy's relationship, even the bad part of it. When she asked Andy to talk to her, he felt some anxiety, but he knew some time in the future, he was going to have to really get into this with Mary. He started off saying, "When I met your mother in college, I was a young man with big ideas. I was in the agricultural part of the college studying ranching and business management. I won't go into the reason why, because I just want to focus on your mother and me. We were going to the University of Texas, and your mother was majoring in literature. She was in the fine arts college. I had gotten in line at the cafeteria behind this attractive young lady. We were in a long line so we had a chance to talk. By the time we got to the food part of the line, I was trying to get a date with her. She didn't seem very responsive to that idea, so I followed her to the table where she was eating. We continued our talk. It took several meetings at the cafeteria before she agreed to have a date with me. It didn't take us long to realize that there was something special about our relationship. By the end of that year, we were talking about being engaged. Before we went to our homes for the summer, Nancy wanted me to come by her house and be introduced to her family. At that time I was introduced as a dear friend, and she wanted her family to meet me. Going to her house the second time was quite different. It was one year later, and we were definitely going to be married. Her parents were concerned about my ability to support her, but it was Margaret who really opposed it. Your mother stood up to all of them and said, 'This is my life, and we are going to be married regardless of your objections.'

Mary, I want to impress upon you, your mother was not a weak person. When she loved a person, she stuck with them with a loyalty that was beyond my comprehension. Our first few years were difficult financially. She had left a well off family to live with a person that was only marginally capable of supporting her. I was desperate to have income, and I joined the National Guard. You know how that was a disaster. I wasn't around you and your mother for 3 years, and when I came back, I was a vicious man. I had left a ranch that was the envy of the county, and I found on my return, a ranch that was grown up in weeds with no cattle. I had lost three years of my life. I was furious about my circumstances. I had no one to blame except your mother, and did I load her with all my despair. Mary, you were a stranger to me. You were told that I was your father, but we made no connection. I was not interested in developing one. Your mother quite early started demanding that I pay more attention to you.

Any demand from anyone at that time enraged me. I want you to understand one thing, Mary. I had been under command to do terrible things for three years. I was bitter about all those years. I had gone into the army with friends, and in the battle for Sicily, I lost half of them. By the time I got to Anzio, I had only one friend left and that was Jacob Wright. You know, Jacob is the father of Don Wright who is an intimate friend of Jonathan's. I've often wondered why Jacob came back with such a better frame of mind than I did. Anyway, getting back to your mom and me.

I began to try to salvage the ranch. I seemed to blame everything on your mother. She didn't tolerate this, and we had many arguments. You were never around when we had these arguments because she didn't want you to know we were having any difficulty. On several occasions, she left with you and went to Margaret's. She told you that you were just visiting your aunt, but she went because she told me she would not tolerate my abuse of her. She would stay there until I came and convinced her otherwise. It didn't take me more than a week for me to try to get her back. In fact, if your mother had not become ill, I think we would have gotten a divorce. I don't know why she thought her being ill was the reason to stay with me. I know she wanted you to have a father, and I guess she thought if she tried to stay with me, I would be different. I remember thinking when she was obviously dying how much I loved her, but I seemed to be unable to express it. I defeated myself by being angry and cruel with the only woman I ever loved. My coming home that night, and your sitting there in a frozen, despaired position by your dead mother utterly destroyed me. I don't think you remember that, but I just sat down by my wife and cried bitterly. You know the rest of what happened to us. I want you to know one thing very clearly. Your mother was a fighter, and she never gave up on me or you."

Mary sat still as he went through all this. Then she got up and went over to Andy and hugged him. She said, "I have denied you as my father for a long time. By doing this, I have denied myself of having a father, and I have denied the memory of my mother. I have no idea why I did this, but I want to change it now. I want to try to have a better relationship with you. I don't know how we are going to do this, but I want you to know I don't hate you anymore. I want to be around you more and try and learn to love you or at least, have some close relationship." Andy got up and said, "I love you, Mary.

Mary's next few sessions with Doctor Joseph were around this issue of why she had remembered her mother and her father in such a way that she would hate her father and not respect her mother. It seemed like she kept drawing a blank to this inquiry. Her actions seemed to change in her behavior towards others. She seemed to become more sensitive and gentle. The hard shell of her C.E.O. personality seemed to be weakening.

All during this time she was struggling with this inquiry, Liz and Henry were actively planning their wedding, and Liz was depending heavily on Mary. In many ways, Mary was the mother of the bride. Liz and Mary both wanted this to be a memorable wedding. Mary would be the maid of honor and since Henry had no close friends, he wanted Jonathan to be his best man. So, the wedding was drawing Jonathan and Mary back together.

Chapter XXVIII

Mary was excited about the wedding and wasn't observant about how it was affecting Jonathan. To Jonathan, here was another couple being married, and he was still left out in the cold. He felt that he was not going to get anywhere with Mary. They were always just going to be good friends. After the wedding and the celebration that followed, Jonathan decided to leave early, as it was too painful to be sitting around with others who were so happy. He had no hope of experiencing the same thing.

Again, he left without saying goodbye to Mary and returned to his ranch. Canela and Fremont were looking for him and when they couldn't find him, they asked Mary where was he. It was the first time Mary became aware that he was gone. When all the festivities were over and Mary was alone again, she began to wonder about what was going on between her and Jonathan. She knew he was withdrawing from her, and she wasn't too sure what this meant to her. She knew she had moved from a business- friendship relationship with him, but she still hadn't really considered him in any other role. She felt that it was time for her to really address Jonathan in her sessions with Doctor Joseph. She felt she had uncovered all she could about her mother and father, and her inquiries into why she distorted reality were fruitless. She did know that her life was changing concerning sensitivity, and she believed she could be something other than just a hardnosed C.E.O. She didn't feel like she could be like Virginia just copying her mother as the mother she knew as a child didn't lend itself to that. She was going to have to be her own maker of her femininity.

When she talked to Doctor Joseph about the changing relationship with Jonathan and his withdrawal, he encouraged her to look carefully at that relationship. He said, "This man has been very diligent in trying to help you, and from my experience with him, he has a lot to offer you." It was surprising to her that he would make such a positive statement as he was inclined to let her get to those positions. She asked him why he was doing this. Doctor Joseph said, "Mary, you spent almost a year-and-a-half resolving your memory, and then dealing with your situation with your parents and its effect upon you. You have clarified many issues, but you still seem to struggle with having an intimate relationship with a man. As you have approached the resolution of all these other conflicts, all you seem to be doing is withdrawing from this vital issue. We both know that you have been lonely all your life, and at one time, you thought that finding a man to love was your answer. It seems the failure of that experience continues to dominate you. We don't talk about this, and I think this is the final part of your treatment that we need to resolve."

This refocusing of Doctor Joseph troubled Mary, and she found herself experiencing a strong resistance to deal with it. She said to Doctor Joseph, "I have a great reluctance to get into this area. I know now I really wasn't attracted to Tom Carlson. I was just seeking an escape from the loneliness and hate of my father. His rejection and my feeling of rejection by my father were more than I could stand. I think possibly this is why I am so resistant to consider intimacy with any man. I am going to have to think about this stuff. I am very reluctant to even talk about it."

Jonathan drove home from the wedding quite depressed. He realized that Mary had paid very little attention to him, and she was not moving towards her wanting to have a wedding of their own. He said to himself, "I have been a stubborn fool. I thought I could convince Mary to love me. All I had to do was just be there and caring and somehow she would start loving me. I know now this is not going to happen. I need to break away and start my life anew in other directions. Out of this entire struggle, I know one thing very clearly; I want to have a wife and a family. I want to have someone who really loves me and wants to be a part of my live as well as I want to be a part of theirs." With this statement, his mind drifted off into trivial things, and all he had was a feeling of despair. It was late afternoon when he arrived back to his ranch, and he sat down and occupied himself with what he had always wanted to do. He was going to explore for gas on his ranch property. He put a note on Fremont's desk saying," I want to talk to you tomorrow about a project. Come to my office immediately when you arrive."

Canela and Fremont stayed to the end of the wedding feast and thoroughly enjoyed knowing Liz and Henry. They had talked with both of them for a long time during the wedding feast. Plans had been made that they would connect up again, and both couples were hopeful they could develop a close friendship. As they were driving back to the ranch, they were talking about Jonathan's behavior. Canela was saying that she thought Jonathan was withdrawing from Mary. She was puzzled why Mary wasn't doing something about it. There was a silence for a period of time, and they started talking about the question of whether to buy her uncle's bank. Canela was saying, "I don't want anything to do with a bank. I just want to have my ranch back and maybe build a nice house but being involved in a banking business would take too much of my time away from our relationship. I don't want to be a business woman. I want to be a wife and a mother. Fremont, did you hear that last word? I want to be a mother. I expect you to do something about that." Fremont smiled.

Jonathan could not sleep that night. His mind kept going back to Mary and his lost hope about their relationship. He was repeating these thoughts over and over again, compulsively. Finally, he said to himself, "Stop this! Think of something else. You must get your mind on some project that will completely take these thoughts out of your mind." When he said this to himself, immediately the bank in Santa Fe came to mind. Certainly, taking a bank out of bankruptcy would be a pretty consuming business. That business plus getting a gas field started on his ranch would be a time and emotionally consuming event. With those decisions, he found himself dropping off to sleep. For now Mary was definitely on a back burner, and he was going on with his life.

He got up early the next morning and was very active working on his business when Fremont came in. Canela didn't work in the office anymore and said that she was now a housewife and didn't want to have anything to do with the business. With this being the case, their first order of business was finding a new secretary. They knew it would be a difficult task because Socorro didn't offer many prospects. Fremont suggested that they consider going to the campus at New Mexico Tech and see if they had any courses on business. His idea was that they needed a business administrator, not a secretary. They could hire anybody to type, but they needed someone who could perform like Canela. She was a business administrator. Jonathan said, "I don't want you involved with that, Fremont, because I have two projects for you. Do you think Canela would help us in that regard?" As he was saying that, Canela walked in and heard her name. She said, "What are you all talking about?" Jonathan replied, "Canela, would you go to the campus of New Mexico Tech in Socorro and find out if we can hire somebody who has training in business administration?" Canela liked this idea and was eager to accept that task.

Jonathan turned to Fremont and said, "Here are my two projects. First, I want you to start actively searching the geology of the ranch for us to start a trial drill for gas in the Pennsylvania Strata at a level of about 6,500 feet. Now, before you start objecting, Fremont, I want you to understand I am going to do this regardless of what you say. I know you have resisted this idea ever since I bought this ranch, but I am determined to do it now. Fremont, you are my dear friend and colleague. I need to do something now to distract me from my deteriorating relationship with Mary. Will you help me?" Fremont was very surprised by this statement, and he quickly swallowed all of his objections to this plan. He replied by saying, "I will start immediately on the geology, and I will work on getting a testing well started. What was your second task?" Jonathan replied, "I have been thinking about what would really keep me involved over the next few months. I think that we should buy the Santa Fe Bank from the Bankruptcy Judge. I will leave later on this morning and go to Santa Fe to negotiate the purchase of this bank. That means that I will be spending considerable time in Santa Fe over the next several months. I will depend on you to be taking care of the first project, i.e. the well. I will be gone approximately four days a week, and I will be on the job here for three days. I will expect you, and Canela to hire this business administrator."

While Jonathan was driving to Santa Fe, he passed through Albuquerque where he would turn to go to Mary's house. He felt a tug at his heart as he passed that intersection. He quickly suppressed that and moved on. He arrived at Santa Fe about 2:00 in the afternoon, and he had called ahead to the Bankruptcy Judge requesting a conference. He had picked up Donald Wright in Albuquerque as he was going to be his legal representative as he went through this negotiation. On the way to Santa Fe, he and Don talked about their past. Don asked him how things were going with him and Mary. Jonathan didn't want to get into any discussion about this, so he said, "We are both backing off and seeing what we can do as time passes." Don was not satisfied with this response, and he started telling him about Mary's visits to Virginia. He said, "Jonathan, did you know that Mary has been seeing Virginia once a week? They have become good friends. Virginia tells me that Mary has real concern about her personality. She feels that for ten years she has been a C.E.O., and she had learned more of a man's attitude than a woman's. Mary wants always to talk about how does a woman think. Virginia tells me that she doesn't know how a woman thinks, and she tells Mary the same thing. She says to Mary, 'I am just me. I don't consider myself as a woman thinking. I just think of me as thinking.' So far Mary seems to be very dissatisfied with this answer." Jonathan didn't respond to that information and thought, "I am not going to think about Mary. I am not going to think about Mary."

As soon as they arrived at the bankruptcy office, they were immediately ushered into the Judge's office. After the usual introductions, they got down to the business of acquiring the bank. The Bankruptcy Judge asked them if they had any experience in banking. Jonathan said, "I have a degree in business, but finance was not part of my degree. I have developed a successful business, and I do know how to add figures. I think I am perfectly competent to manage a bank. If there are any technical issues in running it, I will hire a person to handle it. What I think is important in this negotiation, is whether I am willing to put up the necessary capital to restore this bank. I don't mean to brag, Sir, but I am a wealthy man, and $5 Million is not significant to my income. Do you have any problems with what I have said?" The Judge was somewhat startled by his frankness, but he liked the clarity of it. He turned to Don and said, "I think you represent him legally, is that correct?" Don replied with a yes. He continued saying, "I want you to go over these papers and advise your client as to the risks of this purchase. I would like to meet with you in five days and either settle the purchase of this bank or move on." They parted and drove back to Don's office in Albuquerque.

For the next five days, they worked intensely over the records of the bank, and the problems it had. Jonathan was amazed at the carelessness of Canela's uncle. He had a solid bank, and he let it go by irrational loans and almost a gambler's spirit. Both thought that the bank was a real asset and even though Jonathan was buying it for the wrong reason, they thought he would be successful in his ownership.

During those 5 days, they worked late at night. Jonathan went to his hotel. Don noticed that he made no effort to contact Mary. On Friday of that week, they drove back to Santa Fe and met with the Bankruptcy Judge. Don had prepared the papers of purchase and presented them to the Bankruptcy Judge. In the papers Don had written down what they had decided was the right amount of money to resolve the cash problems of the bank. They came up with a figure that was less than $5 Million. They said in their report that if the Judge disagrees with this figure that they would ask him to check the figures again as they were standing firm on their offer. They left the meeting with the understanding the Judge would get in touch with them as to his decision.

Jonathan drove Don back to his office and continued down to his ranch. When he arrived, he was surprised to find a very attractive young lady sitting in the business administrator's seat. He introduced himself as the president of this company and told her he would like for her to come into his office as he would like to talk to her. She was a professional woman and very intelligent. As he was questioning her about her ability, he became aware that they had found a very important person for their company. He inquired about Fremont's work. She said, "He is out in the field now, and they have already negotiated with a driller and that drilling is supposed to start next Monday." He then asked her what she knew about his oil business. She said, "I have been working with Canela on this, and I feel like I am getting an understanding about what my duties are in that regard." He told her that he tried to work his employees on an 8:00 to 5:00 schedule, but in times of emergency, she would have to work late. Was this agreeable to her? She said, "That is fine." He inquired if the salary she was being offered was adequate for her expectations. She replied, "Yes, and I feel it is quite generous. I feel very fortunate to have this job as there are no similar paying jobs in Socorro." This ended their interview, and he went to work on the papers that were piled on his desk. Late Saturday afternoon he received a call from the Bankruptcy Judge accepting his position.

On Monday morning, he picked up Don, and they drove to Santa

Fe. The paper signing was an anticlimactic event, and they both went to the bank. The Bankruptcy Judge had kept the bank open and operating. Jonathan wanted to meet with the staff to see how they should proceed. He was surprised to find that Mr. Gonzalez was still in the office of the President. Jonathan sat down opposite him and began to inquire why he was there. Gonzalez was stuttering and stammering and told him that the Judge had told him to stay on the job until he had a replacement. Jonathan said, "I won't need your services, and I want you to vacate this office immediately. You are not to take anything from the office as I want to evaluate everything that is here." He called the security officer and asked him to escort Mr. Gonzalez from the bank. If he had any keys, the security officer was to get these, and he wanted the lock on the front door to be changed immediately. Gonzalez protested at first, but when he looked into the eyes of Jonathan, he knew he had better get out of there. When the banking staff saw how Jonathan handled Gonzalez, they were glad and more hopeful about their future. They didn't think that Mr. Gonzalez was the right man for this job, and he had been a tyrant in his relation with them.

Jonathan called the staff into his office, and he told them that he was their new president. He said he had made a large investment in this bank, and he wasn't in the mood to lose any of it. He expected all of them to perform their duties, and if there was any failure on their part, they would be terminated. He told them that he was bringing a banking adviser into the bank. This advisor was going over the records and was going to review all the people in the bank and determine their qualifications for their positions. "If you meet the standards of this person, you can be assured that you have a position. I will see that you are adequately reimbursed for your services. I want you to understand one thing about me. I am a task maker. I don't put up with any nonsense, and I do not hesitate to fire; but if you are loyal and work diligently, you will have my complete support." With that he told them to go back to work. That afternoon his bank administrator arrived, and he started his evaluation of the bank. Jonathan rented a condo in Santa Fe and planned to work at the bank for at least three months.

Chapter XXIX

It had been several months, and Mary had not heard from Jonathan. She had been spending that time working with Doctor Joseph with the issue of her reluctance to engage in a man-woman relationship. Nothing was coming forth in these sessions. She was beginning to feel lonely for Jonathan. For some reason, she didn't want to be the one to initiate their talking to each other, and it took several weeks for her to finally decide to call him. When she called his office in Socorro, a young lady answered the phone, and she asked to speak to Jonathan.

The young lady said that he was not there, and she would have to make an appointment if she wished to talk to him. The young lady continued, "I do not give out information about Mr. McCandlish over the phone. I suggest you make a formal request, and I will advise him of your request." Mary was shocked. She felt that she had been completely excluded from Jonathan's life. Who was that woman anyway? She wondered what she could do, and she immediately thought of Canela. She knew that Canela had moved to Socorro, but she did not have her telephone number. After spending some time, she did find her number and called Canela.

Canela was delighted to hear from Mary as it was three months since the wedding, and she still had fond memories of the activities. It didn't take Mary long to get down to why she was calling. She said, "Canela, I called the office and a strange woman refused to give me Jonathan's telephone number. She had the gall to tell me I needed to make an appointment with him." Canela smiled and said, "A lot of changes have happened over the last three months. Jonathan is not in his office now. He is working out of a bank in Santa Fe. He has purchased the Santa Fe National Bank and is actively reorganizing it. He has told us that he will probably be there for three months. He comes back every Friday to his office here and spends Friday and the weekend going over other problems of his business with Fremont and his secretary. If you would have called Monday or Tuesday, you would have gotten no answer from the administrator. Business is closed down on those days because they work Saturday and Sunday." Mary said, "Canela, I feel something is wrong between Jonathan and me. He doesn't call me anymore and doesn't particularly want to have anything to do with me." Canela didn't know what to say. Her primary loyalties were with Jonathan, but she liked Mary. Mary had been her boss for a number of years. She said, "Mary, I don't like to be involved in a personal relationship. I like both of you very much. Fremont and I have noticed that Jonathan rarely mentions you, and as far as we know, he doesn't call you. We don't understand this, and we hope things will get better between both of you." Mary said, "Canela, you are my only connection with Jonathan now, and I hope you will let me call you and find out where he is and what is happening." Canela said she would.

When Mary hung up, she felt a strange emptiness inside her. For the first time, she was feeling a loss that seemed to penetrate deeply into her. It was a despairing loss. She couldn't understand what had happened in this conversation that had made her feel such despair and loneliness. Was the possible loss of Jonathan that important to her? It didn't take her long to figure out what it was, but she still had a great reluctance to engage with him.

In her session with Doctor Joseph, she talked about what had happened, and this sense of loss and what it meant. Doctor Joseph inquired as to what she lost. She couldn't answer the question by a name such as Jonathan's. It seemed to be something deeper than that. What had she lost? What flashed to her mind with that pressure of thought was the word "caring". She pondered that word. "Caring?" Doctor Joseph questioned her, "Can caring from a meaningful person be important?" There was no "aha" from that statement; she just continued to think. As the months passed Doctor Joseph realized that Mary was becoming too comfortable with being lonely. He was seeing her slipping into being a perpetual patient role and not having the desire for a conclusive ending of her treatment. As he continued to push her, he noticed that she was moving more into a masochistic position in response to his demanding position. He knew he would have to continue to pursue this and would have to break through this defense if she were ever to live a meaningful life. He was fearful that he would not be successful. He finally decided that the only way to force her to address this, was to say that he was going to stop her treatment at a specific time. He told her the reason for this was because she was enjoying her dependency and helplessness, and as far as he was concerned, she was getting too much pleasure out of suffering. He said, "I am not in the business of indulging people who enjoy suffering. I will not allow you to do this with me. Hence, in two weeks, if we do not make any progress, and you continue this behavior, I am going to terminate the treatment." Mary was shocked and left the session wondering what she was going to do.

Jonathan found himself enjoying the bank work. Working with his bank adviser was a new experience for him. He found the banking industry was very interesting, and he wondered why he had never thought of owning a bank. He was constantly borrowing money for projects, and he was giving business to another bank. Why not give his business to his bank? When he thought of this, he realized that this was what Mr. Gonzalez had done. He talked to the banking administrator about the feasibility of doing this. The bank administrator said, "It's not uncommon for industries like Wal-Mart to buy banks." He didn't have too much information on how they used the bank, but he thought it wasn't an uncommon event. He felt that if the loans were short termed and backed heavily with collateral, there would be no question by the bank examiner. He suggested that he get in touch with the bank examiner and see what his feelings were about that.

His relationships with the staff of the bank were becoming more and more pleasant. After his bank investigator had studied their abilities and reported to him, he felt he could be more trusting of them. At least, he felt he didn't have to go through a long period of "on guard". As he relaxed his pressure on them, they seemed to relax with him, and he began to feel a harmony in the bank. The first quarter report of the bank as to earnings was remarkable. The bank had made a 15% profit on its capital. He didn't know if this was a fluke or not, but he was certainly encouraged. By the end of the second quarter, he felt he should find a bank president, and he would become its chairman.

In his past experience in acquiring qualified people, he had found that going to prosperous businesses and finding their best person was the best way to get the most qualified person. What he had learned by this process was that many businesses neglect important employees, and by offering an adequate salary increase, it was easy to bring them into his organization. Using this technique, he found a very competent person, and now he decided to go back to his office in Socorro. He had been coming every weekend and going over all of his other workloads, and he was looking forward to having an easier time. He didn't think of Mary very much anymore and hadn't heard from her in five months. During the past month he had been dating his business manager. He was finding that she was an uncomplicated person, and that was a great relief to him. He enjoyed her company, but he just couldn't seem to get more interested than that.

Chapter XXX

CANELA AND FREMONT WERE CONCERNED about Jonathon dating his business manager. They didn't talk to him about it, but they both felt he was on the rebound and not really seeking a new relationship. They knew he was concerned about his own age and not having a marriage and a family. Finally, Canela told Fremont that she was going to call Mary. When she made this call, Mary had arrived home from her session with Doctor Joseph where he had told her he was terminating her sessions in two weeks. Mary was upset about this, but when Canela told her that Jonathan was actively dating another woman, she really became upset. She didn't know what to say to Canelo about this information. She just felt shocked.

After Canela hung up, she began to seriously look at her life and what was happening to her. Jonathan became the center of her thoughts again. Before this, she had just played with the idea of his being gone. Now she had to consider the real possibility that he would be gone forever. She didn't know what to do about it and waited until she talked to Doctor Joseph the following day. When she told him about the information she had gotten from Canela, Doctor Joseph didn't respond immediately. She had become dependent upon his interfering and now she heard nothing from him. He was forcing her to think and feel for what she really wanted. Finally he said to her, "Well, Mary, you really have a good case. Now you can really suffer. Now you are going to lose the one man that really loved you because it's better to suffer than to have a loving relationship."

An anger arose in Mary when she heard this. She found herself angrily saying, "You have no right to talk to me like this. I can suffer if I want to." She was shocked by what she had said. For the first time, she realized what she had been doing. She had been enjoying her suffering. She didn't say anything. She just spent the rest of this session in silence. Doctor Joseph knew he had a breakthrough. The next three sessions were filled with her making up her mind about her life and working toward their conclusion of her therapy. She knew then that she loved Jonathan, and she wanted him to be her husband. She wanted to have a family by him. When she openly stated that to herself and Doctor Joseph, she said, "I don't need to come here anymore, Doctor Joseph. I can take control of my life, and I am going to find some way to get Jonathan back; I don't need your help to do that."

The next few days she was constantly thinking about Jonathan. She finally decided the only way to do it was to go down to Socorro and have it out with him. She didn't make an appointment. She got in her car and drove to his ranch. When she got to the gate of the ranch, she was not admitted as the gateman had never heard of her. She had him call Canela and got her to request that she be let in. Canela told the gateman to let her in and give her directions to her house.

Canela was living in a house Jonathan had built for them, and they used it while their own house was being built on their ranch. When Mary arrived, she told Canela why she was there. Canela said, "Mary, you must realize that it has been six months since you and Jonathan have had contact. Jonathan is a man who is determined to go on with his life, and you have shown no interest in him over the last six months." Mary became impatient with Canela. She said, "Canela, I know all that. It has taken me a long time to get where I am today, and I am determined to get Jonathan back. I don't care what has happened in the last six months. I want Jonathan now." This thrilled Canela as she wanted them to be together. She asked, "Mary, what are you planning to do?" "I have decided," Mary said, "I must go to Jonathan and talk to him about my changed feelings and see if I can persuade him that I have really changed." Canela said, "I have to go to the office now. Why don't we go over there and see if we can find Jonathan." When they walked into the office, Jonathan was at the administrator's desk talking about going out that weekend.

When Mary walked in, he was in a state of shock. Mary walked up to him and gave him a big hug and kissed him firmly on the mouth. He found himself embracing her. He was surprised. After he broke free from their hug, he told her to come into the office. He found himself still on guard and put himself behind the desk and put Mary in the chair in front of the desk. Mary recognized that he was still holding back. She knew she was going to have to be aggressive if she was going to be successful at all.

"Jonathan, I have finished my treatment. I am now on my own, and I am a whole person. I know what I want, and I want you. I realize that I have been neglectful of you, and I have been so consumed with my own self-interest that I have not paid attention to the important things in my life. I know now that I have loved you from the moment you walked into that hospital room and was so afraid that I would reject you. Your caring then was so meaningful to me that I know it was a vital force in my getting well. I have no idea why it has taken me so long to get to this point in my life. I hope it is not too late for us."

Jonathan said, "Mary, when I left you at the wedding of your friend, Liz, I felt that we would never have our wedding. I have written you off. That young lady out there and I have been dating for over a month. She didn't have all the garbage that you carried around. I don't know if I am willing to reengage with you. I kind of like dating a person that has no problems." Mary had been prepared for this kind of response. It reminded her of the time when she was trying to get loans for her new business and being rejected. When that happened back in those circumstances, she just fought back, and she was going to do it now.

She looked at Jonathan and said, "You may think you are going to escape me, but I have you know right now, I don't give up when I want something." To Jonathan, this was a different Mary, and he thought, "Am I willing to take another chance on her?" They talked for awhile and parted with the understanding that he would come to Albuquerque on the weekend, and they would talk further.

The weekend arrived, and Mary was waiting for Jonathan to arrive. When he didn't appear at the appropriate time, she called his office. He was just leaving. She asked why he wasn't in Albuquerque. Jonathan replied, "Mary, I am very reluctant to get involved with you again. I just can't make myself come there and talk with you." Mary said, "Jonathan, if you won't come to me, I am going to come to you. I am on my way now. I am getting in my car now, and I should be in your office in an hour-and-a-half. If your stupid gateman won't let me in, I will crash the gate, and I am going to see you regardless of your reluctance." She hung up. She did not give him a chance to respond. Again, Jonathan was surprised over Mary's aggression. He sat down in his office and waited for Mary to arrive. He called the front gate and told the gateman that Mary McGregor would be arriving at his gate in about an hour, and he was to let her in. Mary made it from Albuquerque in less than an hour. In other words, she drove 70 miles on a bad road in less than an hour. She was prepared to be very defiant with the gateman, but he rapidly acknowledged that she could enter, and she had no trouble getting to Jonathan's office. She entered and said very quickly, "Jonathan, you may think you can get away from me, but there's not any way that you are going to escape me."

They started talking. Jonathan told her of all the times he had tried to be close to her. Now she was saying it was entirely different. She was ready to be close to him. Why was she so conceited that she thought that he would change at an instant notice? He said, "You can't walk into my life and tell me that you love me and expect me to believe that you love me when all you have done for the last six months is to ignore me. When I left in despair from that wedding party, you didn't even call me, and wonder why I had left so early. You just went on with your business as if I didn't exist. Frankly, Mary, you are not very convincing."

Mary knew she was in for a tough sale, but she was determined to break through his resistance. She didn't defend herself against his anger. She didn't plead the fact that she needed time to work out her own problems before she could find him again. She just simply said, "Jonathan, I love you, and I am going to do whatever it takes to convince you that you really love me." They talked on, but the outcome of it was that Jonathan was still angry and not accepting of her. Mary said, "Jonathan, I am not going back to Albuquerque. I don't belong there anymore. I belong here with you. Before I came here to see you, I was visiting with Canela, and she told me that she had an extra bedroom. I am staying with her for as long as I need to. I brought my things with me, and I am moving in with her today. You are not going to get away from me." With that she left and went to Canela's, and Jonathan was left pondering what to do. One thing he was sure of was that he wasn't going to run back into her arms. He was still very angry at how she had treated him. It concerned him that she was going to be on the ranch, but he had no way of dealing with it.

During the next week, Mary used every opportunity she had to be with him. She irritated his administrator because she interfered with the flow of business. The administrator complained to Jonathan about her being in the office all the time. Jonathan knew he had to make a decision. He called Mary into his office and said, "Mary, this is not the way to resolve the situation between us. I want you to go back to Albuquerque, and I will come there, and we will talk about our future." Mary said, "I will go back, Jonathan, but if you don't show up, I am going to come back, and you can count on it."

She left and returned to Albuquerque, and Jonathan came to Albuquerque that weekend. Mary had asked Margaret and Andy to go someplace else as she wanted to be alone with Jonathan. When Jonathan arrived, he didn't hesitate to engage Mary. He started off saying, "I am so angry with you that I can hardly stand it. I keep saying to myself, 'Why am I tolerating any kind of contact with you?' I spent over two years worshipping you, and all I got from it was your stating you felt like I was like a brother and a father. You don't know how insulted I felt about that comment. I had no desire to be any one of those people in your life, much less your father. I was passionately in love with you at that time. I would have given anything for your love. Now I don't think it's worth a continental damn." He raved on for a few minutes and then just sat down frustrated about being there. Mary ignored all his anger. She said, "Jonathan, may I get your something?" He couldn't believe what she was saying. He raged, "Mary, don't you understand that I'm mad as hell at you, and all you do is calmly say 'do I want anything?' Yes, I want something. I want to get the hell out of here and get you out of my life." Mary didn't respond. She let him stew awhile because she knew this was the only way to get passed his anger. She didn't want to inhibit his anger because the sooner it was out of the way, the better chance she had of getting close to him. They sat quietly together for a while and he said, "Mary, do you have any coke in the house?" She got up quickly and got it for him. When she brought it to him, he said, "Mary, I don't know what is going to happen to us. I have a lot to deal with in thinking about reconnecting with you. I am reluctant to experience wanting you and being rejected." Mary said, "Jonathan, I am not going to ever reject you. I don't know how to convince you of that except by my determination to never let you go. I feel the only way we can break through this, and I know now that I am the only one who wants to, is by being in constant contact with you. I know you have every reason to be angry with me, and if expressing that will help us, I am perfectly willing to endure with whatever you have to say." Jonathan with a sigh responded, "Mary, I get no pleasure in being angry with you. I just know that I don't want to reengage with you. I don't want to feel the pain again of loving you. I thought I had my life back in order again. I was dating a nice, uncomplicated woman. I didn't have to deal with any garbage. Now you come along and say you are well and able to love me. How am I going to be convinced that it really is so? Mary, I have known you since high school. I worshipped you from afar, and I have used every chance I had to be with you. Now you are telling me you want to be with me forever, and I just can't accept it." Mary said, "Jonathan, I'm tired of talking. Come here. I want to hug and kiss you." Jonathan didn't move. "Okay, Jonathan, if the mountain won't come to me, I will come to the mountain." She gave him a firm and passionate kiss. It was nothing less than a kiss that a lover would give their lover. He found himself responding to it. All of the resistance that he had vanished. He held her close and said, "Oh, Mary, I have loved you so long, and it's just impossible to grasp all that is happening now." Mary didn't answer; she just kissed him again even more passionately. They just sat there clinging to each other.

They didn't talk any more about the past; they just sat next to each other and let time pass. Neither one of them was trying to consummate their relationship. They just were sitting there and thinking about what had passed in their lives, neither one of them telling the other what they were thinking, but both came to the same conclusion. They loved each other. The rest of the weekend was rather quiet for them, and they enjoyed each other's company. Towards the end of the weekend, Jonathan said, "I am going on next Thursday to Calgary, Alberta, Canada. I have been asked by the officials there to participate as an honorary guest in their rodeo. I am flying up in my jet on Thursday. Will you go with me?" Mary said, "I am ready to go now." He thought that was a good idea, and they left that night for Calgary.

They arrived early, and the officials were delighted to have him. They participated in the early activities, and he introduced Mary as his fiancée. On Thursday, the active rodeo began, and he was scheduled to ride a bronco. Mary was in the officials' section of the rodeo and was anxious about him doing this. Before he went to the chute to mount his bronco, he went out into the arena and raised his hat to the crowd. There was a tremendous roar of approval. Jonathan was a legendary hero in rodeo history. What he had done in New York City would be in their lore for generations to generations. All of the participating rodeo cowboys walked out onto the field and surrounded Jonathan and raised their hats to him. He was, not only the crowd's hero, but also he was their hero. He left for the chute, and it opened and out came a bucking bronco like they had never seen before. Jonathan had not lost his skill, and he had the crowd shouting with joy as they were seeing a champion repeating another brilliant ride. Here again the crowd insisted he be allowed to ride further. They didn't want to give up this moment. After a few seconds he was taken off the horse, and he walked to the center of the arena waving his hat to the crowd. It was impossible to describe the joy with which the crowd greeted him. All of the rodeo cowboys ran out, lifted him on their shoulders and carried him off the field. Mary was in ecstasy. She had her man who accomplished many great things. It wasn't just the ride that impressed Mary; neither was it the expression of the crowd and his fellow cowboys. It was his ability to excel in anything that he did. She said to herself, "How did I ever miss seeing the value of this man?"

That night, they started talking about marriage. Mary said, "Jonathan, I don't want a big wedding, I just want to be married to you as quickly as possible. Let's go home now, and I will be down next Tuesday with a solution for our marriage." She continued, "Now, don't you try to run away again because I mean it." Jonathan smiled and kissed her a lovingly goodbye as he drove from Mary's home to the ranch.

For the next two days, Mary was actively preparing her wedding. She called Liz and Henry, Don and Virginia, Andy and Margaret, Lillian and Jake, and Canela and Fremont. She told them at 2:00 p.m. on Tuesday, there was to be a wedding at Jonathan's ranch. They were just simply to arrive casually and surprise Jonathan. They were to say they were there for a party. Mary had arranged a place for them. Tuesday came, and they all arrived as directed. Jonathan, thinking there was going to be some kind of announcement of their coming wedding, told the staff to leave as he had other things planned for that day. At 2:00 p.m. the gateman called, and told Jonathan there was a caravan of vehicles at the gate being led by that woman -- Mary McGregor. Jonathan said, "Let them in." The whole caravan proceeded to the ranch house. In the caravan was Mary's minister, and he had all the necessary papers for a wedding. The rest of the caravan was a catering service. They had been instructed to set up the main room at the ranch house for a wedding, and they brought all the necessary equipment to do this. They were also instructed to have the best wedding feast that they could conceive.

Mary had planned, while she was dressing to make her wedding entry, to have refreshments brought to the group that was on the patio. She told them they were to meet on the outside patio and enjoy themselves until the props for the wedding could be put in place. Jonathan couldn't believe what was happening, but he had no objections. In a short time the minister came out and said, "We are ready for the service." All came in to the sound of the wedding march. When the wedding march was sounded, Mary came out and walked towards Jonathan who was standing in front of the minister. Jonathan was overwhelmed by Mary's beauty. The wedding ended very quickly, and they were man and wife. Everybody was excited about what had happened, and for two hours there was wild excitement. At exactly 9:00 p.m. Mary told the group that it was time for them to leave; that from here on she wanted to have her husband alone.

After the crowd left, Mary took Jonathan's hand, and they walked into their bedroom. They stood looking at each other. Without a word being said, both started taking off their clothes. When they were completely naked, they looked at bodies that were heavily scarred, but that wasn't what they saw. They saw two beautiful bodies that brought only joy. They both walked calmly to the bed and lay down beside each other. As they were embracing and kissing, Jonathan rose up on his elbow and said, "Mary, before we consummate our marriage, I need to tell you something." She responded, "What is it, Jonathan?" He said, "Mary, I have never had sex with a woman but I know how to do it." Mary responded, "Jonathan, I haven't had sex with a man but I also know how. So let's have it." And, so they began a new life together. THE END

Epilogue

JONATHAN DISCOVERED A LARGE GAS field on his ranch.
Jonathan and Mary had five children, three boys and two girls.
Fremont and Canela had three girls and one boy.
Liz and Henry had two boys and one girl.
Don and Virginia had a boy and a girl.
William and Suzanne loved all of their grandchildren
Margaret and Andy were celebrated grandparents of all.
All families would meet every three months and celebrate their friendship.
All of the children were claimed as cousins.

Charles Samuel Betts lives in Little Rock, Arkansas. He is a retired psychiatrist. He has written genealogical books and this is his second novel. He travels with his wife to many continents. He is eighty-five years old and lives an active life. He expects to live another ten years.

Manufactured By: RR Donnelley
Breinigsville, PA USA
January, 2011